001379030

D0426360

DATE DUE   1 / 02

JUL 08 02

Also by Laurali R. Wright

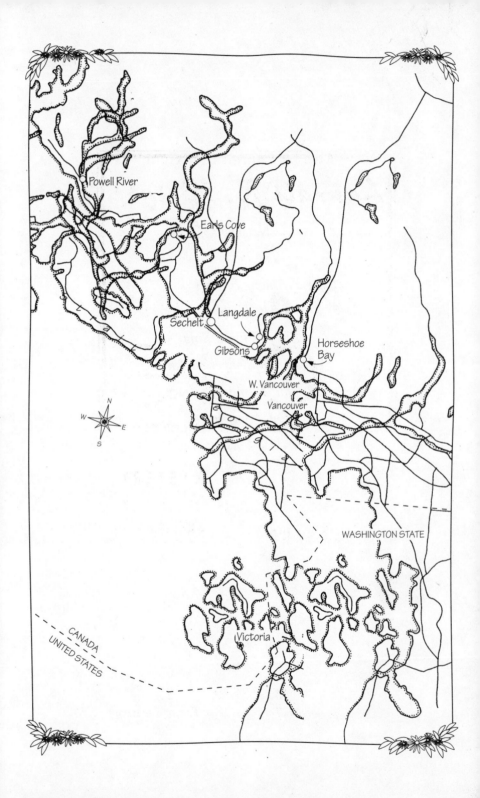

Laurali R. Wright

Mother LOVE

A KARL ALBERG MYSTERY
WITH
CASSANDRA MITCHELL

SCRIBNER
New York London Toronto Sydney Tokyo Singapore

SCRIBNER
1230 Avenue of the Americas
New York., NY 10020

SCRIBNER and design are trademarks of Simon & Schuster Inc.

Manufactured in the United States of America

1 3 5 7 9 10 8 6 4 2

Library of Congress Cataloging-in-Publication Data
Wright, Laurali, 1939–
Mother love: a Karl Alberg mystery with Cassandra Mitchell/Laurali R. Wright.
p.   cm.
I. Title.
PR9199.3.W68M68   1995
813'.54—dc20   95–5593   CIP

ISBN 0-684-19673-5

This book is for my friends
Nancy Hardy and
Bill Banting

Acknowledgments

Thank you, John—
for the eleventh time.
Greece beckons. . . .

Author's Note

There is a Sunshine Coast,
and its towns and villages are called by the names used here.
But all the rest is fiction. The events and the characters
are products of the author's imagination,
and geographical and other liberties have been taken
in the depiction of the town of Sechelt.

Prologue

*I*t was a few days before Christmas. She woke in the night, shivering with cold, from a fitful sleep. She tried to guess the time without looking at the clock ticking from the orange crate that served as her bedside table. The clock sat in the center of a lace doily she had crocheted herself, in front of the coal-oil lamp and next to a box of wooden matches. She lay on her back, the covers up to her chin, next to her sleeping husband and watched her breath make the air in front of her face visible.

It wasn't the first night she had awakened. It was the third, maybe the fourth night that week. She carried exhaustion into each day; each morning it was deeper and more profound. She knew where it could lead her, and she was afraid.

Stretched flat on her back, she clutched the bedclothes in both hands and struggled with escalating panic. She focused her mind upon comfortable, comforting things, trying to soothe herself. She thought about the rag rug on the floor beside the bed, and her slippers sitting there, and the chenille robe that was hung over the back of a wooden chair next to the dresser.

She had been advised to take deep, slow breaths on these occasions, and she did this, concentrating on the expansion and contraction of her lungs.

But the tension remained. It was in her limbs, caught there in bone and muscle. And it was in her head, too; it had seized her brain, had taken hold of it like her own fist around an orange, or a child's hand.

She fought to keep control of her breathing, a tiny island of self-dominance that with concentration she could perhaps make larger, and larger, until her entire physical body would be under her command and she could force herself to sleep, to be calm, to be loving. . . .

Terror scurried through her blood. She found herself sitting upright. She swung her legs out of bed, and in an instant she was out the bedroom door.

She made her way along the hall, touching the walls with outstretched hands, her bare feet cold on the bare floor, passing the bedrooms of her children, and went quickly and soundlessly down the stairs and into the kitchen.

The stove slumbered, banked for the night but still glowing, and in its faint light she saw her breath like tattered fog. She walked back and forth across the braided rug that lay between the stove and the wooden table where the family ate. She was rubbing her palms together and then making washing motions, all the while pacing, pacing. Then she stood still and touched her cheeks, and discovered that she was weeping.

She sat at the table and rested her head on her hands. "Please, please," she whispered, "help me, please. . . ."

She was aware of the instant of her capitulation. It did indeed feel like the final link breaking. It was like letting go of a tree branch, or ceasing to cling to a rock face: it was acceptance of failure, and with it came a precious instant of relief.

This was followed by utter blankness.

She would not remember, later, the things she did then.

THE PRESENT

Chapter

1

ABBOTSFORD, B.C.

Maria Buscombe's eyes opened and she looked, unseeing, at the ceiling, cautiously assessing the day. The light coming through the curtain at the small, high window in her bedroom shone with the bright confidence of an unclouded sun. There was an expectant quality to this morning light, a brittle anxiety.

She turned her head to look directly at the window. And in the second it took her to move her gaze, Maria captured the moment, the day—and all traces of slumber vanished. She became rigid. Breathless. It was the twenty-eighth day of September; and she had made a decision in the night.

Maria came from the prairies and remembered from her childhood red geraniums on a kitchen windowsill and a snowy landscape beyond. Maria grew up in Winnipeg, a city in the middle of the province of Manitoba, in the middle of Canada, halfway between the Atlantic and Pacific coasts.

She realized that she had been immersing herself on a regular basis, lately, in childhood memories that were fraudulent yet real; burrowing into a far-off past in the ever more futile hope of continuing to avoid the nearer one.

She threw back the covers and sat on the edge of her bed for a moment. Her left foot was bisected by a sliver of light cast upon the rough, green indoor-outdoor carpeting by the space between the window ledge and the bottom of the curtain. It was a half day of waiting, that was all. There was no cause for anxiety. She had had other days just like it.

But this one was different. This one had made itself significant.

She washed and dressed herself and combed her hair and made some breakfast, which she couldn't eat.

Maria, waiting, watching the clock, noting the slow rise of tension in her body, remembered summer hollyhocks taller than she and bees drunk with pollen, bumping dizzily in and out of the blossoms.

She lived now in a small, dim apartment in the basement of a house in Abbotsford, a town forty miles east of Vancouver. The house was owned by an elderly woman who, along with her large, kindly dog, occupied the upstairs. Maria liked it that she was elderly and had taken a motherly interest in her tenant—it made her feel young by contrast.

She moved around her apartment, picking things up and putting them down, trying to divest herself of a gathering excitement. She must not allow herself, yet, to think ahead. Once again she nudged the future aside with remembrances.

In Manitoba September was an eye blink. Leaves felt the chill of autumn and turned in confusion, turned red and gold, turned to admire themselves, became detached from their trees, and fluttered to the ground, dead.

And new clothes for school. Maria remembered that about September, too. In Winnipeg in grade two she had had to wear a uniform. A navy blue jumper, a long-sleeved white shirt, navy blue socks, a navy blue tie—even navy blue bloomers. And a Red River coat, which was navy blue with a red lining and had a hood.

As the morning passed, Maria could almost see the accretion of her anticipation, building upon itself like layers of oil paint upon a canvas or plaster upon a wall.

Sometimes in Manitoba Easter came late enough to coincide with spring, and she could wear her new black patent-leather shoes with buckles to church on Easter Sunday. Then Maria sprang along the street, bootless, her feet light as sparkling dreams, dancing between the puddles and getting not a single spot of mud on her shoes, which her mother had cleaned with Vaseline. . . . That was perhaps not a genuine memory, the Vaseline, but something she had just now invented. It was very difficult, sometimes, to separate real things from events she had partially manufactured, things she had made neat, or meaningful, in retrospect.

Maria's apartment comprised a long, narrow living room with no windows, the bedroom, and a kitchen with a table and two chairs at one end and stove and refrigerator and counters at the other. The kitchen, like the bedroom, had one small window. A door led from the living room directly outdoors into the backyard, where sidewalks extended from either side of a small patio and curved around the house to the street. The sidewalk that Maria used passed beneath the elderly woman's bedroom window. A second door in her apartment gave access to the basement laundry room. The elderly woman kept her outside doors locked, but not the one at the top of the basement stairs. Maria kept both of hers locked, always, even when she was at home.

Oh! those geraniums on the windowsill! They had had thick stems and had lived for years in the same pots. Even when they weren't blooming they were comforting, a familiar presence, a greening, breathing piece of life looking out upon the winter and pronouncing it temporary. They had a smell, too, of earth and cultivation—not a fragrance, but a smell to be inhaled with gusto, like the commonplace aromas of kitchen and dust—life-affirming counterpoints to the dry and foreign odor of winter.

Maria looked at her watch.

She sat down at the desk in her living room, turned on the lamp, and took from a drawer a piece of paper on which was written a list of chores: "dust with feather duster, dust with oiled cloth, dust walls with dry mop, scrub toilet, scrub bathroom sink, scrub kitchen sink, clean out fridge, sweep floors, vacuum carpets, change bed, polish windows," etc., etc. The idea was to pick one, at random, whenever she found herself with time on her hands.

Today, though, looking at the list only increased her impatience. She folded the piece of paper and put it back in her desk drawer.

In Winnipeg the school playground had been made of cinders. She had fallen there once, while playing a running game and had skidded on her side, badly skinning her left arm and leg. She ran home screaming and her mother put her in a warm bath and gently, gently, squeezed the washcloth over Maria's damaged flesh, adding hot water whenever the bath cooled, talking, soothing. Gradually all the black cinder-flecks and all the red blood-bubbles disappeared into the water. Maria had believed that day that her mother loved her.

Maria got up from the desk and went into the bedroom, where she knelt before a straight-backed chair that was wedged into the corner nearest the window. On the chair sat a large doll that had been given to Maria on her fifth birthday. She had twice during Maria's childhood been to the doll hospital. She looked now, at age fifty, almost as good as new.

"It's over, Bonnie," Maria whispered to the doll, which had curly brown hair, large blue eyes that swiveled, and pink-painted cheeks. She was wearing blue-and-white-checked overalls and a white blouse.

"I've decided," said Maria, sitting on her heels, examining the doll's face intently. With two fingers she stroked its cheek, and the upturned nose, and the pink mouth that looked like a rosebud.

The school principal in Winnipeg had had an artificial hand, fist-shaped, that always wore a glove—a leather-covered lump at the end of his arm that was the result of a war injury. The principal wore no expression. Not even when he called for a fire drill. The fire escapes were big round chutes. The teacher sent the children down one by one. It was perfectly dark in there. Maria had wondered, what if somebody behind her were to go too fast and crash into her? What if she went too fast herself and crashed into somebody ahead of her? What if she stalled in the middle and she was the last one down and everybody forgot about her and she had to spend the night in the fire escape? But none of those things ever happened. Sliding fast on her seat in the dark down the fire escape she sometimes felt like she was flying and sometimes like she was plummeting into hell. When she got to the bottom, breathless and triumphant, another teacher hauled her out and she waited with the other children in the cold, in the snow, shivering, until the whole class had caromed out of the fire escape, one by one, like blind docile bats.

Maria stood and looked down at the doll, resting her hand for a moment on its springy brown hair. Then she went into the kitchen to finish her waiting.

It was very quiet upstairs. She heard no murmurings—only silence from the old woman. And the dog, who spent most of his time sleeping, as far as Maria could tell. Her landlady had explained that this was because he was deaf. Maria tried to imagine herself deaf—a terrifying prospect. She was certain she would sleep a great deal less, not more, if she were to become deaf.

The furnace and the refrigerator turned themselves on

and off with soothing regularity. The house creaked and groaned a bit, suffering from arthritis in the rafters or rheumatism in the joists: that was soothing, too. Yet Maria's mouth was dry and her skin prickled with tension.

There was no wind today, and she couldn't hear any birds. She heard no sounds from the street, either, but then she hardly ever did, since her apartment was at the back of the house.

Maria placed her hands on the tabletop and spread them like fans. Her fingernails were painted with pink polish. She thought about the man who owned the stationery store on Essondale Avenue where she had for the last couple of years been working part-time, the young man with the limp, whose black hair had been invaded by a disfiguring thatch of white. She imagined her hand with the pink nails reaching out, the fingertips resting lightly for just a second on his white hair, imagined his hair turning black again and his limp disappearing.

Someone crunched along the walk at the side of the house, passing the window above her head. Maria got up and went to the door, stood with head bowed until the courier knocked, signed for the envelope, closed the door. She took the envelope back to the table and sat down. Her name and address were typed on the front. She opened it and took out the bank draft. "Pay to the Order of Maria Buscombe," it read, "Twenty Thousand Dollars."

Next she took out the photograph. She held it in her two hands, staring at it hungrily. She saw a young woman wearing shorts, standing just outside a shop, looking toward it, shading her eyes from the sun. Dark brown hair fell down her back. Her left leg was supporting most of her weight; the knee of her right leg was bent. Another person stood just inside the shop, a streak of sunlight illuminating trousered legs, the rest of the figure in shadow. Maria kissed the photograph, weeping, and set it down on the table. Then she picked up the check and tore it in half, then quarters, and threw it into the trash.

SECHELT, B.C.

Belinda Hollister went into the bedroom to snatch a sweater from the closet and on her way out of the room glanced through the window. She stopped. Looked. Threw open the sliding glass door that led to the crumbling patio and the backyard and stared in disbelief. Trash littered the weedy lawn. At first Belinda thought a dog must have gotten into their garbage. But Raymond had put out the garbage the previous evening, and it was picked up early in the morning. Besides, she thought, walking hesitantly across the patio, she didn't recognize anything in this mess. There was an old iron, its cotton-covered cord mangled. A man's shirt, striped blue and white, with a hole in the elbow. A crumpled orange juice carton, a multitude of eggshells and coffee grounds, several wire hangers, some magazines. Belinda seized a broom from the patio and began poking around in the clutter, looking for ripped-open envelopes. But she found nothing to identify whose garbage it was.

Belinda's father operated an unconventional shop that was actually the front half of a house, a bungalow that had once been his parents' home. He had rented it out during his years as a teacher, most of which had been spent in Vancouver, and had intended to live in it when he moved back to Sechelt. But a house on the hilltop overlooking Porpoise Bay, at the southern end of Sechelt Inlet, had caught his fancy. Soon he had decided that being retired wasn't very interesting, and he'd had the idea to turn his parents' house into a shop.

Behind the store proper was a kitchen, a dining room now furnished as a sitting room, and a bedroom that was used as a storeroom.

Belinda's father refused to sell lottery tickets, but he did carry tobacco products. "If you're intent on catering to people's addictions," Belinda had once said, exasperated, "you oughtn't to be selective about them." He would sell beer and wine, too, he had retorted, if that were allowed, but never lottery tickets.

A sign hung from a rose-covered trellis that arched over the sidewalk by the front gate: "The Jolly Shopper." There were no signs in the windows, no advertisements plastered on the glass.

The shop had unusual hours, too. It was open from ten in the morning until only four in the afternoon, and it was closed on weekends and holidays.

But Belinda's father carried, at his customers' requests, things that were hard to get elsewhere in Sechelt. Bread and milk were available at the Jolly Shopper, but so was caviar. And sun-dried tomatoes packed in oil. And hearts of palm.

Although he wouldn't accept credit cards, her father did extend credit, keeping track of what people owed him in a spiral-bound notebook. In this respect, he told Belinda, though not in any other, his shop was like a corner store he had worked in during the summers when he was a boy living in Sechelt.

He didn't make any money—but he didn't lose money, either—and as Belinda liked to say, the store kept him off the streets. She helped him out sometimes, on the weekends, and he hired a couple of neighborhood teenagers, too.

It was two o'clock by the time Belinda had cleaned up the back lawn and walked through the village to the store. On the way she greeted several people she knew and was struck again by the smallness of the place. It was beautiful, Sechelt, sure it was—but it was also killingly small.

Inside the Jolly Shopper, sunlight streamed onto the black-and-white-tiled floor and slid along the aisles, which were unusually wide. Wooden signs hung from the ceiling—"Cleaning Supplies," "Canned Goods," "Magazines"—written in the same flowing script as "The Jolly Shopper" sign outside: Belinda's father had had them done by an acquaintance, now retired, who used to teach shop at the local high school. They were carved, polished, and laminated.

He was behind the counter, talking quietly to a small woman wearing jeans and a white sweater who was listing to her right side because of an enormous denim bag that sagged from her left shoulder.

"Okay then, well—*you* tell *me*," the woman said. Belinda's father removed several items from the red wire basket that was sitting on the counter between them: cigarettes, a bag of chips, a copy of the *National Enquirer*.

"That's it?" said the woman.

"That's it."

"Okay then." The woman pulled a string bag from her pocket and packed it with the items that remained in the basket. Belinda saw cans of vegetables go in, and a loaf of bread, some tins of tuna and salmon, a carton of cottage cheese.

She studied her father carefully while he wrote in the credit book. He was definitely aging. The skin of his neck was loose. Behind his face lay the shadow of the crumpled face he'd wear ten years from now. His fringe of dark hair had become almost completely gray. His shoulders were slightly bent, he had no waist, and there was a plumpness upon his once elegant fingers that caused her particular sorrow.

The woman left the store, carrying the string bag in her right hand and listing considerably less.

Belinda's father turned his smiling blue eyes upon her.

"What are you staring at?" He said it good-humoredly, though. He was used to Belinda's gaze, which she knew others sometimes found intrusively direct.

"Nothing," she said. "You need to get some exercise."

"I do. In my garden."

"No, I mean seriously."

"So do I."

Her father perched on the tall stool he kept back there and rested his feet on the top rung. On a shelf below the counter, out of sight, a radio tuned to the CBC's FM station played softly. There was no one in the shop but Belinda and her father. He was gazing at her expectantly, but now that she was here Belinda was reluctant to tell him her news.

She leaned on the glass counter and looked through it at a neat display of gum, chocolate bars, and candy. "It's a good thing you didn't have this place when I was a kid."

"You want a chocolate bar?"

Belinda shook her head. "Dad—how come you didn't have any other kids but me?"

Belinda knew exactly what would happen now. Her father lifted his left hand and smoothed it over his head, carefully stroking front to back, over the bald spot and down across the fringe, and then he grasped the back of his neck and kneaded it. Performing this action required him to look down, away from Belinda.

"We were afraid we might not get it perfect twice in a row," he replied, as he had every one of the dozens of times she had asked the question. There was some weariness in his voice.

Belinda turned her head to look out the window. A feeling of unutterable melancholy had seized her. It was sickening, how profoundly life could change. It had been like having a volcano or a tornado happen. A natural disaster of some kind had picked her up, held her upside down, shaken her energetically, and then dropped her on her head. The world had not been the same since.

"You have to put it behind you, Belinda," said her father softly.

"I have. I did. But it keeps coming back."

Belinda could see an inch of white, almost hairless skin between the gray sock on his left foot and the bottom of his pant leg. There wasn't a similar gap on the right leg.

"I'm pregnant, Dad."

A look of awe blossomed on his face. He slid off the stool and reached across the counter to take her hands. It was a completely spontaneous gesture, so tender, so uncharacteristic, that Belinda, laughing, began to weep.

"Oh, honey," said her father. "Sit down."

"Where?" Belinda laughed again. "Dad, look at me." She freed her hands and held her arms away from her sides. "I'm as strong as a horse. Listen. I haven't told Raymond. I don't know if I'm going to have it."

He seemed bewildered, as if he hadn't understood her words. And then he did understand. "Belinda," he said urgently. "Please quit your job." He kept on talking, raising his voice over her protests. "Nothing has happened the way it was supposed to." He wiped the back of his hand across his forehead as if he were sweating, but the day wasn't warm enough for that. "Nothing. Nothing!" He ignored Belinda, who was shaking her head, having heard this before. "You weren't supposed to end up answering phones in a damned hospital," he said. "You were supposed to go to university. And then you got married. Far too young, *far* too young, *and* you married beneath you."

"Oh, Dad," Belinda said impatiently. "Don't be silly. I don't deserve Raymond, for heaven's sake. He's too good for me."

"Now—at least do this thing right, Belinda."

"It's all this—stuff." She felt so strong, outside. Yet inside, she was all mush. "This leftover—crap. I'm not ready to be a mother." She lifted her eyebrows. "It's totally ridiculous."

Her father came out from behind the counter and put his arms around her. She rested her cheek against his shoulder and let her eyes close. She put her arms around his middle, resting them where his hips ought to have been. She could have counted on her fingers the number of times in her life that her father had hugged her. "You haven't put it behind you, either, Dad."

"I've started to." He pulled away. There was eagerness in his face and a freshness that made Belinda resentful and surly. "I've been thinking about taking some action," he said. "And this news of yours—"

He looked at her curiously, with busy eyes. His cheeks were flushed. Trepidation stole over Belinda, and she wanted to go home.

"Come on," he said abruptly.

He led Belinda through the shop and into the sitting room. There was a sofa in there, and two chairs, and a desk and a filing cabinet, and a worktable. On the table were several of the cardboard cartons upon which years earlier he had wielded a savage felt pen: they were labeled "chest of drawers," "night table," "closet," "desk."

"I thought you'd gotten rid of this stuff." Belinda was surprised that she could speak: her throat had closed at the sight of those boxes.

"Couldn't. Wasn't ready." His eyes were blazing. "But I'm ready now."

Belinda stared at the boxes. She almost expected to be able to see right through the cardboard. She remembered a soft white sweater with pearl buttons. Black ankle boots. A green-and-black-plaid woolen scarf.

"Dad." Belinda's heart began to hammer in her chest. She put her hands over her mouth.

"I'm going to go through them all," he said. "Every single box."

"Dad." She thought—inexplicably—of the garbage strewn across the lawn.

"And then I'm going to find her."

Belinda moved to stand face-to-face with him. "Dad. No." The bell over the front door jangled as someone came into the shop. Belinda's father nodded, affirming his decision, and left to wait on his customer.

Alone with the boxes, Belinda was paralyzed with fear. She struggled, broke free, and backed out of the sitting room.

"Belinda!" called her father at the edge of her vision, but she hurried past him, her eyes fixed on the street beyond.

ABBOTSFORD

Maria Buscombe knelt again in front of the doll. I have nothing to lose, she told herself. It was a brand-new thought.

She took her rising excitement into the kitchen and made a pot of coffee.

She saw herself as radioactive. Potentially contaminative. So she would have to be fastidiously cautious.

But she could do it.

Twenty thousand dollars a year for ten years, in exchange for her absence. That was the agreement.

Only seven years had passed.

But Maria was opting out.

Chapter 2

The Sechelt Peninsula lies along the southwestern flank of British Columbia, sheltered by the coastline against which it nestles on one side and by the lumbering presence of Vancouver Island to the west. It is almost completely surrounded by the waters of the Pacific Ocean, linked to the mainland at its center by a strip of land less than a mile wide. Here the village of Sechelt is located, halfway along the stretch of shoreline that is known as the Sunshine Coast. It is bracketed by the waters of the Strait of Georgia to the south and Sechelt Inlet to the north.

The highway that passes through Sechelt ambles northeast to the end of the peninsula, where a ferry travels across Jervis Inlet to Powell River, and southwest through Gibsons to Langdale and another ferry route, this one to Horseshoe Bay, near Vancouver.

Autumn sunshine glints from the red bark of arbutus trees, strikes sparks from the blue sea, and bathes the islands dotting the Strait of Georgia in a dreamlike haze. The days grow shorter, their summer-warm afternoons sandwiched between suddenly cool mornings and evenings. But gardens continue to produce tomatoes and roses, zucchini and chrysanthemums, cucumbers and dahlias: the fruiting and the flowering won't stop until frost, which might come in November, or in December, or not at all.

Chapter
3

Karl Alberg was thinking about early retirement that Wednesday morning. Sometimes, like now, these were cheerful thoughts. Having a whole lot of spare time, for travel and . . . whatever; it might not be so bad, he told himself, pulling away from the RCMP detachment. As he passed the Jolly Shopper it occurred to him that he might even get himself a second career, like the schoolteacher. Maybe he'd open up a ship chandlery somewhere.

Not here, though.

As Alberg drove along the highway next to Davis Bay, he tried not to admit how difficult it would be, after twelve years here, to leave the Sunshine Coast.

It was midmorning when Alberg and Cassandra Mitchell, on the *Queen of New Westminster*, wrapped their jackets around them and went out on deck. The mountainous coastline and the hilly islands thrusting skyward were swathed in green that held glimpses of red and gold, and a shallow fog bank skimmed the surface of the sea.

Alberg put his arms around Cassandra and rested his chin on the top of her head. He felt protective of her, and for the moment she was allowing this. She habitually stood closer to him, now, than she used to, which both pleased and worried him.

From Horseshoe Bay the highway wound southeast toward Vancouver, passing north of the city through the municipalities of West Vancouver and North Vancouver. It crossed Burrard Inlet as the Second Narrows Bridge, bisected the city of Burnaby and skirted New Westminster, then swept into the Fraser Valley.

Alberg and Cassandra were on their way to Calgary. They were driving a rented car, which they would leave at the Calgary airport on Sunday. Cassandra wasn't looking forward to the flight home—she would feel claustrophobic, she knew it. But at least it was only for an hour.

In the valley, a median separated the east- and westbound lanes, a wide strip of rolling land, elegantly treed, where daffodils proliferated in the spring. It was nearing noon. They had driven forty miles inland. The mists had evaporated, the sky was a deeper blue, and the sun was hot.

They edged past the towns of Langley, Fort Langley, Aldergrove, and Abbotsford, and Alberg peered with new interest at what he could see of each place. Could he and Cassandra live here? he wondered. Or there? They were pretty towns. He tried to imagine them occupying one of the houses that sprawled up the mountainside near Abbotsford. But couldn't.

On the way to Chilliwack Cassandra gazed out the window at fields of corn and blueberry bushes and expansive dairy farms. The land stretched rich and languid to the mountains, fertile land where once had sprawled an enormous lake.

From Chilliwack the highway ascended and for the first time looped close to the Fraser River, wide and silver, and then it veered away at the town of Hope and offered drivers a choice among the Fraser Canyon Highway, the Coquihalla, or the Hope-Princeton.

Alberg chose the Coquihalla, which soared and swooped northeast through the mountains, traveling high. Halfway to the town of Merritt, Cassandra spotted in the rapidly approaching distance a small bear standing transfixed by the side of the freeway; by the time they reached him he had turned and run, and as they sped past he was scrambling up the mountainside, displaying, thought Cassandra, the traction of a small tank. From Merritt they continued on to Kamloops, a small city on the Thompson River surrounded by brown hillsides and sagebrush, where they would spend the night. Alberg had been posted there before getting the Sechelt assignment. His marriage had ended in Kamloops. It seemed like another lifetime.

They found a motel room that had glass doors opening onto a grassy bank from which they could look down upon the river, and after dinner they sat out there, on lawn chairs provided by the management.

"This is good," said Alberg, his hands behind his head. "This is very good." He knew he would miss the sea, but maybe a river would do. Or a lake. He'd learned to sail on a lake, after all. Admittedly, that was Lake Ontario, which was damn near big enough to be called an ocean.

His left arm was burned, Cassandra noticed, despite the sunblock. "Have you decided on a present yet?" she asked him.

Alberg sighed. "Nope."

"Karl. For God's sake. The wedding's in three days." It was the wedding of his elder daughter, Janey.

He opened his eyes to gaze at the river and the rapidly darkening western sky.

"Did you talk to Maura?" The name of Alberg's ex-wife felt awkward in Cassandra's mouth, like a foreign phrase she wasn't sure how to pronounce.

"Something's come over Maura," said Karl regretfully, "since she got married again. She's not as nice as she used to be."

Cassandra laughed.

"How the hell am I supposed to figure out what to get for them?" Alberg complained. "She's marrying a total stranger."

It became very hot in Kamloops in the summertime. It had been very hot that day, in fact, even though it was late September. But now the air had cooled, and Cassandra smelled autumn. "I think I have to go inside, Karl." It was a request. She could not yet bear to be alone.

He stood immediately and pulled her to her feet. He put his arms around her and held her close. She knew that he took it for granted, now, that they'd be getting married eventually. She wondered if this was true.

They went inside together. Cassandra closed the door and pulled the curtains, and Alberg turned on the television.

"Maybe you should give them silver," she said.

Alberg looked confused. "Silver?"

"Flatware. Knives and forks and spoons."

"Do people do that anymore?" he said doubtfully.

"I think so."

He sat on the edge of the bed and thought about it.

"It'll be from the two of us, of course," she said. "I'd like to pay half."

"You mean, in a wooden box?" Where the hell had that come from? he wondered. And then remembered such a box sitting on the buffet in his parents' dining room. In fact, it still sat there. Only it was just his mother's dining room now.

"Maybe," said Cassandra. She was bent over slightly, arranging things on her night table: her diary, the special ballpoint pen she used to write in it, the three books she'd brought from the library.

"Did you check those books out on your card?" said Alberg curiously. "Have you even *got* a library card?"

She shot him an indignant glance. "Of course I have."

"I thought it might be a perk," he said. "I thought maybe you got to sashay out of there with any book you wanted, whenever you felt like it."

"Fix your mind on the subject at hand." She straightened and ran her hand through her short, curly hair, and Alberg smiled at its springiness and the silvery glints in it. "How about it? Flatware. What do you think?"

Alberg tried to imagine Janey and the musician years from now, having a house, and a dining room, and family gatherings. Having kids. He and Maura hadn't had any silver. "I don't even know this guy she's marrying," he grumbled.

"I'm becoming impatient with you," said Cassandra. She gathered up her nightclothes. "I'm going to have a bath."

She hesitated, and he smiled reassuringly. "Don't worry. I'll be here." He would make a point of calling out to her, casually, every so often, so that she would know that he was there, and she was safe.

As he prepared for bed, Alberg was pleased with himself. Seldom that day had he thought of work. It would be difficult to leave, sure. But not impossible. Here he was, hundreds of miles away from the detachment and perfectly happy. Of course, he knew it was in good hands. And there wasn't much going on, at the moment. Although the vandalism bothered him. That's why he'd gone in that morning, before he and Cassandra headed for the ferry. He'd been thumbing through the reports when Sid Sokolowski had loomed into view in his office doorway.

"What are you doing?" said the sergeant, exasperated. He had recently acquired reading glasses and enjoyed peering over them. He was peering now, and an expression of disapproval was establishing itself firmly on his face.

"Take a look at these, will you?" Alberg handed over the reports, and Sokolowski flipped through them. Alberg took off his own glasses and slid them into his jacket pocket. "It's getting more frequent and more aggressive," he said.

"I'll look into it," said the sergeant heavily.

Alberg looked at him more closely. "You're sure you're going to be all right?" Sokolowski's wife, Elsie, had recently left him, a state of affairs the sergeant found as bewildering as it was painful.

"Yeah," he said. "I'll be fine. Work's the best thing."

Not always, thought Alberg now, listening to Cassandra splashing in the bathtub. Sometimes a holiday was the best thing. And retirement—who knows—might be even better. "How're you doing in there?" he called out.

"Fine," she called back.

Maybe she'd start to sing, he thought hopefully. That would be a sure sign of recovery.

He kept listening but heard only splashing and then the sound of the tub draining.

The next day they drove east through range after range of mountains. In the national parks a small white flag had been planted wherever an animal had blundered onto the highway, been struck by traffic, and blundered off, to die: there was a forest of small white flags. High wire fences had been raised wherever possible to keep elk and moose and mountain goats and mountain sheep from wandering onto the road. Yet twice Alberg pressed hard on the brakes to avoid elk, who moved regally out of the woods and across four lanes of pavement, in front of several cars that had managed to stop in time. "Christ," said Alberg, watching the huge animals disappear into the forest on the opposite side of the highway.

From the eastern boundary of Banff National Park the

land descended rapidly, becoming rolling foothills and then prairie. It was late afternoon and the sun slanted rich and golden upon Calgary. Alberg observed again that there was something different about the light in southwestern Alberta. More than mere illumination, it had substance and texture. It existed in and of itself, as tangible as if it had taste and fragrance.

He had suggested that they stay in one of the downtown hotels, but Cassandra, although she at first agreed, had changed her mind by the time they reached the city. "I want to stay in something that's only one story high," she said firmly.

"You got it," said Alberg, and he headed for a motel on Sixteenth Avenue.

When they were settled in their room Alberg called Maura, to ask if anybody else was giving Janey silver, and learned that his attendance was required the following afternoon at a wedding rehearsal.

"The stores are open late tonight," he said to Cassandra when he was off the phone. "I guess we better go shopping."

They bought a sterling silver service for four, in a pattern the salesperson assured them would be available throughout eternity.

Chapter

4

ABBOTSFORD

Probably she was no longer watched. Not after seven years. But if she ever was, thought Maria, this was the most likely time—right after the arrival of the check.

So for a couple of days she did nothing. This was extremely difficult. She felt a strong sense of urgency.

(The knock on her door had reverberated through the house like thunder. She had looked through the window—and there he stood: her unlikely nemesis.)

On Friday morning Maria sat on the sofa with her photo album. She studied each page intently, as if she'd never seen it before, and then she added the new picture.

(He had come to threaten her, or that's what he thought; but instead he had brought salvation.)

Maria closed the album. For a few seconds she looked at the wall, at nothing.

Sitting in her small apartment, seven years having vanished like early morning mist, Maria looked blindly into the past and acknowledged that she had done wrong. She had tried to protect herself and her daughter, but she had failed them both; she knew that now. She had had a failure of courage. Realizing this, it was now as though she had awakened from a troubled sleep, relieved to escape a nightmare, only to be told that she had murdered in the night.

SECHELT

In front of a small house on a large lot on the outskirts of town, Belinda's husband, Raymond, was washing the maroon-and-silver cab of his Mack truck, whose name—"Buster"—was written in elegant script on each of the doors. Raymond, who was twenty-five, was a couple of inches short of six feet tall and had long legs and broad shoulders. He was wearing a T-shirt, baggy sweatpants, and running shoes, and he was scrubbing that truck, making it gleam, making it shine, polishing it for the trip to Penticton later that morning.

Raymond, laboring, was getting hard, as usual, which was why he was wearing the baggy sweatpants. He wondered if anybody else in the world got turned on by washing his goddamn truck. He tried to think of something else, but no dice. The sunlight fractured itself in the chrome, blinding him for an instant, and Raymond polished harder—and then the front door of the house opened and Belinda came outside, wearing jeans and a denim shirt, carrying a tray.

Raymond stopped, startled. "What's this?"

"Coffee and a cinnamon bun."

"For me?"

"Who else?"

Raymond sat on the front step. "Thanks, hon," he said, and started eating, taking glances at Belinda, who had sat down on the lawn, just out of his reach. She pushed her long brown hair away from her forehead and stretched out her legs in front of her. Raymond liked to look at Belinda in profile. He liked to be able to look at her and think about her at the same time, which wasn't really possible when she was looking back at him. There was something disconcerting about the way Belinda regarded people. Her gaze was so direct that it was alarming even to Raymond.

"What're you going to do while I'm gone?" he said.

She drew her feet toward her and sat cross-legged, plucking at the dry brown grass. "You're only going to be away for a day, Raymond. And I work tonight."

She sounded preoccupied, and this worried him. Belinda's powerful directness was something easily used as a shield. She was reticent—Raymond was the talker in the family. And he often felt that his reach, when he tried to get her to open up to him, was clumsy.

He slid to the end of the step and put his hand on her back, firmly, wanting her to feel reassured. A few seconds passed before she turned to him.

"I don't want to cause you distress, Raymond."

He nodded, as if he understood. He felt cold, despite the warmth of the day, and found that this time he didn't want her to open up.

Bewildered, Raymond put his arm around his wife and pulled her close.

CALGARY, ALBERTA

At lunch that day Cassandra said to her brother, Graham, "What's it like, being in your fifties?"

He ate some of his linguine with clams and then laughed. "That's right. It's coming up in a few weeks, isn't it? The big five oh."

His face was a touch florid, she noticed, and more wrinkled than when she had last seen him; but his hair was still thick and dark. Maybe he dyed it.

"You worry about your retirement, your old age," said Graham. "That's what the fifties are all about."

"It sounds like a hoot," said Cassandra dryly, dragging her spoon through her clam chowder. She imagined she heard her mother's voice, telling her not to play with her food. A very old memory.

Graham looked at her more closely. "I hope it's okay to ask this, but—are you all right now, Cassandra?" He was eyeing her uneasily across the table. "It's hard to tell, just talking on the phone."

He looked concerned, she granted him that. And he probably *was* concerned, since he'd driven all the way down from Edmonton to see her. But he also looked furtively curious. It was an expression Cassandra had seen on other faces. He was wondering exactly what had happened to her.

"Yes. I'm all right." There was no need to tell him that she couldn't be alone.

"What an awful thing," said Graham, shaking his head.

Cassandra, when she had to refer to it, told her story in one sentence: "I was abducted by a psychopathic librarian." Abducted, kept prisoner, bizarrely courted by a person of wealth and intelligence who also happened to be insane. Now, watching her brother eating his pasta, she thought Graham was probably one of those people who couldn't help but think that whatever had happened to her had been in some measure her own fault.

"Are you getting therapy?" her brother asked.

Cassandra ducked her head to hide her anger and concentrated on her salad. "I don't need therapy," she said flatly. "What I need is to see the son of a bitch thrown in jail for the rest of his natural life. Which I'm sure will happen. When are you coming out to see Mom?"

"We thought we'd invite her to come to us for Christmas."

"A good idea whose time has passed," said Cassandra. "She's afraid to travel alone now."

"Oh, come on, Cassandra. You'd take her to the airport there, we'd pick her up here—nothing to it."

"You think her heart condition's gone into remission, after eighteen years?" she snapped.

"I think she's found a way to live with it," he said. "I don't think you give her enough credit."

Cassandra put down her spoon. Graham and Millie hadn't been to Sechelt for three years. Her mother hadn't been to Edmonton for five. Cassandra brushed at her lap and looked at her watch. "I think I'd like a martini," she said to her brother.

ABBOTSFORD

Maria took only one precaution: she left in the middle of the night. In the afternoon she cleaned out her bank account and rented a car, no longer concerned about being traced, and parked it a couple of blocks away. She packed her things in bags and boxes during the evening. Shortly after midnight, when she knew the elderly woman would be asleep, she moved the car to the front of the house and loaded it. She left a note and a check on the kitchen table and at 2:00 A.M., Maria drove away.

From her bedroom window, the landlady watched her leave.

It was shortly after three when Maria left the Upper Levels Highway and weaved her way south down the mountainside into West Vancouver.

She parked in a narrow street and sat still for a moment, collecting herself and visualizing this collection process, which was a gathering together of her several lives. She would live them all concurrently, for once, and then bring them all to a tidy, concurrent end: it was what she should have had the boldness to do seven years earlier.

She started to get out of the car—then thought: What if he's moved? What if she knocked on his door in the middle of the night and roused somebody else, roused a stranger?

Maria closed the door and hugged herself. There were bound to be snags, unforeseen events around which she would have to improvise. She would wait in her car.

Such tunnels of danger she must push herself through. Like the fire escapes in Winnipeg, she thought.

Later, in the gray beginning of the day, she stepped out of the car. She went through the gate and across a wide lawn, leaving a trail of footprints in the silvery dew, and down to the house. Nobody responded when she knocked on the door. But everything she saw through the windows was familiar, so at least he still lived there. He must be away, she thought. She would have to do things in reverse order, that was all. She retraced her steps, climbed into her car, and headed back up to the highway and the ferry terminal at Langdale.

She didn't notice the small blue car that followed her.

SECHELT

Three hours later, Maria collected the key to her new apartment and moved her bags and boxes inside, stumbling frequently on the stairway in her haste. When the last item had been unloaded she leaned against the locked door and closed her eyes, profoundly weary. Then she set to work, unpacking.

The suite was bright and sunny. From the living room balcony she could glimpse Trail Bay, and the bedroom looked out across rooftops to the wooded hillsides flanking the inlet. Maria wasn't interested in the view, however. She had never liked Sechelt.

The place was clean, too, and furnished just as the agent had described over the phone. Maria first laid the photo album on a shelf in the bookcase. Then she took a kitchen chair into the bedroom. She put it in a corner and carefully placed the doll on it, where she would be able to see it from the bed. She whispered to it for a moment, before putting her clothes away.

Maria was in the small kitchen, digging in the last remaining box in a search for the coffeepot, when she looked back at the doll, and the reality of what she had done struck her, hard. She was flooded with exultation and robbed of breath. She leaned heavily against the countertop, both hands pressed upon it, staring at the floor and seeing her daughter, seeing Belinda, glimpsed through windows, followed on the street. Belinda. Striding on strong brown legs, the sun igniting sparks of gold in her dark brown hair. Belinda. Twenty-one years old last month.

Maria turned and slumped against the countertop, wiping tears from her cheeks.

Chapter 5

Belinda, housecleaning the next day in preparation for Raymond's return, paused, several newspapers in her hand, and listened. But no. It was too early. She picked up another paper and dumped the pile of them in the recycling box.

She did the bathroom next. And then she dusted.

She stopped in the middle of her cleaning to acknowledge a fondness for many aspects of her present life. It was like the sixty seconds of silence offered up on Remembrance Day, though: a self-conscious moment of synthetic mourning. A mere pause, her attention elsewhere. Life really was a killer, she thought. One second there was still time; an instant passed—and it was too late.

Belinda rubbed her palms on her jeans, drying them, and lifted her hair away from her neck for a minute. She was sweating, even though it wasn't a hot day.

Their rented house was very small. It had a kitchen with a tiny eating area, a cramped living room, a bathroom, and two bedrooms, one of which Raymond occasionally referred to as the nursery—certainly a crib was about the only kind of bed it could have accommodated. They were using it now as a storage room. Poor Raymond, she thought, gazing in at the jumble of boxes and empty suitcases that lived there.

She closed the door on the clutter and started to work on the kitchen. When she'd cleaned the counters and the sinks and the top of the stove, she began polishing the window— and stopped again, to listen intently, her heart hovering somewhere between her chest and her throat . . . but no, she hadn't heard his truck.

The best thing about the house was the main bedroom, which was actually a sunporch. It was long and wide, and the top half of each of its outside walls was made of glass. One of Belinda's favorite things was making love with Raymond while lying in a pool of summer sun, with more sunlight streaming in upon them, licking at their skin: hot flickers of light and passion. She put her hand palm down in the middle of the mattress, let it rest there like a water lily on the blue sheen of the bedspread. She wondered who would be the next lover in her life.

She decided to pick up something at Earl's Café for dinner. Something Raymond would particularly enjoy.

Through the windows Belinda looked out upon their large backyard, fenced high on all sides. Fruit trees grew at the bottom of the garden: two cherries, an apple, and a plum. There were lilac bushes along one side and climbing roses along the other. Doors from the sunporch and the kitchen led out onto a disintegrating cement patio, next to which grew an acacia tree. The garden was overgrown, the grass was too tall, the flower beds near the house were flopped over and weedy.

Belinda, gazing from the sunporch, was impatient with this mess. She belonged in a small apartment somewhere in Vancouver. It would have a window overlooking a busy street, and maybe there'd be a decent Italian restaurant nearby. She'd put a desk under the window so that while she was studying, or whatever, she'd be able to glance up and watch life on the street below for a minute. . . .

She was suddenly invaded by a memory. It flooded into her head, evicting present and future, leaving only this fragment of the past.

She saw herself opening the door to her parents' bedroom. She must have been very young, for the door handle, which was made of glass, was above her head. She grasped it, turned it, pushed the door open a few inches, and peeked in. The big brass bed was on her right. Straight ahead was a window, with sheer white curtains hanging on either side. The window was halfway open, and a breeze made the curtains move. Belinda remembered a feeling of tranquillity, watching the curtains move. In front of the window was her mother's desk, a small one, made of mahogany, with a matching chair. Her mother was sitting on the chair, her back to Belinda, head bent, writing a letter. Belinda, clinging to the door handle, said, "Mommy." She had to say it again. And again. And still her mother had not heard her. Finally she said it very loud, with tears in her voice: "Mommy!" Her mother turned quickly around, and stared at Belinda for what felt like a very long time. Belinda thought for a minute that her mother had turned into a stranger—or else Belinda had: they didn't seem to know one another. And then something in her mother's face shifted, and Belinda's heart pounded with relief.

She didn't remember what had happened next.

Belinda passed a hand in front of her face, as if she'd collided with a cobweb.

She hauled out the vacuum cleaner and plugged it in. But then she had to sit down for a minute, because her legs were suddenly too weak to bear her weight.

Raymond, she thought, staring down at the carpet. Raymond.

★ ★ ★

He got home an hour later.

He bounded into his house and knew almost immediately that something was wrong. Maybe not wrong, he thought, staring at Belinda, but out of kilter.

It was the way she wasn't quite looking at him. She was standing in the kitchen doorway, and for a minute he thought there was somebody behind her. A vivid image entered his head of Belinda on her back, on their bed, with a faceless son of a bitch fucking her, and her legs were up over this guy's shoulders. This picture was so real that Raymond could for a long moment neither speak nor move. And then Belinda came close and laid a kiss upon his cheek. He smelled her shampoo and thought, She's washed her hair for me, and he buried his face in it.

"Hi," he said.

"Hi, Raymond."

Dinner was good—spaghetti and meatballs and garlic bread from Earl's—and afterward he lay on the sofa with his head in Belinda's lap while she watched the television news. He had told her all about his trip while they ate. He had also asked what she'd been up to in his absence, but she hadn't had much to say.

When the news was over he sat up and looked at her. "What's going on, Belinda?"

"What?"

"What's on your mind? Something is."

Belinda rubbed her hands together. Raymond had never seen her do that before. "I'm just preoccupied, Raymond. Thinking about stuff."

"What stuff?"

"Oh, I don't know."

Raymond was aware of the evening sun shafting through the living room window. He felt charged with vigilance, as if he would at any moment be called upon to protect his family. Belinda. He put his hand gently on her thigh. She was wearing jeans, and he couldn't feel the warmth of her body, but he felt its firmness. "What stuff, Belinda?" Finally she turned her head and looked directly into his eyes. He didn't turn away. He groped for courage, found it, clung to it, and said again—because he had to: "What stuff, Belinda?"

She picked up his hand and examined it. Raymond waited, helpless, wondering how to protect himself.

"The future," she said.

She was his true happiness.

Raymond, decisive, appropriated the moment. He said confidently, "In the future we will have kids." He was watching Belinda, utterly concentrated on her, meticulous in his observations. "Not too many. But not just one, either."

Belinda's shoulder lifted slightly in an expression of distaste. "That's not the kind of future I've been thinking about."

She was still holding his hand. Raymond made himself keep that hand relaxed. He wanted to open it and turn it over and take harsh hold of hers—but he kept it still, a willing captive.

"At times like Christmas, for instance, kids are good," he said. "Did I ever tell you about when I got a bike for Christmas?"

Belinda pushed his hand away and stood up. She knew that if she could just get it out, say it, he'd accept it. Men take you at your word, she thought. It's women who assume that there's a next step, which is negotiation.

"I was about eight," said Raymond. He was lying full length on the sofa now, his hands behind his head, looking up at the ceiling. "I had a room in the basement," he went on. "Did I ever tell you about my room?"

His voice was so full of tension, Belinda wanted to weep.

"I had this big tall chest of drawers," he said. "And an old moth-eaten bear rug."

Belinda sat on the end of the sofa, shoving his feet to one side. "Why are you doing this? What are you doing?"

Raymond lifted his head to look at her. He'd invented a hurt expression to put on his face, but behind it something else was happening. Belinda, seeing this, wondered: Does he know?

"I'm getting around to Christmas," he said. "And the bike. Okay?" He reached out and with his fingertips stroked Belinda's forearm, resting along the top of the sofa. "There I was, trying to get to sleep on Christmas Eve. My old dog Moe curled up fast asleep on the end of my bed."

"I never heard about your dog Moe," said Belinda irritably.

Raymond said, "There's a lot you don't know about me yet."

"Get to the damn bike," she said, standing up again.

"I'd been saving up for it," said Raymond. "But it was gonna be about 1982 before I had enough money, and by then I'd be ready for a car. So I told my old man I was going to ask Santa Claus for the bike, and use the money I'd saved to buy accessories for it."

"Is that what you said? 'Accessories'?" said Belinda.

"I was a smart kid," said Raymond. "I don't know what I said. So here's Christmas Eve and I'm in bed not sleeping." He was wearing a short-sleeved blue cotton shirt and the moccasins Belinda had given him. His eyes were brown, with lashes longer than Belinda's. She loved his eyes. And his mouth. She would never pretend that she didn't find him attractive. That wasn't why she was going to leave him.

"And then I heard a noise," said Raymond. "Feet, tiptoeing down the stairs. Jesus, I thought. It's Santa Claus."

Belinda, with a sigh, sat down on the old brown rocking chair.

"Then there was a lot of whispering out in the basement,"

said Raymond. "And somebody swore. So I got up and went over to my door and opened it just a crack."

"What was the damn dog doing?"

"Sitting on the bed, with his ears up. I peeked through the crack and there was my old man, trying to get a blue bike up the basement stairs. A pedal had got stuck underneath one of the steps."

Belinda wondered how long he would go on talking if she let him. He'd have to stop eventually. His voice would get hoarse. Or he'd tire himself out. Or he'd have to go to the bathroom.

"He'd hidden it behind the furnace," said Raymond. "It was the only place in the house I wouldn't go. Do you want to know why?"

"No." Belinda got up from the rocking chair and sat next to him on the sofa. She kissed the side of his face until he turned to her, and then she kissed his mouth, opening it with her tongue.

A reprieve, he thought, his hands slipping under her T-shirt. It's only a reprieve.

Chapter

6

CALGARY

The weather in southwestern Alberta defied accurate prediction. Alberg had once had another Member tell him that in his first tour of duty there it had snowed every month of the year. Not much in July and August, the guy had conceded. And it hadn't stuck to the ground.

But Chinooks happened, too, in southern Alberta: warm winds from the west that created a fleeting, midwinter spring.

And so did Indian summer.

Early Sunday afternoon Alberg and Cassandra drove east on Sixteenth Avenue, south on Deerfoot Trail until it ended, and then east again, beyond the city limits, along a two-lane highway straight and purposeful, and south once more, past bright yellow fields of fragrant canola and meadows where horses grazed. In the west, seventy-five miles away, the white crags of the Rocky Mountains paraded across the horizon like well-ordered sentries, shoulder to shoulder.

Alberg eventually pulled into a long driveway that led up a slight rise to a large house made of cedar: this was the home of the groom's parents. To the south, a row of poplars grew along the fence, their yellow leaves shuddering and sometimes relinquishing themselves to the breeze. The house was large, encircled by a wide deck that was crowded with people. Alberg groaned at the sight of them, and Cassandra, who was usually impatient with his lack of sociability, squeezed his hand sympathetically.

They left the car in a field that had been turned into a temporary parking lot and made their way up the driveway toward the open front door of the house.

Inside, the foyer was crowded with people holding glasses and talking animatedly. Alberg, uncomfortable in his tuxedo, looked through the foyer and the living room beyond, out to the deck, and there he saw Maura and the accountant she'd married. Cassandra was already moving through the crowd, and he followed her. In the living room they accepted glasses of champagne from a tray being ferried about by a smiling person in a waiter's uniform.

"Come on," said Alberg, heading for the deck. He went through the sliding doors and waited for Cassandra to catch up. "There's Maura," he said.

"Ah," said Cassandra. She had discovered that there was nothing like having been abducted by a psychopathic librarian to firm up one's perspective on life. Not only had she not been dreading this moment, she had actually been looking forward to it.

She followed Alberg to the edge of the deck, where his ex-wife and her husband were leaning on the railing and looking out at the garden, the lawn, and the fields of pale green grain beyond—Cassandra had no idea what kind of grain it was, but it seemed to be spreading all the way to the far-off mountains.

"Maura," said Alberg, with a heartiness that made Cassandra grin, and the woman turned, lifting a hand to hold back her hair, which the breeze wanted to blow across her face. She was taller than Cassandra and considerably thinner: an elegant woman, well dressed, stylishly coiffed, with green eyes that reminded Cassandra of the picture of his elder daughter—the bride—that Alberg kept on his dresser, along with one of Diana.

"Karl," said Maura warmly.

Cassandra felt a gleaming in her heart. She had been reluctantly respectful of this marriage-that-was. Now she knew a wistful affection for it, too.

"I'd like you to meet Cassandra Mitchell," said Alberg. "Cassandra, this is Maura Sullivan, who is the mother of my children."

He said this with such awkward solemnity that Cassandra knew he had given the moment a great deal of thought. She imagined him rehearsing in front of the bathroom mirror, moving his lips soundlessly so that she wouldn't hear.

"How do you do," they murmured to each other, she and Maura, and shook hands firmly.

"And this is my husband, Des," said Maura. He had a stocky, athletic build and an open, friendly face and was probably younger than his wife.

"Glad to meet you," said Alberg, stretching out his hand. "This is quite a day," said Des Sullivan. "Are you nervous?"

Alberg had been so preoccupied with the inevitable meeting between Cassandra and his ex-wife that he hadn't had time to worry about his role in the wedding. It was pretty straightforward, he thought, going through it in his mind. He just had to escort Janey up the aisle and stand there until—shit. He couldn't remember his cue to back off.

"You're damn right I'm nervous," he said fervently.

Soon his daughter Diana came to get him, wearing pink, with pink flowers in her hair. On the way to the room where Janey was waiting, she reminded him of the sequence of events. "You're not nervous, are you?" she asked, giving him a sideways glance.

"Of course not," said Alberg.

The bride wore a silky-looking dress of pale yellow and a tiara of tiny yellow flowers. Alberg, looking at her, couldn't speak. Janey put her arms around him, and he smelled an unfamiliar perfume. "Your gift is gorgeous, Daddy, absolutely gorgeous." He nodded at her, trying to smile.

From then on it was as if he were having an out-of-body experience.

The ceremony took place outdoors, on a large patio, beneath a trellis. There were huge vases of flowers, despite the ones still blooming on the trellis, and chairs had been set up for eighty people.

Alberg's responsibility ended early. He stepped back and allowed himself to relax. He was pleased with himself for getting it right. He began to feel like a kind man—magnanimous, even; possessing an abundance of love, tenderness, and generosity of spirit.

The sky arched gloriously blue above them, the benevolent sun lavished warmth upon them, and the music provided by four of the groom's colleagues swelled while the couple kissed, with a chasteness Alberg approved.

As Daniel Silverman escorted his new wife down the makeshift aisle, he caught Alberg's eye, held it, and gave him a slow, expressionless wink.

Chapter

7

Belinda was in her father's living room Saturday afternoon, watching him sort through the box marked "chest of drawers" that sat on the coffee table. There was a curious excitement in the air, created by her father's absorption in his task, an almost prurient excitement that Belinda found repellent. She was struggling to accept his bizarre behavior with detachment, but this was not possible: it endangered her. She had grown a skin over the hole torn in her life by her mother's departure, but it was thin, fragile protection.

He was sitting on the sofa, picking through her mother's clothes, taking his time about it. On the floor another box awaited his ministrations: Belinda couldn't see what was written on it.

She took her coffee mug into the kitchen and refilled it.

She still missed the china and cutlery familiar from her childhood. Even though this was not the house in which she had grown up, even though she had helped her father choose the contents of his kitchen, even though this had been accomplished years ago—still Belinda missed that everyday china, which had had some kinds of flowers splashed upon a white background. There were matching cream and sugar containers: the lid to the sugar bowl had a chip out of it, and two of the dinner plates were cracked.

The everyday cutlery was stainless steel. One soup spoon and two salad forks had gone missing over the years.

Then there was the best china, navy blue and gold, Royal Albert. It had remained intact and unbroken because it was used only on special occasions like Christmas and birthdays. The good silver was used then, too. Belinda had always loved cleaning the silver.

Her father had gotten rid of all of it, one way or another, immediately after her mother left. Belinda had thought he'd gotten rid of the personal stuff then, too.

Belinda was looking out the kitchen window, from which she could see her father's front lawn, the gravel driveway, and the winding road that led down the hill to the isthmus and across to Sechelt. Rosebushes bordered the driveway. When she'd arrived a couple of hours earlier, she had found her father leaning on a shovel, contemplating the roses.

He didn't own any casual clothes. In the garden, going for walks, he wore dress pants and shirts that had grown old or become worn, and narrow gray suspenders. And tennis shoes.

He had turned swiftly, startled, when he heard her sneakers crunching on the gravel. And then smiled, at Belinda in her khaki pants and red sweater. "Hi, sunshine," he said, and returned his attention to the garden. "I think I'm going to dig up the damn roses."

"Why?"

"Look at them. They've got black spot, they've got powdery mildew, they've got aphids."

"They've got a lot of flowers, though," said Belinda. "Aren't you supposed to spray them or something?"

"I've sprayed them every week since March," he said, and tossed the shovel to the ground.

Maybe I'll take some roses home, thought Belinda.

She returned to the living room.

Her father folded nightgowns. Handkerchiefs. Scarves. He worked in silence, deftly, adding to the neat piles he had created, one for the Salvation Army, one for the garbage.

"Dad."

"What?"

"I want to leave Raymond."

He looked up at her quickly. "Don't be silly. You're pregnant."

"For the moment, I'm pregnant."

Her father's face flushed so red that Belinda became alarmed. "I don't want to hear that," he said. "This is a human life you're talking about."

"Not yet, Dad. You can't call it a life yet."

"A human life. And it may be your child, but it's my grandchild." He struck his chest. Belinda felt embarrassed for him; and for herself, too.

The piles of clothing sat to his left and right, on the cushions of the sofa, which was upholstered in large red-and-white checks. Belinda, when she first saw the sofa, had thought it revolting. But now she admitted that her father had been right: it was a splotch of cheer that welcomed casual sprawling.

He picked up the pile to his left—panties, bras, slips, half slips, teddies, and panty hose in various colors—and dropped it into a plastic garbage bag. Belinda had recognized nothing so far. When he started going through stuff she recognized, that was when she'd be out of there.

Now she saw him pull from the box a pair of socks. He glanced at Belinda, and she knew he was going to ask her advice, but he changed his mind. He put the socks into the garbage bag and several more pairs as well. Then he turned the box over and shook it. A sachet fell upon the coffee table.

"What's that?" said Belinda's father.

She picked it up, sniffed but smelled nothing. "I made it for her. It was lavender." She tossed it into the garbage bag.

"Maybe there's a genetic defect operating here," said her father, studying her face.

"It isn't the same thing at all," Belinda said.

"No, it isn't. Instead of deserting your child, like your mother did, you plan to kill yours."

"That's not fair," said Belinda, steeling herself. Her father was not a person who became less articulate with anger. It was important not to quail before him.

But his anger passed, this time, as quickly as it had flared, leaving him pale and defenseless. He smoothed his bald head and tenderly stroked the fringe of hair that had been left him.

"It's made me sick to hear you talk this way," he said quietly. "I don't think what's going on here has anything to do with Raymond, with your marriage."

Belinda went to the big window and pressed her cheek against the glass. Tears leaked from her closed eyes. She concentrated on suppressing them—did the visualization thing, imagined two little taps, one in each eye; imagined turning them off. Then she opened her eyes and wiped her cheeks dry.

Through the window Belinda watched the long grass move in the breeze and saw a few golden leaves flutter to the ground from the birch trees that marked the edge of her father's property, and down at the bottom of the hill the sun flashed from the rough blue waters of Porpoise Bay.

A man climbed out of his car at Porpoise Bay, near where the seaplanes landed. He was of average height, with gray hair; middle-aged, but slim and athletic. He had a look on his face of total concentration as he crossed the parking lot and turned up the road that paralleled the inlet. The woman he had followed here was perhaps fifty yards ahead.

The man kept close to the brush at the side of the road, which consisted almost entirely of blackberry vines. He flinched the first time the thorns scraped his flesh but stayed where he was, only raising his arms to protect his face: he was wearing jeans, a long-sleeved shirt, and sneakers.

After a while he stepped out of the brush to glance up the road: the woman plodded on, oblivious. With a grimace, he pushed back into the blackberries.

Scratches soon appeared on the backs of his hands, his neck, and one side of his face. Chunks and fragments of blackberry vines clung to his clothing. Sweat broke out on his forehead.

Once more he pulled free and looked—the woman had stopped walking. She was leaning against the trunk of a maple tree about forty feet away.

Swiftly he propelled himself backward into the blackberries and stood completely still.

Several minutes passed. A car drove by, heading toward Sechelt. The midafternoon sun coaxed fragrance from the blackberries. A breeze muttered in the vine leaves, and birds chortled high in the maple tree.

Eventually the man turned, slowly, and squinted through the foliage. The woman was still leaning against the trunk of the tree, doing nothing. Then he saw her straighten and step out from behind the tree to stand at the edge of the road, looking northward, not moving.

Belinda was walking home from her father's house, back to Sechelt, when suddenly a woman appeared on the road from behind a huge old maple tree and pulled off a scarf that had been tied over her hair. Belinda stopped. The woman was about fifty yards away.

Belinda's body went into shock. She felt disoriented. Terrified.

She took a step backward. Her mother didn't move. Just stood there, staring at her—and Belinda saw brokenness in her face, and pain, and she saw that her mother, too, was terrified.

It was her mother all right. But Belinda had remembered her as being more commanding. This woman was small and thin to the point of frailness. And her mother had had black hair, but this woman's hair was almost completely silver.

The woman remained motionless.

Belinda turned around and hurried back up the road, back toward her father's house. She took fifteen long strides and then whirled around. Her mother still hadn't moved.

"Go away!" Belinda shouted. She felt enormous. She thought about Michelangelo's *David* and his hands, disproportionately large, capable of miracles. What would she do with her size, her strength?

Her mother was speaking.

"I can't hear you. Go away!"

Her mother spoke more loudly. Belinda heard "love," and "reason."

She turned around again and ran back up the road, pelted up the road, wishing she could fly. She sprinted around a corner and stopped, leaning forward to catch her breath, her hands on her thighs. Tears began dripping from her eyes, and fury clogged her throat.

Belinda got some tissues from the small zippered bag that was belted around her waist and dried her eyes and blew her nose. Then she marched determinedly back toward Sechelt. If her mother wanted a damn confrontation, well, Belinda would damn well give her one.

The edges of the road were dusty. Belinda noted this and was aware of the sun warming her back and the smell of ripe blackberries that tempted her from the roadside. But she disregarded dust, and sun, and blackberries. She had thousands of questions for her mother, and the fact that Maria had shown herself, Belinda was belatedly realizing, meant that she was prepared to answer them. Belinda was in a turmoil of rage and eagerness, and she began to run again, racing around the corner, and saw the road ahead, empty. She stopped. She heard birds calling, and a child shouted, somewhere far away. Belinda walked to the maple tree and looked behind it, but nobody stood there waiting for her.

Belinda leaned against the tree and looked up, through its many-layered branching, to the winks of sun and sky at the top. After a long time she began walking home.

The man in the blackberry bushes didn't breathe as she approached, slowly, her eyes on the ground. He thought she hesitated when she passed the place where he was hidden. He thought her body half turned toward him. He thought he would have to do it now, here on this public road. A cyclist whizzed by, heading up the hill. The girl glanced across at the cyclist and continued walking, out of the man's sight.

He stayed where he was.

The shit was well and truly in the fan.

But he was serene and confident, and looking forward to doing what had to be done.

He waited, enmeshed, scratched and sore, for several minutes. Then he shoved roughly through the vines, brushing leaves and thorns and crushed berries from his clothing, and returned to his car.

Chapter

8

Alberg and Cassandra had been home for three hours and in bed for two when the phone rang, at one o'clock Monday morning: Alberg was being called to a crime scene.

"I'm sorry," he said to Cassandra when he'd hung up. "It's a homicide. I have to go."

"Don't apologize. It's your job, for God's sake." She threw back the covers and got up. "I have to go with you, though." Furious with herself, and humiliated, she dressed quickly. She would wait in the car until Earl's Café opened at six.

"She got pushed a little bit, by the door, when I opened it," the woman kept telling them, not looking down the hallway.

"I know, ma'am. It's all right," said Sid Sokolowski. "You just go back inside there and get yourself a cup of coffee."

The woman turned to Alberg. "I heard a scream, you know? At first I thought, It can't be a scream. But then I heard it again, you know? And so I knocked at the door, and—" She made a faltering, pushing gesture. Hilda Makepeace was small and bony, wrapped in a dark green bathrobe. "And—there she was. Couldn't believe my eyes at first. It's not a thing you expect to see. I've lived here eighteen years, never seen a thing like that, never expected to, either. So then I called you guys."

"I know, ma'am," said Sokolowski patiently. "You told us. I wrote it down." He held up his notebook.

"Would you like some coffee?" said Hilda Makepeace, who was a widow. Every few seconds she rubbed industriously at her thinning gray hair, which was standing up in startled wisps all over her scalp. "I could make you some. It wouldn't be any trouble."

"No, thank you—" said Sokolowski, but Alberg interrupted.

"That would be very kind of you," he said.

Mrs. Makepeace, looking relieved, retreated behind her door.

"I want a minute, before we let the troops in," Alberg said to the sergeant, and before Sokolowski could reply he was down the hall and inside the victim's apartment.

Walking from my car, I am innocent, I am in the fullness of my innocence. Everything I have ever done wrong is in these remaining moments expunged from the record. My innocence blossoms within me, as I stride toward my crime.

Alberg saw that a circle of glass had been cut from the balcony door, to accommodate a reaching hand: the door was unlocked. He stood in the middle of the living room, his back to the balcony.

My feet are firm on the floor. There is no weakness in my knees. My heart is calming, as I stand in the silence. I am wearing gloves. My clothes are black. In my hand there is a hammer.

Alberg saw a photo album on a bookcase shelf. A lamp lay on the floor, its shade detached and crushed, the brass base dented. A trail of blood led from the body across the living room, down the hall, and into the bedroom.

I will do it neatly, silently; with respect. I will slide her into another world in her sleep. She has dozed off here—she will awaken somewhere else. I know exactly where to strike her.

Hands in his pockets, Alberg stood in the bedroom doorway, looking in. A large doll sprawled on the floor at the end of the bed. The bedclothes were crumpled. The victim had scrambled out of them: she had not had time to throw them aside.

There was blood here; she had received the first blow here.

As I go down the hall I am in a delirium of poetry, never before so alert, so talented. Into the bedroom. Up to the bedside. I lift my weapon—but a splotch of white in the corner seizes my eye and my heart lurches, my knees lock, she moves in her sleep, and the hammer blow glances irresolutely off her temple. And instead of dying, she awakens.

She ran for the door, thought Alberg. And he chased her. She ran for the door, bleeding—but before that, she hit him: the doll's head was smashed. Alberg could see blood on it. And he'd bet that it wasn't the victim's blood: she had been struck with something much harder than a doll.

She falls in the hallway, slipping on her blood, and I hit her again. Her hands claw at the floor, and my head is spinning, cracking with pain. It is a poem of horror. She gets up again and runs again. In the light from outside she looks demented—I have an instant of fear.

Alberg went back down the hall, careful to avoid stepping in blood. He looked down at the body, which was that of a woman in her mid-fifties, of average height, thin, with shoulder-length gray hair, who had been bludgeoned to death. It was a messy way to kill someone. He noticed pink polish on her fingernails.

"Okay, Sid," he called out to the sergeant, who was waiting impatiently in the hall. "They can take the body."

He called in the evidence team and pointed to the photo album. "I want to have a look at that as soon as you're finished with it. I'll be next door." And he went down the hall to get some of Hilda Makepeace's coffee.

She scrabbles at the door, trying to get it open. I lift the hammer and bring it crashing down. The side of her head crumples, and she falls to the floor—so fast does she drop, so obediently, it is as if she had been waiting all her life for this special blow.

One down.

One to go.

1987

Chapter
9

Maria rushed Belinda and Richard through breakfast on that Saturday morning in March, responding to them absently, her mind already outside in the garden. Gardening and driving her car; these were the only activities she could count on being permitted to do alone. Being alone was important, from time to time.

As soon as Richard put aside his napkin and began to rise from his chair, Maria said, "Look after the dishes before you leave, will you, Belinda?" And ignoring Belinda's half-hearted protest, she hurried outside.

It was a gray morning, still and silver. She crossed to the toolshed for a rake and began raking the lawn, accumulating piles of leaves and pieces of cedar branches, debris that had been blown into the yard from the trees surrounding the house. Maria raked vigorously, restoring order, finding within herself a small pocket of serenity and striving to make it bigger.

She was dressed in jeans and a sweatshirt with a T-shirt underneath, and she had on a denim jacket, too, but after half an hour or so she took this off and tossed it onto the

71

picnic table. She scooped up the piles of debris and stuffed them into black plastic bags until the lawn was bare again.

Maria couldn't tell whether it was raining or not. Perhaps the silkenness upon her face was moisture from yesterday's showers still clinging to the air. She ignored Richard when he appeared at the door, watching her, seeming to hover there, indistinct but palpable, behind the screen. She continued to rake, scraping at the patches of bare earth that sprawled here and there in the grass, and imagined she could feel the lawn tingle, like a vigorously scratched scalp.

When her husband eventually retreated from the door, Maria, on her way back to the toolshed, stopped for a moment to bow her head and take stock. Her pocket of serenity was ashudder, like a rainpuddle swept by a passing breeze.

She replaced the rake and began cleaning up the gardens, wrenching yellowed sweet pea vines from netting that was nailed to the fence on the west side of the yard, uprooting them, stuffing them into another plastic bag, a job she should have taken care of in the fall. She ought to have a compost heap. Maybe she would, this year. She pulled the dead leaves away from the lilies, whose new leaves were already several inches high. It was the beginning of Maria's favorite time of year, when spring hung bright in the nearby forest, an infusion of green. Her face was moist and glowing. Yes, this year she would have a compost pile. And maybe a raised bed or two, for vegetables.

Eventually she sat back on her haunches, her hands cold, earth beneath her fingernails. She could no longer pretend that it wasn't raining. Her face was no longer moist, or even damp, but definitely wet with rain. She stroked rain from her warm cheeks, stroked rain from her hair, and saw phantoms, black swirlings of unknown origin.

Maria held fast to thoughts of spring, pictured the clematis that would soon bloom on the trellis by the front door, white flowers on one side, purple on the other. But something out there was holding its breath. She was aware of nausea, of pinpricks of dread. Maria pushed herself to her feet and stumbled indoors, rain-wet and shivering.

That night in bed she and Richard sat reading. They were close together—only maybe a foot of mattress separated them—but it was as though Richard was in another room. She was to blame for this mood. She had chosen to spend her day alone, and Richard had in retaliation created distance between them, fashioned it from nothing, a heavy, reproachful distance. She imagined him sitting in the dark somewhere, spinning distance on a cerebral loom.

Maria would have liked to stretch her arms across that distance, to embrace him, hold him close. She wanted to kiss his closed eyes, stroke open his mouth, explore the terrain of his plump but sturdy body with fingertips and tongue. It was love that prompted these yearnings, not lust; but lust would have been the result.

She couldn't do it, though. Couldn't reach for him because he would retreat, couldn't beguile him sexually because he would reject her. Richard seldom allowed himself to be seduced.

Maria, her eyes on the book she was pretending to read, compelled herself to be artificially calm, knowing that if she imagined something long enough and hard enough, it could sometimes become real.

They were neither of them uncomplicated. Both were sometimes difficult. Each could be stubborn, uncompromising, intractable. But Maria thought these things were perhaps more true of Richard than of her.

She heard him turn a page and realized that she hadn't turned one for far too long.

She leaned her head back against the bunched-up pillows and closed her eyes. "Sometimes," she said aloud, "I have little hope for us, Richard."

She let her book drop to her lap. Outside, an unequivocal rain was falling, a harsh rain that occasional moments of windblown acceleration turned into rough, martial music. Richard said nothing as Maria listened to the rain. Then she heard him switch off his lamp and felt him suddenly close to her, and his mouth was on hers. She opened her eyes just as he turned off her own lamp.

He pulled her down onto the bed and continued to kiss her, his hands on the sides of her face, now sliding down her body to lift her nightgown. She felt his hands on her breasts, his thumbs teasing her nipples, and now his lips were there, his tongue on her breasts. He was pulling down her pants, and she helped, kicking them off. She touched him, lightly, wishing she had a feather. When he entered her she reached behind to stroke his balls. He began talking to her now, and she answered him: "Yes, please," she whispered, "oh yes, please. . . ."

Maria came first this time, and later she felt like a firmament as he thrust into her again and again; she was space and time and the earth itself.

Chapter
10

On Sunday afternoon, Hamilton Gleitman fired up his printer and rolled his office chair from the computer to the desk. He took a file folder from his IN basket, opened it, and examined the form it contained. He smoothed it with the palm of his hand. Picked up a pen. Checked the box next to the word *Writing*.

Hamilton Gleitman was a streak of silver, a stealthy streak of silver, gray-haired and lightning fast, compact, dressed almost always in easygoing denim, usually wearing hiking boots. Several chains hung from the waistband of his jeans, one from almost every loop, and each chain held something—keys, a calculator, a bottle opener, a Swiss Army knife. He jingled, faintly, as he walked.

He was a freelance magazine writer who also wrote poetry. It was the latter that he considered his life's work.

Hamilton had begun to write in jail, mostly because he was so bored there, he was afraid he'd go crazy. It turned out, though, that he had a knack for it, so he'd kept on writing when he got out.

"Year of Writing:" Hamilton wrote, "1939."

He had found that articulating his life made it clearer. It

was as though writing and thinking were simultaneous; he didn't know which came first. He had come to see his life as a stylus, writing itself—a cursive life, an interlocking series of black curves and swirls, some broad, some narrow. His task was to sketch for the world his own interior monologues, which at one and the same time made sense for him of what he saw, and created poetry.

He filled in his address, which was an apartment building on Bellevue Avenue in West Vancouver. Next to "Employment:" he printed, "Writer. Self-employed." He mulled over the next question on the form, trying to settle on a figure.

The printer stopped. He gathered up the pages of his piece on collectors of hockey memorabilia and stuffed them into a manila envelope, which he tossed onto the table in the hall. Then he stood for several minutes in the living room, looking out the huge window, which faced southwest. He had a one-hundred-and-eighty-degree view that swept from Burrard Inlet on his left to Stanley Park and the Lions Gate Bridge and across English Bay to Point Grey.

In his dedication to his art he felt linked with the poets of all the ages. But the subjects about which people wrote poetry varied, of course, according to the person doing the writing. All poets were not the same. They had specialties, which developed naturally out of their personal preoccupations. Some poets wrote about the natural world, for example. Or love, in its many variations. The fear of dying, perhaps. Madness. Hamilton's preoccupation, poetically speaking, was shame.

He had recently decided that it was time to devote himself full-time to poetry: he would write his first book. A series of poems, a collection, differing in length and tone and style, linked only by a common theme.

It was an exceptionally clear day. Gazing away out to the

west, Hamilton glimpsed the Gulf Islands and, beyond them, the long purplish rising that was Vancouver Island. He spent a lot of time looking at his view, feeling like a bird in a nest up there. In strong winds he imagined he felt the building move. Someday, he knew, there would be an earthquake, and he would die in it. Not many people knew how they would die, but Hamilton Gleitman did. It had come to him in a dream several years ago. He had awakened covered in sweat, his heart thrashing around in his chest: he had felt the earth fracture beneath his feet and fall away and vanish. After a while, when he had calmed himself enough to deliberate upon the dream, he had decided that he was glad to have been given this knowledge. With it came an immense amount of freedom, because knowing how he would die, he also knew how he would not.

He lived up there, yes, like a bird in a nest, isolated and private.

Hamilton went back to his desk and the application form.

"Amount requested: Subsistence (maximum of $2,500 a month):" Hamilton wrote, "12 months at $2,500 = $30,000."

He had to find three references, which he figured he could do. There were a couple of magazine editors who could be depended upon to say good things about him. And of course he'd ask the guy who'd taught the writing course in prison.

He grinned to himself. The Canada Council would love it that he'd learned to write in the slammer.

Several blocks away, an acquaintance of Hamilton's named Harry was sitting in the sun in his living room with the TV on, watching a rerun of *Magnum, P.I.* on the Arts & Entertainment channel. It had become hard to see the screen, because the sun was shining almost directly upon it, and it was shining on Harry in his easy chair, too, making him warmly, cozily sleepy. He got up to close the curtains. He stretched, scratched his belly, and lay down on the sofa. He managed to focus on *Magnum* for a few more minutes and then dropped off to sleep.

Harry was thirty-seven.

There wasn't much furniture in his apartment, which he considered only temporary accommodation. In fact, it seemed that his had always been a life in waiting. He had grown up rich—or at least knowing he would be rich eventually. And for a long time he didn't clue in to the fact that despite this, his parents expected him to exhibit a certain amount of ambition. They displayed an insistent curiosity about what he was going to do with himself that Harry at first found sweet. Touching. But while he was still in high school he had realized that they meant it, that he was seriously expected to come up with some kind of career goal. So he had poked around halfheartedly at school, looking for something he liked and was good at. He took English and French and history and biology and math. One year he tried physics, which he found frighteningly incomprehensible. Cutting open a frog in biology turned his stomach. He couldn't get the accent right in French. Mathematics was a foreign tongue. He was just barely able to remember enough stuff in history to pass the exams, stuffing his head full of facts until it bulged, then vomiting them out upon the examination paper, regurgitating just barely enough to pass and instantly forgetting it. English was boring. Virtually everything was boring.

Once he told his parents that he was going to be a doctor. His dad never did swallow that, but his mother tried hard for a day or two, until she recalled his marks. "Well, geez," he'd said in his own defense. "Geez."

He started looking around among the extracurricular activities—nothing athletic, he didn't have the body for athletics. The only thing he sometimes did well was volleyball, and then it was just good enough to get by. He joined the choir because any fool could sing, right? Apparently not, Harry discovered. Next he tried out for a couple of school plays. He got cast and made people laugh, which at first gave him an excellent feeling. But he was never given any other kind of part, and he got tired of being laughed at after a while.

He managed to graduate from high school and he went on to college, because his marks weren't good enough to get him into a university. Even at college, though, Harry always felt that he was marking time. Waiting for the day when his life could really get going, get off the ground. He'd fantasize about what he'd do when he was well financed. Saw himself paying cash for a brand-new BMW. Putting himself in the hands of an experienced salesman at some fancy men's store. Buying himself a forty-foot powerboat, maybe. Getting a big-screen TV: he'd have a VCR, a big-screen TV, a pile of rented movies, and an enormous bowl of popcorn. His wants were few.

As an adult, Harry continued to have an ambivalent relationship with his father. In a perfect world his old man would have been the one to die first. Harry would have moved back into the house then and looked after his mother in her old age. Taken over everything for her. Hired somebody to clean, hired somebody else to look after the grounds, kept her financial affairs in order.

But he had almost stopped thinking this way now. More than two years had passed since his mother's death, and Harry had more or less accepted his lot. The old guy couldn't last much longer, and in the meantime Harry was really a pretty happy fella. Everett said he watched too much TV, and maybe he did, but so what? There was a lot to learn on TV.

Harry awoke after a twenty-minute nap, refreshed. He stretched, catlike, on his warm sofa and noticed the glow the sunlight created in the middle of the dark green curtains. *Magnum* was over and *The Rockford Files* was about to start, but Harry was too restless now to watch TV. If his old man had been any decent kind of a father at all, it would be time for Harry to go over there for Sunday dinner now. But no.

Harry decided to head over to Everett's place. Everett Danforth managed a bookstore, and he was also kind of an actor. But the most significant aspect of his personality was his love of gambling. It was fortunate for him, Harry thought, giving his face and hands a cursory rinse, that Everett wasn't gambling at the moment. When he was in the thrall of his addiction, you couldn't talk to the guy about anything but the horses.

See, he thought, going out into the hall, locking his apartment door behind him, that was another aspect of TV that was very useful. It distracted a fellow from stuff that could screw up his life. He had tried to get Everett to watch more TV, but it had been too late by the time Harry met him: Everett was hooked. The problem was, Harry thought, descending five stories in an otherwise empty elevator, that sometimes Everett actually won—and this just fed the fire. A lottery ticket here and there turned out to be a winner. Or else he'd go to the track and bet on some damn horse that had his mother's maiden name or some damn thing, and once in a blue moon the damn horse would actually win, and there you go, Everett would be in the money again. These things didn't happen often. Just often enough to keep Everett hanging in there for the big score.

Fortunately, Harry acknowledged, crossing the lobby toward the street, Everett was (unlike Harry) extremely frugal, except when it came to gambling. He lived, oblivious of his surroundings, in a cramped and gloomy basement suite that would have driven Harry nuts. Harry was not happy at the prospect of inviting himself for dinner in that place. He would drag Everett out of there, to Flora's, probably, even though he knew he'd have to foot the bill. A guy just didn't feel right eating alone on a Sunday, when he had a father whose house he ought to be going to.

Jesus, he thought. When the fuck was the old guy finally going to croak?

Chapter 11

What would her mother do, Maria wondered, if she were to stand right in front of her, make sure she had her attention, and then say, "Mother. Help."

It was late Sunday afternoon, and they were driving to her mother's house.

Richard began humming to himself. Maria imagined that she felt the vibration of his humming in the cushiony part of her own lips, closed upon themselves. It was an aimless, tuneless creation that he was humming. Maria thought it a pity that they weren't a family that sang together. Instead they took turns, while driving: Richard would hum for a while, then Belinda would sing to herself, gazing out the side window and daydreaming about fame, fortune, and what she would call love, although it was really sex. Then it would be Maria's turn, but by then she would no longer be in the mood, or the other two would have decided they wanted to talk.

She didn't know what kind of help she would ask of her mother, were she to ask.

Maria shifted on her seat and leaned close to the window. She didn't like riding in a car that was being driven by somebody else. Driving was one of her favorite things. Why was it that male people, most of them, anyway, always assumed that if there was driving to be done, they were naturally the ones who'd be doing it?

Ignoring Richard's humming, Maria began to sing. " 'Moonbeams shining,' " she sang, " 'soft above, let me beg of you; find the one I dearly love, tell him I'll e'er be true.' "

Richard glanced at her, and even though she didn't look at him, she knew it was a look of surprise that was about to become disapproval.

" 'Fate may part us,' " she sang more loudly, " 'years may pass, future all unknown.' " He had stopped humming now. " 'Still my heart will always be faithful to him alone.' "

"That's pretty, Mom," said Belinda from the backseat.

Maria turned to smile at her and aimed the rest of the song in her daughter's direction. " 'O wandering wind, won't you quickly find my dear one where'er he may be. And give him a message I fain would send; I know that he's dreaming of me. Fate may part us,' " she sang (and Belinda sang along, " 'La la la-la, la la la' "), " 'years may pass, future all unknown. Still my heart will always be faithful to him alone.' "

"You pick one now, Dad," said Belinda, leaning toward the front seat.

Maria, looking again out the window, had a spasm of heartache. She touched the inside of the glass, following with her fingertip the trail left on the outside by a drop of rain. It was probably some hormonal thing, this apprehension that had come to afflict her.

" 'There was a man,' " said Richard. "This isn't a song, mind you. Because I don't sing."

"I know, Dad," said Belinda. "It's a recitative."

"Precisely," he said. " 'There was a man' "—Belinda joined in—" 'whose name was Mertz.' "

Maria gazed at him in astonishment. He hadn't sung this in years.

" 'His wife bought him. Some colored shirts. He bought a goat. To please his kids. And this is what. That poor goat did. He ate the shirts. Right off the line. But Mrs. Mertz caught him in time. She tied him to. The railroad tracks. And swore she would. Those shirts get back. He coughed and kicked. With might and main. Coughed up the shirts. And flagged the train.' I don't know if we got that altogether right," said Richard to Belinda. He reached across the seat and took Maria's hand. She let him hold it; they were pulling up in front of her mother's house.

Maria's mother lived in the Dunbar area, not far from Forty-first Avenue, in the house in which Maria had grown up after they'd moved to Vancouver from Winnipeg. Her mother's name was Agatha. She was an angular woman of sixty-nine who had recently taken up speed-walking. Her husband, Thomas, Maria's father, was dead.

Agatha kept very busy with her speed-walking (she was a member of a club) and volunteer work with Mothers Against Drunk Driving. She had once been a teacher and enjoyed conversations with Richard in which he would tell her about innovations in education and she would say that these weren't innovations: innovations had to be new.

She met them at the door, wearing tights, a long black cardigan over a white T-shirt, and a headband. On her feet were clunky black walking shoes. "You're early!" she exclaimed, but they weren't. Maria knew that Agatha had just wanted to be sure they saw her in her speed-walking gear.

"We can drive around the block a few times, if you like," said Richard. Maria's fondness for him was never greater than during visits with her mother.

"No no no, come in, come in." Agatha kissed Belinda on both cheeks and bent to do the same to Maria.

They were all crowded together in the tiny foyer, from which a narrow staircase led upstairs. There were three bedrooms and a bath up there, plus a large square hall.

Agatha ushered them into the living room. "I have to dash upstairs and quickly shower and change," she said. "Sit down, sit down."

"Mother, how about if I make some coffee?" said Maria, and not waiting for a reply, she went through into the kitchen.

It had been years and years since she'd lived with her mother, but it still surprised her that Agatha lived alone apparently happily, and quite differently from when she'd had a family. Maria pondered this, staring into a cupboard. Things were put away differently. The house was messier. There was a patina of carelessness over everything. But maybe her mother was more carefree than careless, Maria thought, brooding. Agatha was to Maria an inscrutable person. There was more to her than that which Maria was willing to know. She wondered if Belinda felt the same way about her.

She put the coffee on, then sat at the table in the sunny alcove that overlooked her mother's backyard. She was thinking about what life with her parents had been like when she was a child, a teenager, a coming-and-going adult, a married person. The life she studied was, of course, a Maria-centered life: it was mildly shocking to realize that things had been going on in her mother's life, too, all those years. She felt slightly guilty not to have thought about this much earlier. And slightly irritated that her mother had not thought to tell her. The point was, did she really know her mother? Where had all this speed-walking come from? Did Agatha miss having sex? Maria stared thoughtfully out the window, absently noting the mess that was her mother's overgrown back garden. She herself thought that she would be able to do without sex quite well. But maybe that was only because it was, theoretically, always available to her.

In the living room, Belinda was playing the piano. Richard would be standing, hands clasped behind his back, watching his daughter's hands on the piano keys. But soon he would move to the front window and then out the front door, to check something in the car or to walk to the corner and back. Richard hated to be idle. Idleness soured his digestive system. Which was why he had a problem with holidays. Christmas was especially bad. Maria had established several rituals for Christmas Day, most of which were designed to keep Richard busy, to give him a sense of purpose. Richard really wanted to feel a sense of destiny, but purpose would do.

Agatha came downstairs smelling like Pears soap and Yardley's lavender. Maria could just see her, standing there on the bathmat, vigorously toweling herself dry, spreading deodorant in her armpits and slapping talcum powder all over her aged body. She was surprised and depressed to realize that she envied her mother, who was active and fit and, as far as Maria could tell, without a care in the world. Maria felt wan and driven by comparison.

"Have some coffee, Mom," she said, but Agatha opted for fruit juice.

They sat in the living room, making conversation, and it felt to Maria that the three of them had dropped in unannounced: you'd never know, she thought, that the woman had invited us for dinner.

Upstairs there was a bedroom that used to be Maria's. Now it was what her mother called her "ideas room." It was full of projects, some new, some old, some abandoned. There was a sewing machine in it, and a knitting machine, and a computer.

Maria would have liked to have a nest somewhere—a

den—another home—a refuge, for her imagination as much as for her self—a hidey-hole—a place to which she could flee. She thought about this, idly watching her mother drink her orange juice, and noticed that Agatha had lost more weight.

She looked more closely at her mother, and Agatha must have felt this, because she gazed back at her. Richard was talking, Belinda was yawning and taking peeks into the kitchen, as if wanting to find out whether dinner were actually happening. Maria studied her mother's face, and Agatha looked back, steadily, calmly. And Maria knew in that moment that Agatha was dying.

Chapter

12

She was actually waving to him from the porch. Hamilton Gleitman glanced back at the house as he unlocked his car door, and there she was, waving. He imagined that he could see tear traces on her cheeks, silvery, like slug trails, and as he returned the wave he marveled, thankfully, at the naiveté rampant in the world around him.

He drove a block or two away from the woman's house before pulling over to the curb to jot a few things in his second notebook: the vulnerable arch of her neck when with head bowed she made her confession; the powerful fragrance that had emanated from a pot of dark blue hyacinths; the tired wail of the child she had put down for a nap; her bitten fingernails; and the way she pushed her hair away from her face and tucked it behind her ears.

Most of the people he interviewed for his magazine pieces were pitiably trusting. Most didn't even ask him for any identification. But even the few who did were no problem because he was legitimate; he was always working on an actual story and could always refer them to an actual editor to verify this.

Usually they were women. If they were working women,

he'd arrange to see them on the weekend or during an evening. He didn't care if there was a husband around, or kids; it was amazing how happily people chattered away when you were taking notes. He took two kinds of notes, one set for the story he was writing (how Family A were managing to exist happily on a single income or how B has made a success of going into business for herself or how C organizes life as wife/mother/employee/amateur actor— Hamilton wasn't particular, he'd take any assignment going: it was this that kept him in steady work) and a second set for Hamilton the poet.

He didn't look for anything in particular. He simply opened all his senses and let the place and its occupants flood into him, and in the course of the interview he would usually find little soft spots, small areas of rottenness, places that hurt when he touched them. A failed marriage. A failed business. A personal humiliation. A dead child. He would, of course, back away at first, with delicacy and tact, when he found these life blotches, these hurtful patches of inadequacy. Sometimes, however, he was wordlessly encouraged to go on probing.

He and today's candidate, a woman named Aileen Churley, had been well into the interview by the time Hamilton got what he'd been patiently waiting for. She had given him a tour of her prize-winning rosegarden, which was the subject of his piece, and then she made coffee and he continued the interview in the living room, taking copious notes, turning the pages in his notebook impatiently, his pen flying, laughing appreciatively at her jokes, and leaning forward in a demonstration of eager interest every time he asked a new question. He was in his late forties, pleasing to look at, but not handsome enough to titillate or threaten.

Every so often the interview took a rest and real conversation bubbled through, and after three or four of these leisurely interludes she made an apparently casual reference to her husband, and Hamilton realized it was the first time she'd mentioned him. He saw in her, then, a physical tension that was most obvious in her face but was probably also present in the rest of her: she'd be as rigid as a tree trunk, he thought, sweeping his gaze up and down her body.

"Does he share your love of roses?" said Hamilton of the absent spouse, whose presence he now felt, sullen and brooding. His notebook and pen were resting harmlessly on the coffee table, and he was sitting back, relaxed, his body language assuring her of his sympathy and understanding.

She shook her head. Her suffering was palpable. He almost felt sorry for her.

"You're unhappy," he said, soft and tentative. "I can come back, if you like, another time."

She gave a little wave of her hand, holding her face averted from him until she had it under control. "No," she said, swallowing a sob. "I'm fine." She flickered a glance at him, wiped the palms of her hands firmly on her jeans. "I just found out," she said, "that he's having an affair."

Hamilton had let his eyes widen, and assumed an expression of disapproval, and leaned forward slightly, to listen to her tale.

Like a fastidious collector of butterflies, Hamilton now pinned her into his notebook with the phrases that would resurrect her and her shame when he needed them. And then he drove home to write his story.

The next morning, a Wednesday morning in late April, a small event occurred that would change the course of Hamilton Gleitman's life.

He took the elevator down to the parking garage in his

apartment building and stepped out, his sneakers silent upon the concrete floor, and started walking toward his car, which was one of only three in the whole garage: most people were at work in the middle of a weekday.

Suddenly the door to the stairs flew open and a young woman hurried out. She didn't see Hamilton, who was behind her. She raced toward a blue Honda and started fumbling at the lock.

Hamilton didn't know why he did what he did then. He slipped behind a pillar, detached his keyring from his waistband, and let it fall. He remained perfectly still as the flat, grating sound reverberated throughout the garage. Then there was absolute silence.

Hamilton was intent upon this silence. He sniffed it, he was almost trembling, as he waited for it to be broken. She will call out, he thought. But no—she's afraid of a quiver in her voice. How do I know this? he wondered. Finally her key scraped against the lock—and once more—and then it found the opening. Hamilton tasted the relief that flooded her mouth and felt the urgency with which she stuffed herself behind the wheel and locked the door. The Honda roared out of the garage.

Hamilton leaned against the pillar, thinking. Finally he picked up his keys, loped over to his car, and drove downtown to deliver his story to the magazine.

That evening he wrote a poem that followed the woman out of the garage. It echoed with the self-deprecating laughter of relief; there had been nobody there after all, no danger after all . . . except, of course, there had been. Danger on soft, silent feet had crept close, dark and pungent, had persisted, briefly, in the murky shadows: Hamilton, invisible yet perceived, had created an acrid stink of terror.

He considered, lying that night in bed, in the dark, that there was a wide spectrum of fright. Like an alphabet, or the vocabulary of music, once you knew the basics you could probably make it sing for you forever, you could create an endless variety of tunes, of moments.

He would revise the program of work he'd do when he got the Canada Council grant. He would write a collection of poems about fear. They would be streaks of moonlight—rivulets of blood—bursts of thunder.

Each would re-create a moment of terror.

Hamilton smiled in the dark and felt his eyes gleam.

Chapter

13

Agatha had admitted to Maria, privately, that she was ill and that her illness was terminal. She had made Maria promise not to tell anyone else. Agatha would do that herself, when she thought the time was right.

It was the Easter weekend now, and she hadn't yet done so. Richard and Belinda knew that she was ill, but they didn't know she was dying. She was still at home and wanted to stay there. She wouldn't let Maria look after her. She preferred to have this done by home care nurses.

On Saturday afternoon Maria took a walk down the lane behind her house. It was a very neat lane, bordered on either side by back fences and the bland closed faces of one-car garages. A dog made noises at her from behind one of the fences, an unusually tall fence, much taller than Maria, made of wide wooden planks with half-inch spaces between them. The dog snorted and snuffled, trying to stick his nose between two of the planks. He sounded friendly, Maria decided. . . .

She stopped in the middle of the alley and hunched into herself, her hands over her face, unable to breathe. She was panicked by the extent of her pain. It was an apocalyptic moment: remorseless. Was the world ending? Was she dying?

Were these the same thing? Maria remained unmoving, eyes closed behind the palms of her hands, feeling their ineffectual defense. And like a tongue imprudently probing an aching tooth, her mind returned to the dog, scrabbling and whining behind the fence, fearless and impatient.

The moment passed.

That evening she tapped on Belinda's door, waited a moment, pushed the door open. "Belinda."

Belinda lay on her back on the bed, her hands behind her hand, ankles crossed. Maria wished she could talk to her about Agatha.

"You were very quiet at dinner. What's wrong?" said Maria.

"Nothing."

"May I come in?"

"I don't care."

Maria entered and closed the door. "I hate to see you unhappy."

Belinda's gaze focused on her mother's face, and Maria felt her guard go up—an involuntary response, but necessary. "Do you?" said Belinda.

Maria nodded.

Belinda looked away. "He won't let me take the job at McDonald's."

"Did he say why?"

"He says I'm too young. Too young!"

"Fourteen is pretty young, though."

Belinda glared at her.

"Is that all he said?"

"He says I get a big enough allowance. He says if I had a job, I wouldn't have time to do my chores. He says he doesn't want me"—she put this next into quotation marks—" 'wandering around town on my own at night.' "

Maria leaned against the door and looked around her daughter's room. Lots of books. But dolls from childhood sat in a line on the top shelf of her bookcase. A desk, piled with school stuff. Posters of musicians and other entertainers on the walls; the only one familiar to Maria was James Dean. There was a dressing table, littered with makeup. Flouncy white curtains edged the windows, which were open, admitting cool breezes, the fragrance of roses, and the sound of rain. It was growing dark outside. Belinda had turned on her bedside lamp, and in its glow sat an alarm clock, a diary, and a charm bracelet.

Maria's daughter had thick brown hair threaded with gold and a firm, square jaw. Her eyes were blue, but a different blue from Richard's. Belinda's eyes were the color of the sea on a sunny day, warm and dark and glowing. They did not reveal her soul. They coaxed others to reveal theirs. Belinda had not yet begun to know this.

"I'll talk to him," said Maria.

Later, in the bathroom, she brushed her long black hair, glinting now with silver. It accumulated more silver every month, saving up, thought Maria, for her old age. And she tied her pink robe around her. Turned out the light and went into the bedroom.

Richard was in bed, reading, as usual.

Maria climbed in next to him and picked up a library book from the stack on the floor next to her night table.

She said, "I would like us to give Belinda permission to take that job."

Richard didn't say anything for a minute. It was up to him to decide which way they went from here, and he was thinking about this, she knew.

Maria learned quickly. She had clashed early and often with her husband, and although these encounters had left her feeling bruised and as if her ears were ringing, they'd been exhilarating, too. She had to admit that she'd rather enjoyed them. But later, when they had Belinda, it was different. She would do no ineffectual flailing around when it came to her daughter. A compromise, of sorts, was reached. Richard usually had his way in decisions about the raising of Belinda. But when Maria absolutely disagreed, she was implacable. She had acquired the kind of flexibility that was necessary in order to prevail. She developed many strategies and, most important, a continuing capability to create more.

Really, then, when she spoke, she had already won. She knew this. Richard knew it. But the conventions had to be observed.

"Why?" said Richard finally. It was debate he wanted, then.

Maria talked about money earning, of the lessons it would offer Belinda in budgeting, saving, making wise spending decisions. Working would teach her responsibility, accountability. She would have to be on time, reliable, she would have to serve customers politely even when she didn't feel like it. If Richard was seriously worried about his daughter's safety, Maria would pick her up whenever she had an evening shift. Although, she pointed out, Belinda used buses and the sky train almost every day and frequently at night.

They discussed the matter courteously for fifteen minutes or so. Then:

"All right, Maria. We'll allow it for a three-month probation period."

"Good," said Maria. She opened her library book and closed it again. She got out of bed to phone her mother. But it was late, after eleven. Better not disturb her.

★   ★   ★

At breakfast the next morning, Richard gave Belinda the good news. She beamed, hugged him, hugged Maria, and rushed out of the house to stop by McDonald's on her way to school. Richard left soon afterward.

Maria took the breakfast dishes to the sink and started to wash them. The kitchen was flooded with sunlight. From the window she could glimpse the house next door through the lilac hedge on the other side of the fence. On this side, rosebushes presented themselves to the morning sun.

Maria tried to hum something but couldn't think of a single tune. It was almost a relief when her hands, swathed in soapsuds, began to shake. "It's all right," she said to herself—or to her mother—out loud, soothingly, and she stood at the sink in a strange state of docility as she was shaken, violently, by a familiar rage.

Chapter

14

Two months later, on a wet and gloomy day in June, Harry was prowling around his father's living room, hands clasped behind his back, inspecting paintings and sculptures. He had made himself thoroughly familiar with his father's extensive collection, some of which was on display, with the rest stored in boxes in the attic. Harry was a regular visitor to the Vancouver galleries, keeping up with who was hot and who was not and what their stuff was worth. He had a notebook, four inches by six, in which he had surreptitiously listed every artwork the old man owned—or at least every one that Harry knew about. He wouldn't be surprised to find out when his father kicked the bucket that there were still more, stashed away in safety-deposit boxes or someplace.

This was as close as Harry could get to his father's wealth, which was actually mostly his mother's. When she died she'd left a little bit to Harry and all the rest to his father, which had made Harry tremendously angry. And still did, when he allowed himself to think about it. He'd sure as hell like to rummage around in his old man's investment portfolio, but his father reacted with hostility every time Harry suggested that it might be a good idea for him to become familiar with these things.

But it was worth another try, he thought now.

"What if you start going gaga?" he said to his father, who was sitting across the room, watching him suspiciously. "You're an old man, for chrissake—these things happen."

His dad hugged his chest and stared mutinously at the floor.

"Be realistic," said Harry, exasperated.

"Everything's taken care of," said his dad sullenly. "Go away. What are you doing here, anyway?"

"What am I doing here? You invited me for supper."

"I did not."

"See, Dad, now that's the kind of thing I mean," said Harry. "You've forgotten."

"I have not forgotten. I did not invite you."

"Okay, okay," said Harry. Well, next time it might work. "I'm just trying to help out."

"I don't need your help."

Harry was still circling the room. He had put the notebook away, but his interest in the paintings and the sculptures was as bright as ever. "I made my will recently," he told his father.

"Did you, now?"

"Yeah. Everything goes to you, Dad, if something happens and I crap out first." He could see his dad's eyes wanting to roll around in their sockets. "I admit it's not very likely, but stranger things have happened." He was stroking one of the Inuit carvings, made of soapstone, a large walrus, soft and warm, as if there were real flesh there, frozen in time, frozen in an instant of introspection, a walrus contemplating mortality, unaware that in that instant he'd become immortal. Harry looked around at the paintings, many of which were of wildlife, of wilderness, as if his father gave two hoots about the damn environment. He stared at his father. He felt cheated and reproachful. Obviously the old man hadn't cared a hell of a lot about Harry's mother. Her death ought to have resulted in his rapid decline, but no, oh no, life went on like business as usual as soon as he'd gotten her planted.

Maria backed out of her mother's ideas room, turned, and walked in a daze down the hall to Agatha's bedroom. She stood in the doorway, looking with a stranger's eyes into a room full of familiar things, including an old four-poster bed with a heavy chenille bedspread that was worn almost through in places. It had been a wedding gift to Agatha and Thomas from Thomas's parents. But what does that mean to me now? thought Maria. She thought about the boxes of slides stored in a downstairs closet, pictures of family and friends spanning decades, the photographic record of her personal history. A counterfeit history.

Maria sat sideways on her mother's dressing table stool. Upon the glass top was a silver-backed hand mirror, a gift from Maria on Agatha's last birthday. She opened drawers containing jumbles of cosmetics, and brushes and combs, and makeup remover, and various bottles of perfume and cologne. Then she lifted her head and saw her reflection in the swing mirror attached to the dressing table.

Maria leaned closer. She touched her face with her fingertips, feeling the cheekbones, the jawbones, the bones beneath her eyebrows. She stroked the hair back from her face, this stranger's face; she was immersed in scrutiny. Her heartbeat had become a thick, heavy, urgent pounding. Her mouth was dry, but the palms of her hands were sweating. Terror tried to consume her.

Maria stood and walked swiftly from the room, down the steps, out of the house, and quickly around to the backyard, where she stood beneath the cherry tree, her back pressed to the trunk, hugging herself tightly.

Rain was falling, listless but steady, from a sky painted battleship gray. Maria stood beneath the bare branches of the cherry tree until she was drenched and shivering but herself again, aware of things outside herself again, until her heart had steadied and terror had waned.

Her mother's illness had spanned four months. Maria could see those months in the garden that surrounded her, in the weed-ridden vegetable patch; in the overgrown lawn; in the aphids on the rosebushes. Maria had no responsibility here. The house and its front and back yards now belonged to the bank. She lifted her face, closed her eyes, and opened her mouth: the rain tasted like silver.

Soaked and trembling with cold, she hurried across the sodden lawn to the back door and went inside. She took off her shoes in the kitchen and got a towel from the linen closet with which to dry herself. Then she lit a fire in the fireplace and made a cup of instant coffee, and sat cross-legged on the floor close to the fire, getting warm, getting dry. She was still there an hour later when Richard arrived to pick her up.

He came in the front door and called her name. She heard him go down the hall to the kitchen. She heard him approach the living room. She felt him standing in the doorway, but she didn't turn around.

"Maria?"

Right, she thought.

He walked over to her, hesitated, then sat down next to her. She was leaning back on her hands, legs straight out. The fire was threatening to die. Maria reached for another piece of wood.

"Don't you think you'd better let it burn out?" said Richard.

Maria tossed the wood on the fire. They watched it for a while. She knew his mind was busy. She thought about getting up and closing the curtains, but it seemed like too much effort—and she would need all of her strength, couldn't afford to waste any of it.

"I'll be able to help you with things tomorrow," said Richard. He spoke softly. There was gentleness in his voice, acknowledgment of Maria's pain.

For Maria, truth had blade-sharp edges, silver-glittering, and she was devoted to it. She concentrated for a moment on the greedy crackling and chewing and smacking sounds of fire consuming wood, and noted its pleasant scent. Then she drew up her legs and wrapped her arms around them.

"She wasn't my real mother," she said.

Richard's gaze stroked the side of her face. She felt it, warm and curious on her skin.

"I was adopted." A flooding occurred inside her. She dropped her head and let tears flow down her face—she had no choice; it was weep or die. Richard reached for her, embraced her.

Dearest Maria,

I can see you through the window as I write this. I lean forward, pull the curtain back and look outside, and there you are, sitting on the swing, pushing yourself idly back and forth. You're still wearing your black pleated skirt and the long-sleeved white blouse Daddy and I gave you for Christmas. Do you remember? I still remember a red silk dress with a cowl collar that I had when I was twenty.

It feels very strange to write this letter, not knowing the Maria who will read it. And perhaps after all you never *will* read it. Perhaps I'll eventually find the courage to tell you directly what I can now only write down.

I wouldn't even be writing it down except for Mama's dying.

Today is the day of her funeral, and it struck me suddenly, when we were in there listening to the minister say all those good things about her, that a lightning bolt could strike me, or a speeding car, or maybe some dread disease—anyway, the point is, Maria, I could be dead tomorrow. And Thomas always said that it's up to me to tell you, not him. If I got killed tomorrow, why, then you might never know, and although I am not personally convinced that would be a bad thing, your daddy insists that you have a right—because there are others who know, and maybe someday you might run into one of those people. He's right, I guess. And if you must find out, then I want you to find out from me.

It's very hard, though, because what I'm about to say feels like a lie, although it isn't. The thing I have to tell you is that you aren't our natural-born child. And I look at those words on the page and want to run a line right through them, because you couldn't be more our daughter if you *had* been naturally born to us. You will know, when you read this, however many years have gone by since this day, that we have loved you fully, steadily, happily, for all but the first few months of your life.

It wasn't an official type of adoption. We gathered you into our lives when you were still at the crawling-around stage, and making it all legal wasn't hard to do in a small town when there was a war on. Thomas was away when I first found out about you, but I wrote to him right away and he was as excited as me, and as soon as he came home on leave he looked after all the formalities.

There's nobody else, Maria. You're the only one left.

I found out soon after Thomas and I got married that I couldn't have children. So you see, it was meant to be, you becoming our daughter. It was one of God's better plans.

I love you, Maria.

I glance out the window again. You're no longer sitting on the swing, now you're at the fence, picking sweet peas.

I am greatly relieved to have written this down. Now I can put it away and forget about it, which is the way things should be.

Leave the past alone, Maria. The past is past and done with. The present is where we do our living, and our loving.

Chapter

15

"Why didn't she tell me who I am, Richard?" Maria was standing in the front doorway, about to leave for work. She wore a summer dress and a cardigan and carried a straw handbag. It was a morning in mid-July, but unseasonably cool and gloomy.

"What's more to the point," said Richard, "why didn't she destroy that damn letter?"

"She must have had a reason. In forty-eight years, she never told me who I really am."

Exasperation flickered in his eyes. "Don't be melodramatic about this, Maria. It's not yourself you're unacquainted with. It's your relatives." He shrugged. "And who needs relatives?"

Maria did. She needed relatives. A personal history that went back beyond her birth date. To be bereft of history was to be in some way crippled, she thought.

She drove downtown, where she was office manager for a small public relations firm, and gave notice, effective immediately. She told her employers that a family emergency required her full attention.

She didn't want to go back home yet. Richard would be there for most of the day, and Maria wasn't ready to tell him what she had done and what she was about to do. She stood there in the parking lot, wondering what to do with the morning. After a while she decided that she felt like driving.

She took Georgia Street over the viaduct and followed First Avenue to the freeway, which propelled her through the suburbs and sailed her over the Port Mann Bridge into the Fraser Valley. When she saw the sign for Fort Langley, Maria moved into the exit lane.

Agatha and Thomas had told her that the hospital record of her birth had been destroyed in a fire. It had never occurred to her to question this.

Driving slowly north through the village of Fort Langley, she considered what it might be like to live in such a place—a tranquil, pleasant town, surrounded by green fields and the river, with low, green mountains to the north and Mount Baker soaring white on the eastern horizon: a town that had started life as a Hudson's Bay trading post. She allowed herself to wonder about the town in which her real parents lived. Maria drove over the bridge onto McMillan Island and crossed to the other side.

She had spent hours, over the past weeks, calling people listed in her mother's address book. It was a large leather book, very old. Some of the names entered there had been changed when Agatha's female friends got married. Most had moved a lot. Some names had lines drawn through them. Maria observed that her mother's handwriting had undergone several transformations.

Four cars were in the ferry lineup. She pulled up behind them and turned off the motor. It was very quiet. To the right stood a makeshift fast-food outlet, and although it was apparently open, Maria could see nobody inside. The driver of the car immediately ahead of hers had leaned his head against the side window, maybe sleeping. Somebody was sitting on the hood of the car at the front of the line—a young man with a dejected slump to his shoulders. Maria knew that she was very lucky to have been able to do what she had done today. She whispered this to herself, reverently, looking away, into the forest, where a pile of tires and a collection of unidentifiable paper rubbish occupied a clearing among the trees. Most of the trees were cedar, but there were some deciduous trees, too, heavy with leaves that rustled now and then, in a breeze from the river.

First she had called the people whom she knew or at least had heard of. Most of them lived in B.C.'s Lower Mainland, clustered in and around Vancouver. None could tell her anything useful. All expressed mild surprise to learn that Maria had been adopted.

She saw the top of the ferry approaching, and soon the cars drove off, six of them, and then Maria's lineup made its way, car by car, along the metal-floored driveway that led off the island and onto the boat. The trip across the Fraser River took about five minutes. These were the good old days, thought Maria, gazing out at the river, at a log-laden barge being towed downstream by a tug—the days before the bridge that would surely be built here or near enough to make of the ferry an anachronism.

When the ferry had docked and they'd all disembarked, she followed the other cars to the Lougheed Highway and turned right. She would drive through countryside for a while and cross back over the river at Mission, where there was a bridge. The highway was two lanes for a while, then four, then two again. For a while it followed the river, then it veered inland. The countryside Maria had hungered for seemed solemn and melancholy, painted in shades of gray; even the river glinted a dull pewter in the last tentative rays of a sun soon swept from the sky by brooding tumults of cloud. Mist gathered at the bottoms of the hillsides and at the tops.

Finally, though, she'd spoken to someone who knew something: a woman of about her mother's age now living in Baton Rouge, Louisiana. Her name was Phyllis Mussell, and she had known Agatha at the time of the adoption. She wasn't able to tell Maria anything about her real parents, but she did tell her who could.

Maria had gotten his phone number from directory assistance. When she introduced herself, he was silent for a long time. And then he invited her to come to see him.

Maria had reached the town of Mission. Here the highway turned south, heading for the river, which couldn't yet be seen. Heavy mist moved among the trees that stood in regiments, marching up from the river. It partially obscured them, a thick, heavy mist like God's breath made visible, until it seemed to Maria that it was the trees that were moving, stepping in and out of banks of fog: to Maria they looked like legions of the dead.

She no longer wanted countryside. She no longer wanted to drive. She quickly crossed the soaring bridge and quickly crossed the river valley, seeking the freeway. An hour later she was home.

"There was this old lady," said Belinda. "Sorry. This elderly woman. . . ." She had caught herself because of her grandma, who had been an old person and had recently died. Belinda had been talking with her mouth full, too, she realized, so she paused to chew and swallow before going on. And while she was at it she draped herself in an imaginary shawl of poise and self-possession, which although riddled with holes did work, occasionally. For a minute or two.

"She comes up to my till," Belinda continued, "and I smile at her and she says, 'Just a cup of hot water, please.'" Belinda widened her eyes at her parents and gave a little shrug. "So I didn't know what to do. I mean, was I supposed to say no? Or give her the water? And did I charge her for it, or what?"

"What did you decide?" asked her father.

"First I looked around for Bill, the manager, and he wasn't there. So I say 'Sure,' and I give her the hot water. And she sits down and takes a teabag out of her purse and plops it in the cup."

Belinda cut another bite of chicken, which was cooked in a sauce that had red wine and mushrooms in it. This was her favorite way to have chicken. "It turns out that she comes in every day, and she's never bought anything. She sits there drinking her tea and talking to people. It's, like, her recreation, I guess."

"I'm glad they let her do it," said Belinda's mother.

"Yeah. Me too."

"I've got something to tell you two." Her mother placed her knife and fork on her plate and pushed it away slightly, as if she were finished with her dinner, even though she'd barely eaten anything.

"I've quit my job," said her mother. Belinda was astonished.

"Really," said her father, sounding interested, but not excited, like her mother seemed to be.

"Yes."

"Did something happen?" said her father.

"Richard, I'm going to find my real family." She was clutching her hands together on top of the table, and her face was pink. She had on her face that look of determination that frequently made Belinda's heart sink. But not this time.

"Can I help?" said Belinda.

"Maybe," said her mother. "We'll see."

Her father was staring at her mother, and Belinda could tell he wasn't pleased. "I wish you'd talked to me about this first," he said quietly. "It isn't a good time for us to be trying to do without your considerable salary."

"I did," said her mother. "Or at least I tried to." She stood and began clearing the dishes.

Belinda snatched a glance at her father. He was looking down at his plate, and his face was red. She noticed that his hair had started growing farther back on his head than it used to. He looked calm, except for his red face. His hands were relaxed, one on either side of his plate, resting on the tabletop. But Belinda felt a curious fluttering in her stomach and held her breath, afraid for one awful moment that her father was going to do something completely out of character; waiting, tense and apprehensive, for him to pick up his plate and fling it at the wall. Then her mother returned from the kitchen, and as if she could read Belinda's mind she swiftly scooped up his plate, and Belinda's, and took them away. Belinda's father lifted his head. His pale blue eyes were cool and distant. He smiled at her.

THE PRESENT

Chapter
16

Alberg didn't like the Jolly Shopper much. It made him uncomfortable, with its wooden signs and its eclectic selection of merchandise. The place made a statement that he found incomprehensible; or maybe he just disapproved of it, whatever it was. He hadn't spent any time there to speak of, except when he used to drop in for pipe tobacco during a period when he was trying to quit cigarettes without giving up smoking. The store, he thought now, pulling up in front, was kind of like him smoking a pipe: it didn't ring true.

When he climbed out of his Oldsmobile he saw that the front door wasn't standing open as it usually did in good weather, and as he got closer he noticed the Closed sign. This was exasperating, but not surprising: the store's hours were eclectic, too. He got back into the Olds and headed for Porpoise Bay.

He got to Buscombe's house a few minutes later and pulled up on the roadside across the street. He sat in the car for a moment. His eyes felt as though they were full of sand, and every bone in his body hurt. He was chagrined to admit that he could no longer take a night without sleep comfortably in his stride. He wondered if Cassandra was as wiped out as he was.

He found Richard Buscombe at the back of his house, gazing out down the slope toward the water. His hands were clasped behind his back. He was watching a seaplane that was making a big circle, heading north, turning, coming low and slow, finally landing with a crisp splash at the southern end of Sechelt Inlet.

Richard Buscombe's house occupied a piece of land about a hundred feet above the water. There was some lawn in the front and a few bushes, and Alberg had recognized roses lining the driveway. In the back there was a patio with a gas barbecue, a table and several chairs, and a field of tall meadowgrass that grew down the hillside to the water's edge.

Buscombe was standing beyond the patio, in grass almost up to his knees. He was wearing gray pants and a white shirt and a pair of gray suspenders. He was a man not much older than Alberg, of medium height, somewhat overweight, and he didn't have much hair.

The seaplane had cut its engines. Alberg became aware of birds chirping somewhere—there were islands of trees here and there, scattered among the wild grasses—and the tranquil waters of the inlet washing languidly upon the beach below.

"Mr. Buscombe," said Alberg, and the man turned, startled. "My name is Alberg. I'm with the RCM Police." The man looked at him intently. Alberg knew he was mentally shuffling a lot of material, starting with his nearest and dearest—where were they? was he confident they were safe?—eventually working down to possessions—had somebody broken into his store, stolen his car, whatever? "Are you the husband of Maria Buscombe?"

Richard Buscombe hesitated. "Yes," he said finally.

"I'm afraid I have bad news."

"Is she dead?"

"Yes," said Alberg. "I'm sorry."

Richard turned around now, slowly, facing out toward the sea again, and he folded his arms in front of him. Alberg stayed where he was, watching the man's back. There was a fragrance in the air that he couldn't identify. He stood there for what felt like a long time. He thought he might fall asleep on his feet, lulled by the birds, and the ocean, and the breeze that was stroking the tall grasses, bending them, creating flashes of a different shade of green.

Richard Buscombe faced him again. "I don't know what to do with this."

Alberg nodded sympathetically.

"Was it an accident? What happened?"

Alberg said, "I think we should go inside." Even though the man was obviously in full control of himself, Alberg had a vision of Richard Buscombe pelting down the hillside and throwing himself into the water.

Buscombe looked at Alberg for a long moment, trying unsuccessfully to read his face. Then he crossed the patio and entered the house through a sliding glass door. Alberg followed. Buscombe sat on a red-and-white-checked sofa. Alberg sat on a chair.

"I'm afraid your wife was murdered, Mr. Buscombe." The man's face filled with bewilderment. He said nothing, just stared at Alberg, waiting intently for more information. "When was the last time you saw her?"

"Monday, September twenty-eighth, 1987."

"Uh-huh." Alberg gazed at him. But Buscombe said nothing more; he was still waiting.

"And what were the circumstances?" said Alberg.

"Circumstances?" He made a harsh, painful sound that was supposed to be a laugh. "She was in bed with a cold

when I left for school. And when I got home she was gone."
He leaned forward suddenly, his hands pressing on his
thighs. "She's been murdered? Are you certain?"

"We're certain."

"Wait a minute," said Richard, pointing at him. "I've
seen you around town. Are you with the local detachment?
Sechelt?"

"That's right."

"You mean—" He looked completely confused. "This
happened *here*?"

"That's right. Your wife had rented—"

"Please don't keep referring to her as my wife," said
Richard sharply. "Maria stopped being my wife the day she
left us."

"Maria Buscombe had rented an apartment on Trail Avenue," said Alberg, referring to his notebook. "She moved
in last Friday. September thirtieth." He looked over at Buscombe. "I take it that she hadn't been in touch with you."

"No," said Richard. "She hadn't. Not once, since the day
she left."

"Where has she been for the last seven years?"

"How the hell should I know?" He was sitting literally
on the edge of the sofa. He shook his head. "I'm sorry. She
told me she didn't know where she was going."

"When did she tell you this?"

"I beg your pardon?"

"She didn't tell you before you went to work, or you
wouldn't have gone. Right? And she'd left by the time you
got home. So when *did* she tell you she was going, but did-
n't know where?"

Richard rubbed his face with his hand. There was a rasp-
ing sound—he hadn't shaved. Alberg looked at him more
closely and saw a gray stubble. "She left a note," said
Richard. "It really didn't explain anything at all." He gave

Alberg a weary glance. "She'd gone in search of herself that summer. What she found hadn't pleased her."

Alberg felt his patience, what there was of it, ebbing away. "I don't follow you."

"She'd found out that she was adopted. And she became obsessed with finding her natural parents. That's all. That's what I meant."

"And? Did she?"

Buscombe reddened. "This is going to be a very difficult situation for my daughter and me."

Alberg's eyes stung, his body ached, and now his head had started to throb. "Believe me, Mr. Buscombe," he said softly, "it was a hell of a lot more difficult for your wife." He leaned toward him. "What can you tell me that might help with my investigation?"

"Nothing. I don't know anything about her life these last seven years."

"What about before that?" said Alberg. "What happened when she went off looking for her family?"

"She found them," said Buscombe stiffly. "Her parents. But that's all she told me." He sat erect on the edge of the sofa, looking at Alberg with an unaccountable belligerence.

Chapter

17

"Y ou've lost weight, I think," said Cassandra to her mother at lunchtime that day.

Helen Mitchell lifted a hand toward her face as if to shield herself. The hand stayed there in midair for a moment, then moved to finger the gray bangs that covered her forehead.

"Mother? Are you all right?" Cassandra reached across the restaurant table, but her mother shook her head and put both hands in her lap.

"Of course I'm all right," she said. "No wonder I've lost weight. The food in that place is dreadful." Her face had achieved a sculpted look, cheekbones and jaw revealed in increasing severity by the diminishment of excess flesh. Yet she was as upright as ever and seemed as strong, and her head-hugging bob gleamed silver in the sunlight. Behind her eyeglasses she assembled an expression of bitterness. "I don't want to talk about me. It's too depressing. You haven't told me about your trip. How is your brother?"

"Fine. He wants you to go to Edmonton for Christmas."

Helen busied herself with the small stainless-steel teapot that sat next to her cup and saucer. She removed the lid, pressed the teabag with the back of a spoon, put the lid back on, poured more tea into her cup.

"What do you think, Mom? Do you want to go?" Helen stared at the plate that sat in front of her, which held a tiny pool of melted butter and some crumbs. Cassandra watched her uneasily. "Mom?" She put her hand over her mother's, on the tabletop.

Helen looked up. "Would you come with me?"

"I—I don't know, Mom—"

"Will you think about it?"

No, said a loud voice in Cassandra's head. But, astonished at herself, she said, "Yes, Mom. I'll think about it."

Her mother's expression didn't change. She continued to look at Cassandra steadily, she continued to allow Cassandra's hand to cover her own. Cassandra wanted to hold her breath. She was aware of a tremendous sense of strain, of laboring to see, to perceive. She waited, intense, looking into her mother's eyes with growing panic.

Helen slipped her hand free and removed her bracelet, a wide, gold bracelet with her name and wedding date inscribed inside. "I want you to have this."

Cassandra recoiled, horrified. "No. Don't be silly."

"I'm not being silly. I want you to have it. Now." She took Cassandra's hand and slipped the bracelet on her wrist. "Please, Cassandra."

"But why?"

"I don't know why."

Later, sitting in her car in front of the library, having delivered her mother back to Shady Acres, Cassandra took off the bracelet and looked at it closely. The intricate design etched into the surface had worn down in several places. It was old and seasoned, this bracelet, elegant and burnished. It didn't look right on Cassandra's wrist. But she was surprised to realize that she didn't mind wearing it. She slipped it on and went back to work.

★   ★   ★

Alberg talked to Maria Buscombe's daughter, Belinda, at her home. She was a tall, athletic young woman with long dark hair and blue eyes that were warmer than her father's. She didn't look much like her mother, he thought. Yet it was always difficult to find resemblances between a dead person and anyone living. Alberg remembered the incredulity with which he'd observed his own father lying dead in his coffin: he hadn't even looked like himself.

"It's kinda like a double whammy for her, see?" Belinda's husband, Raymond, was explaining. He was a tall, good-looking kid wearing jeans and a dark red pullover. "I mean, first of all, there she is, suddenly, her mother that Belinda thought was gone forever. And Belinda's mixed up about this, see? Happy and upset at the same time. And before she can get used to the idea that her mother's alive and well and apparently wants to see her, she turns around and the woman's gone again, and this time it really is forever."

"He always talks a lot when he's nervous," said Belinda. Raymond was sitting next to her, with an arm around her, resting on the top of the sofa. The skin beneath her eyes looked transparent, revealing a layer of darkness.

"What are you nervous about, Raymond?" said Alberg.

"He's nervous because you're a policeman, and you're in his house talking to his wife about the murder of her mother," said Belinda sharply. "It may be an ordinary day for you, Sergeant, but it sure isn't ordinary times for me and Raymond." She got up and walked into the kitchen.

Raymond watched her go and for a while watched the doorway through which he expected her to reappear. Then he turned to Alberg, his forehead wrinkled in distress. "What do you think happened?"

Alberg shook his head. "That's what we're trying to find out."

Belinda came back into the room, slowly, sipping from a

glass of water. She sat on a chair adjacent to Alberg's, leaving Raymond in sole possession of the sofa.

Alberg, referring to his notebook, said, "Let's see what I've got here. You hadn't heard from your mother during the years she'd been gone. Then yesterday afternoon—Sunday— she appeared on the road when you were walking home from your father's house. You ran away, changed your mind, ran back to where you'd seen her, and she wasn't there." He looked up over his half glasses at her. "Is that about it?"

"It sounds ludicrous, doesn't it?" She drained the glass and put it down on a coffee table.

Alberg took off his glasses and tucked them into a shirt pocket. "Did you look for her?"

"Nope."

"Did you think about looking for her?"

Belinda pulled her hair to one side of her head and took hold of it in both hands, absently. "Yes. I probably would have looked for her. She had a lot to answer for."

"You were pretty angry with her."

She raised her head, and for the first time she looked at him directly. Her eyes caught his and held them. He experienced this as teetering on the edge of a fathomless depth of blue. It startled him, and he thought of her age, twenty-one—could she really be only twenty-one?

"I was extremely angry with her," said Belinda softly. "She deserted us. She deserted me." She stood up, quickly, and so did Raymond. "Excuse me, please," she said, and hurried from the room.

Raymond turned to Alberg. "She doesn't want you to see her cry."

That day the library was open until nine, so it was almost ten o'clock when Cassandra got home. Alberg was already there, which wasn't always the case on the days she worked late. He opened the door before she was out of the car and stood waiting for her, a tall stocky silhouette against the light pouring through the doorway. Then he turned on the porch light, and she saw his face.

I make him happy, thought Cassandra in wonderment, approaching him.

"Jesus, I'm tired," he said, embracing her. "Sid's here," he said, close to her ear. "Just arrived. I have to talk to him, so I invited him for dinner. Is that okay?"

"As long as I don't have to cook it," said Cassandra. She pulled away, smiling at him. "Hi, Sid," she called over Alberg's shoulder.

"It's all done," said Alberg. He'd cooked a meat loaf from the freezer, mashed some potatoes and opened a couple of cans of peas.

They sat down and served themselves, then began to eat. The light from the fixture that hung low over the dining room table flashed from the gold bracelet on Cassandra's wrist. Alberg reached over and touched it, and looked at her quizzically.

"It's my mother's," said Cassandra. "She gave it to me."

He shook HP sauce onto his meat loaf. "An early birthday present?"

"No. I don't know why she gave it to me. She just did." She glanced across at Sokolowski. "What do you hear from Elsie, Sid?"

"She's doing fine," said Sid. He looked up from his food. "Got herself an apartment. She says it's pretty nice. So I guess it is."

He looked, to Cassandra, less burly than usual, less substantial. It might be that he'd lost weight. But perhaps it was the look of perpetual bewilderment he now wore that made him appear to have shrunk just slightly.

"She's not definite about anything yet," he told her. "I take that as a good sign."

"I think you're right," said Cassandra encouragingly.

They ate in silence for a while. Then Alberg said, "Do you mind if we talk some shop at the dinner table?" She started to answer and he added, quickly, "It can wait, if you like."

"No, of course I don't mind."

"It's the Buscombe thing," he said to Sokolowski.

"Okay," said Sid agreeably, sliding his fork under a chunk of meat loaf.

Alberg pushed his plate slightly away from him, so he could rest his forearms on the table. "Seven years ago this woman left her husband and daughter to go live in a basement apartment in Abbotsford. They don't hear word one from her in all that time. She moved out of there and into the place in Sechelt last Friday. Sunday afternoon she's on the road leading to her husband's place when suddenly there's her daughter, and they scare the hell out of each other and both of them run away. Anyway, she obviously came here because of them. It occurred to me—maybe somebody didn't want her to see them."

"I don't know, Karl," said Sokolowski politely, loading his fork with mashed potatoes. "I tend to go with the obvious. Some cokehead, probably from the mainland, broke into her apartment, and she woke up, and he let her have it with a hammer she'd been using to hang up pictures."

Alberg looked at the sergeant irritably.

"Well, it's possible," said Sokolowski. "More than possible. Likely."

"And then there's the photo album," said Alberg stubbornly. "Either she took those pictures herself—and I don't see how she could have, without being seen at least once— or somebody took them for her. Who? Did somebody help her run away?" He poured more wine into each of their glasses. "I better not have any more of this, or I'm going to fall asleep."

"Eat," said Cassandra. "It's good."

"A few months before she took off," said Alberg, pulling his plate closer to him again, "Maria Buscombe found out that she'd been adopted." He got up and fetched a file folder from the coffee table in the living room. He pulled out a copy of the letter Agatha had left behind for Maria and handed it to Sid. "She decided she wanted information about her real family." Sid took his reading glasses from his shirt pocket and put them on. "So she quit her job and went off to do some research. The husband called it 'going in search of herself,' " he said to Cassandra. "I get the impression he was pissed off about it. Thought she'd be wasting her time." He started eating.

"Huh," said Sokolowski, observing him over his half glasses. "Oh no, she wouldn't be. I mean, how would you feel if you grew up thinking you were—Polish, say. And then years later somebody tells you no, that's wrong. You'd want to find out what the hell you really were, right? And what if it turned out that all along you'd been—English?" He paused to imagine this and shuddered.

"Mmmmm," said Alberg.

"Or you thought you were totally healthy," said Sokolowski, "and it turned out both your parents died in their forties of—I don't know, something genetic that you never even heard of."

"Right," said Alberg, with a glance at Cassandra.

"Or," said Sid, "you thought—"

"Okay," said Alberg, "I get it."

"What did she find out?" said Cassandra.

Sokolowski took off the glasses and put them away, then leaned over to drop the letter into the file folder.

"I don't know," said Alberg. "The husband says she didn't tell him anything when she got back, except that she'd found her parents. I don't know if I believe him, though."

"Got back from where?" said Cassandra.

"Saskatchewan." Alberg got up again, this time for his notebook, and thumbed through it as he walked back to the table. "The husband gave me the name of the guy she went out there to see. I called him this afternoon."

Sokolowski stared at him. "You're not gonna go out there, are you?"

"Are you?" said Cassandra, like an echo. In an instant she relived the moment only months ago when she'd gone to the door, opened it . . . and Gordon Murphy was standing there, brandishing his white teeth, his white shirt so bright it hurt her eyes, his arm slamming the door open, then closed. . . .

"Can you come with me, Cassandra?"

She returned to the present and found both men staring at her uneasily.

"He doesn't have to go," said Sokolowski. "He can get somebody out there to look into it, whatever it is."

"No, I can't come with you, Karl." She looked down at her plate. She'd eaten most of her dinner. Good. She wouldn't have to put any more food in her mouth. "How long will you be gone?"

"A couple of days, that's all. Are you sure you couldn't get away, just for a day or two?"

Cassandra shook her head. "Don't worry about it. I'll—I'll make some arrangements."

Chapter
18

Three days later Alberg was sitting in a living room in a house in Saskatoon. A fire burned in the fireplace, and rugs were placed here and there on the polished hardwood floor. It was the home of Edward Dixon, a man nearing seventy who occupied a worn brown leather chair, its back to corner windows through which Alberg, dismayed, observed that it had begun to snow.

"I've had heart surgery," said Dixon. "I keep myself fit. Golf in the summer. Exercise bike in the winter."

He wore a cardigan sweater, jade green, over a white shirt. His face was remarkably unlined, although he had practically no hair left and what was there was white. His gaze was candid and curious.

"You look after yourself," he continued, "when you've been through a thing like that. You have a lot more respect for your body. You know why?" But he didn't wait for an answer. "Because it's only when you've gotta think about dying that it hits home—doesn't seem right or fair, but there you are—that when the body craps out, there goes the whole of you."

He was a medium-size man. His wife, who returned to

the living room now with a tray, was an uncommonly large person: tall, big-boned, a woman who moved with awkward diffidence. Alberg stood to take the tray from her and set it on the coffee table.

"You gotta have one of her butter tarts," said Edward Dixon, watching, his hazel eyes magnified by his glasses. "Go on, go on," he said, waving an impatient hand in Alberg's direction. He grinned as Alberg took a bite. "Good, eh?"

Alberg turned to Mrs. Dixon, whose first name he had forgotten. He widened his eyes, his mouth full, and shook his head in wonderment.

Edward Dixon chuckled from his easy chair. "People always take one just to be polite. But I've never yet seen anybody remain unamazed. That's absolutely the best butter tart you've ever tasted, isn't it?"

"Absolutely," said Alberg with reverence, eyeing the plate.

"Have another," said Dixon expansively while his wife poured coffee. When she had filled two cups she started to leave the room. "Mavis. Don't go," said Edward Dixon. He had stretched a hand out toward her. She put a finger across her lips and turned again to leave.

"Stay, if you like, Mrs. Dixon," said Alberg.

"I'll just get myself a cup, then," she said.

For the minute or so it took her to fetch a cup and saucer from the kitchen, Edward Dixon stared into the fire, and Alberg brushed crumbs from his fingers; they had apparently decided that their conversation could not commence until Mavis Dixon had rejoined them.

When she had settled on the sofa, Dixon said, looking at Alberg, "This is a police matter. You're a police officer, you said." He peered at the badge Alberg took from an inside jacket pocket. "RCMP. I got mixed feelings about the

Mounties." Next to his chair was a tobacco stand from whose small cupboard he now pulled a white pipe. "We got a big native population on the prairies," he said, talking around the pipe stem.

Alberg was surprised that a man who'd had heart surgery would be smoking a pipe. He wondered if Mrs. Dixon worried about it.

"And those people haven't been well served by the Mounties in a lot of cases."

"I know," said Alberg. He tried not to close himself off from Dixon's frank and thorough scrutiny.

Dixon waited, but Alberg was determined not to have that particular conversation.

"You want to know about the adoption of Maria," Dixon said finally.

"Yes," said Alberg. "Whatever you can tell me."

"Because she's dead."

"Yes."

"Murdered."

"Yes."

Dixon set down the pipe to rub his temples. "Bloody tragedy."

The house reminded Alberg of his mother. There were lace antimacassars on the backs and arms of the sofa and the three easy chairs; not on the leather chair, though. The butter tarts were truly delicious. On the piano behind him he'd glimpsed a congregation of relatives in picture frames. Mavis Dixon probably still had a clothesline out back, he thought, and insisted on pinning up the laundry in fine weather.

"I forget—where do you come from?" said Edward Dixon suddenly, the pipe back between his teeth.

"Where was I born?" said Alberg. "London. Ontario."

"No, now."

"Oh. Sechelt, B.C."

"Is this a small place?"

"Yeah. Pretty small."

"Well, that's good. Because you gotta know small towns to be able to understand about Maria."

He hadn't filled his pipe. He puffed at it, making sucking noises of which he was apparently oblivious, and he gesticulated with it, achieving with this prop an expansiveness that was otherwise absent. But he wasn't smoking it. Alberg was relieved.

"You know everybody, in a small town," the old man went on. "Which is sometimes good, and sometimes bad. But often you don't know people as well as you think you do. You know what I mean?" Again he didn't seem to require a reply. He set the pipe carefully in the ashtray that was built into the top of the tobacco stand and brushed at the knees of his pants. "I was ten years old at the time," he said. "I knew the Gages. There were two other kids, boys, and then Maria came along. I don't think she was planned. Hell, I don't think any of them was planned, I don't think *I* was planned, for Pete's sake. Wait here a minute." He got up and left the room.

Alberg smiled at Mavis Dixon and drank from his coffee cup, which she promptly refilled.

"Mavis?" Dixon hollered from somewhere down the hall. "Where's the photo albums? Never mind, I see 'em." He returned carrying an old album with black covers, his finger marking a place. "There. That's them. Ira and Nadine Gage. Maria's mom and dad."

It was a black-and-white photo that had been tinted, and it showed a couple in their early twenties, standing at the edge of a furrowed field. The man was facing the camera, the woman was snuggled against his right shoulder but had turned to smile at the photographer. The man was wearing gray pants, a white shirt with the sleeves rolled up, and white shoes with black toes. She wore a short-sleeved white sweater tucked into pants whose legs were wide and flowing, and white shoes. Her hair was short and curly.

"This was before they got married," said Dixon.

"And you were related to them how?" said Alberg.

"My mother was Ira's cousin. She'd moved to Saskatoon by the time it happened." He made his way across the room and lowered himself onto his leather chair. "And she'd met Agatha, and knew about how Agatha wanted kids but couldn't have any of her own." He shrugged. "And so that's how it came about. Things could be pretty informal in those days."

Alberg looked at the photo again. The man's head was bent toward the woman's, and her body leaned into his. A slim tree trunk appeared behind them, and leaf shadows were scattered delicately across the photo, faintly obscuring Ira Gage's face and throwing a dainty pattern upon Nadine's elegant trousers.

"Tell me about them."

Dixon picked up his pipe and tapped it gently into the ashtray, emptying nonexistent ashes. "Nadine came from Rosetown. I don't know how she and Ira met up. She was okay until the first kid was born. That was Thaddeus. Born the same year as me, but two months later."

Dixon rested his forearms on his thighs, leaning forward to look into the fire, his pipe held loosely in his right hand. Through the pair of corner windows behind him, Alberg watched the snow fall; there wasn't much of it, but it was definitely snow.

"It's not unusual for a new mother to get the blues," said Dixon, looking at his wife as if for confirmation. "But I guess Nadine Gage got them pretty bad. Had to go to the hospital here in Saskatoon for a while."

Alberg realized as he listened that this was one of the things he liked best about the Job: the stories. He thought it was probably true what he'd read somewhere, that there was a limited number of stories, and they just kept getting relived, repeated, over and over, with an infinite number of variations that were almost inconsequential. But to him, this made them only more fascinating.

Dixon got up and put another piece of wood on the fire, deliberating for several seconds over the selection that was stacked neatly in a brick-lined alcove next to the firebox.

"She had another one almost right away," he said, poking the new log into the middle of the fire. "I'm damn sure that one wasn't planned," he said, glancing over his shoulder at Alberg. He put the poker away and sat down again. "Same thing happened. Ira got his sister to help out, because this time Nadine was in there longer. And even when she got back from the hospital she was in a bad way for a long time." He rubbed at his right eye with his fist, a gesture strangely childlike and poignant. "My mother used to talk about this a lot. She said people weren't very sympathetic—including her. And she used to say, if there'd been more sympathy . . . Ah, well." He looked at Alberg. "I'm gonna just cut to the chase here.

"Years went by, no more babies, which everybody who knew them thought was a very good idea. And then Maria was born."

Edward Dixon stood up and walked behind his chair to look out the window at the darkening sky and the still falling snow. "When Maria was a few months old, Nadine got up in the middle of the night and started killing people. First Ira. They figure he never even woke up. She stabbed him in the heart. And then the kids. Thaddeus first. He never woke up, either." He turned around and put his hands on the top of the chair, leaning there. "But the others did. Geoffrey slept in the same room as Thaddeus. Maria was in a tiny little room across the hall. It was Geoffrey's yelling that wakened the hired man, Art Johnson, who slept downstairs in a room off the kitchen. But by the time he got up there it was too late for Geoffrey."

Dixon looked off into the middle distance, frowning, as if he'd been there himself and was trying to remember exactly what he'd seen. "Art said she came out of the boys' room with a knife in her hand and blood all over this long white nightshirt she was wearing, and on her bare feet, too, and she glanced at him and sort of hesitated, and then she headed across the hall. And that's when he tackled her." A shudder passed over his face. "He got their blood all over him."

Alberg waited. "What happened to her?" he said finally.

"She got locked up. They call it a psychiatric hospital now." He moved around the chair again and sat down.

"Did Maria ever find out about this?"

Dixon nodded wearily. "Same way you did. Sitting in that same chair. Only it was summer. What was it, Mavis—five years ago? Six?"

"More like seven."

"Did she talk to anybody besides you?"

Dixon nodded. "She talked to her mother," he said heavily. "Right after she left here."

1987

Chapter
19

"And as far as I know," said Edward Dixon, "she's still there."

Maria's vision altered. She found this very curious. Light was suddenly sucked away from the room in which they sat, leaving Dixon shrouded in darkness, as though in a cave, with only a single pinpoint of illumination shining upon his face from somewhere. Maria asked him where it was, this place where her mother had been taken all those years ago, and his voice, when he answered, created luminous letters in midair: he opened his mouth, and letters of the alphabet swarmed into the air, glowing in the dark like phosphorescent alphabet soup. Maria studied the letters, but it was not an alphabet she knew.

She nodded politely, smiling, backed out of the house—or felt that she did—and made her way to the rented car parked in front. It was a small silver car, waiting obediently. Maria climbed in and had to tell herself all the things there were to do: close the door, lock it, insert the ignition key, put on her seat belt, turn the key—good. The motor started. Now move the gearshift into the "drive" position.

Maria sat perfectly still for a moment. Then she swiveled

her head slowly to the right. Edward Dixon was standing in the window, looking out at her. Maria felt nothing. He lifted his hand in a gesture that was half wave, half blessing. She kept both hands on the steering wheel. Then she faced front again and drove away.

She turned left at the corner and soon reached a main street beyond which she could see the gray stone buildings of the University of Saskatchewan, where the man who wasn't her father had gone to school. She headed for the center of the city and the Bessborough Hotel, where she was staying because as a child she had once stayed there with the people who weren't her parents. As an eight-year-old she had opened a desk drawer, found a bottle of ink and removed the lid, and managed to spill it. She remembered the blue-black puddle creeping slowly across the bottom of the drawer and onto the hotel stationery. She had closed the drawer, slowly, and then spent an apprehensive evening waiting for one of her nonparents to discover the mess. But they hadn't. She liked to think that somewhere in this hotel even now, today, there was a desk drawer containing a large but faded inkstain.

In her room—where the desk drawer was ink-free—she looked out the window at the South Saskatchewan River and the university rising from the opposite bank. It was a warm summer day. The river was a darker blue than the sky, and a brisk wind tossed the branches of the trees that were clustered along the water's edge.

After a while Maria took a deep, steadying breath, pressed her palms against her chest, between her breasts, and sat down at the telephone table to call the institution where her mother had been housed for the last forty-eight years.

She drove there in her rented silver car with the window open, drove slowly along a two-lane highway. When there was a break in the flow of traffic, she often heard a meadowlark, one of the few birdsongs she could identify, and this sound created in her the singular feeling that was simultaneous pain and joy. It was a melody from her childhood. The flat expanse of prairie, the circular horizon, the thunderheads moving rapidly across the summer-blue sky—these were things from her childhood, too, as powerful, as exultant, as the mountainous, seaside landscape where she now made her home. Through the car window came the song of the meadowlark, the fragrance of canola, the rough prairie breezes—and Maria for a few sporadic instants was almost able to forget where she was going and why.

Eventually, though, she reached her destination.

It was a large, not unfriendly building—except for the bars on the windows—constructed of red brick. Maria wondered, getting out of her car—where did they get the brick?

Inside was a small reception area that felt like a police station. There was no entry into the main part of the building without going behind the reception counter. A Plexiglas wall with wickets cut out of it extended several feet upward from the countertop. Two women were sitting behind it, one working at a computer, the other peering through eyeglasses at paperwork that Maria couldn't see.

Maria leaned forward to speak through one of the wickets. "I'm here to see Nadine Gage." This got her a curious glance from the young, ponytailed woman at the computer.

"One moment, please," the other one said with a smile. She was older and had a pair of crutches propped up in the corner where the counter met the wall. She got on the phone and murmured.

While she waited, Maria turned and looked out the window. The thunderheads were much nearer. By the time she left here the rain would probably have come and gone, a cool delicious shudder expelled by the returning sun.

"May I help you?"

Maria turned.

"I'm Carol Hartley, the director. I understand that you'd like to see Nadine." Her hands were clasped at her waist, and her head was tilted a little. She looked slightly amazed. Well, no wonder, thought Maria.

"Yes. My name is Maria Buscombe. I'm her daughter."

"Really," said Carol Hartley.

"I was adopted when I was a baby." The woman was studying her critically, and Maria tried unsuccessfully to relax. "I discovered only yesterday that—that she's here."

"You're familiar with the circumstances under which she was admitted?" said the director.

"I am. Yes."

The woman's gaze was abrasive. Maria wanted to avert her eyes and shift from foot to foot.

"Why do you want to see her?"

Maria, suddenly composed, considered several replies. "Forgive me," she said finally, "but that's a ridiculous question. The woman is my mother."

"Let me put it another way," said Carol Hartley, unruffled. "Why do you think she ought to see you?"

"Maybe she shouldn't see me," said Maria. "That's something you'll know better than I." She realized that the women behind the counter were listening and felt a flash of anger that this conversation wasn't being conducted in private.

The director sat on a bench near the door, gesturing to Maria to join her. "Nadine hasn't been well," she said, lowering her voice. Maria made no response. "She's had a couple of heart attacks." The director fingered the gold chain around her neck. Her long hair was pinned to her head in a series of tight loops. Maria smelled perfume. There must be people with allergies in this place, she thought. She imagined the director sailing through a dormitory and leaving in her wake elderly mad persons whose sudden sneezes were top-pling them out of their beds.

"Do you think seeing me is likely to provoke another one?"

The director gave her that steady stare again. She was a little older than Maria, an individual who looked strong and confident physically and who had about her an air of impenetrable serenity. She stood up. "Come with me."

Maria followed her down a long hallway with an abnor-mally high ceiling. Then into a long room split horizontally by a thigh-high counter that was itself divided by three-foot walls into ten cubicles, on either side of which was a chair. From the center of the counter a sturdy wire divider rose several feet and was secured to the four corners of the ceil-ing. The room was empty.

"Wait here," said Carol Hartley. "I'll see what she says." She went back into the hallway.

Maria sat down at one of the cubicles.

Her side of the counter faced a wall with a row of win-dows, barred, at the top. Through the glass Maria saw the now darkened sky and a tree being whipped by the wind. There were two doors on the opposite side of the counter, one on either side of the room, near the windows. Maria had placed her handbag on the floor next to her chair. She moved the chair now to align it more precisely in the mid-dle of the cubicle.

She thought she might be having a dream or acting in a movie. Her mouth was very dry—she longed to go outside and lift her face into the rain that had now begun to fall, to let it slide across her lips and into her open mouth. She started when the door behind her opened and Carol Hartley reentered the room.

"She says she'll see you." She was smiling a little. She sat down quietly on a chair by the door.

When the door on the other side of the counter opened, Maria's heart took a tremendous leap. For an instant she thought it had literally stopped, and she wondered how long it would last, this flash of consciousness between death and the brain's acceptance of death. An old woman in gray stepped through the door, followed by a male attendant dressed in white. Maria's heart lurched back into action and assumed a shallow, rapid, but constant rhythm as she watched the elderly person who was her mother make her reluctant, unsteady way across the room. Maria heard the shuffling of her slippered feet and the sound of the rain slapping furiously against the windows: all sounds were echoey in the linoleum-floored expanse of this graceless, charmless room.

As the woman came closer Maria saw that she was thin and frail, dressed not in gray, but in sweatpants and a sweatshirt that were faded blue. She had long white hair in a single braid. Her back was slightly humped, and arthritis had contorted her hands, held hesitantly in front of her, into claws. The attendant pulled out the chair for her, and she sat down, rested her claws on the countertop, lifted her head, and gazed dispassionately through the wire at Maria. Her eyes were rheumy but alert. For what felt like a long time, there was silence.

"Do they still call you Maria?" It was a surprisingly strong voice.

Maria nodded.

Chapter

20

Hamilton Gleitman found his way to a classroom in the Buchanan Building at the University of B.C. He took a seat near the door and dropped his knapsack onto the desk. He took out a pen and a notebook and a file folder and stowed the knapsack at his feet. He looked around him then, at these people who would be the first to experience his poetry.

They were perhaps twenty-five in number. Many of them were younger than Hamilton, but some were older. Some were talking among themselves, but mostly they were sitting alone, absorbed in the summer school course outline, or a paperback book, or jotting things in notebooks.

The desks were desktops attached to chairs, and for a moment Hamilton felt as though he were back in grade school: he wouldn't have been surprised to see an inkwell in the corner. Jesus. He was old enough to actually remember inkwells and pens with nibs.

The instructor entered and began striding back and forth at the front of the room, his hands clasped, elbows raised. He was a big man in his fifties, a novelist and a teacher of creative writing. Hamilton, registering for his class, had been familiar with his name but hadn't read any of his books. He'd found all of them on the shelves of the downtown library, borrowed them all, read them all, and hadn't liked any of them. But by then he'd been accepted into the class.

"Okay, people—let's get to know each other," said the instructor, pushing his glasses higher up the bridge of his nose. He wore a gray vest over a gray shirt, unbuttoned at the throat. His pants were black, and he wore black socks and Birkenstocks. Jesus, thought Hamilton. The guy's eyebrows were black and bushy, his large nose glistened, his thick graying hair was disheveled, but his mustache was sleek. "Okay," he said, pointing. "You first."

Heads craned, aiming glances at the poor sod at one end of the front row. He was a disconsolate adolescent who revealed that he hadn't been able to get into the novelist's regular daytime class. He then ducked his head and went on at some length, in a murmur. Hamilton strained to hear. He caught a phrase or two every time the guy looked up from his crotch: "interested in the narrative form," he heard, and "married to linear thinking," and "the legacy of structuralism." The novelist was pacing, head down, listening hard, hands behind his back. When the young man stopped talking he sat back on his chair, squeaked a look upward, and got an approving nod from the novelist.

Jesus, thought Hamilton. What the hell was he doing here?

"Next!"

A man in his thirties, wearing jeans and a blue T-shirt, moved a disbelieving gaze from the teenager to the instructor. "I'm in advertising and promotion," he said. "I want to learn how to write fiction."

"Some would say that's what you already do," said the novelist. Laughter percolated politely throughout the room.

It was something to do, Hamilton reminded himself, while waiting for the results of his grant application. But Jesus.

The advertising man looked at the novelist wearily.

"Sorry," said the instructor. "Okay. Good! Welcome aboard—you'll be a challenge," he added with a grin. "Next!"

Hamilton's fingers drummed restlessly on the file folder in front of him, which contained the ten pages he'd had to submit in order to be considered for the course.

"I'm a short-story writer," said the woman in the front row. She was maybe twenty-five. She had red hair that hung down her back in a thick braid. Her voice was throaty, assured, and melodious, and she was listing the publications in which her stories had appeared. The instructor was standing in front of her, turned slightly to one side, stroking his mustache with the fingers of his right hand, nodding.

"There is a black joy in sinning," Hamilton's pages began, "that is the real music of the spheres."

". . . and I'm curious about the longer form," the short-story writer was saying. "Whether it offers a bigger challenge, or"—she shrugged and offered a complacent chuckle—"if it's simply a short story that's bigger than it needs to be." She lifted her hand and flicked the braid over her shoulder and stroked it, smiling at the instructor.

The novelist was looking back at the short-story writer, expressionless. Hamilton could see him rummaging through his commodious vocabulary, sorting, selecting, rejecting.

"Next!" he called out, turning swiftly to the second row.

Also, thought Hamilton, he needed to be appreciated. It was time for praise. He needed it like a dying plant needed water.

". . . a historical novel," said the student, an elderly man dressed as if for church in a dark suit, shiny black shoes, a tie, and black suspenders that winked in and out of Hamilton's vision as he leaned forward slightly to get a look at the old man's profile. He was reaching down. Now he hauled onto his desk a large brown paper shopping bag. There was no writing on it. Hamilton wondered where he'd managed to find a shopping bag that didn't advertise something. "I've been working on it on and off over the last ten years or so," he said, taking from the bag a stack of typewritten pages. "Ever since I retired. I'd like your opinion. Your assessment." He beamed around the classroom, twinkling behind his glasses. Hamilton thought for a moment that he was making a joke. Maybe he'd typed out the phone directory. Or copied one of the novelist's own books.

"Well done!" the instructor said heartily. "But we have to assess everybody's work. So we won't be able to take a look at the whole thing, you understand."

The elderly man looked disappointed. There was a flash of sullenness in the glance he cast upon his classmates.

"Next!"

Hamilton, sitting at the end of the third row, pondered his new-hatched need to be read and celebrated.

The person on the seat beside him moved restlessly. He was young, too, another adolescent, and he kept drumming the heel of his right shoe on the floor. It didn't make much of a noise, since he was wearing sneakers and the floor was covered in linoleum, but it was bloody irritating. Hamilton tried to keep his head averted enough to avoid seeing it, that tense shuddering of heel against floor, but this was difficult, and each time he got a glimpse of it his blood pressure rose.

There was laughter in the classroom again, but it sounded comfortable this time, genuinely spontaneous. Even the instructor was smiling. Hamilton leaned to the

side, looking around the bulky man sitting one seat over in
the row ahead of his, but couldn't see the person who'd been
speaking.

And now, "Next!" rang out again.

"I've been writing since I was twelve years old," said a
middle-aged man, balding: that was all Hamilton could see
of him, except that he was wearing a jacket that announced
him as a member of a bowling league.

"I've got a trunkful of manuscripts," he told them. "Novels. I get up every morning at four, regular as clockwork, put
in two hours at the computer." He turned around to address
the class, pushing on the arm that linked his chair to the
desktop. "It's totally amazing what you can accomplish
putting in just two hours a day, five days a week."

A trunkful, thought Hamilton, furious, both hands flat
on his file folder.

The novelist stood at the front of the room, looking
piercingly at the man with the manuscripts. Hamilton wondered if he, too, got up at four in the morning. He imagined
the guy's alarm going off. He'd reach out to quiet the clock
and see 4:00. He would push back the bedclothes, swing his
legs out onto the floor, and get up quickly and quietly, so as
not to disturb his sleeping wife. He'd tiptoe into the bathroom, where he would have left his clothes the night before,
dress, and head immediately for the computer, set up in his
den. No, first he'd probably put on some coffee. And while
it dripped, he'd get to work. And he'd work for two hours.
By which time it would still be only six o'clock in the morning. Ridiculous.

"What are you doing here?" said the teenager at the desk
next to his. Hamilton turned; but the kid was looking at the
man in the bowling jacket.

"Say again?" said the bowler.

"What are you doing here? If you've got all these books

already written?" The kid's face was flushed and angry. "I mean, shit—"

"Now, Kevin," the novelist-instructor said indulgently, and he kept looking at the boy, wearing an almost whimsical expression, until Kevin slumped back on his seat and resumed his heel tapping.

Hamilton thought it unlikely that his work would find among these people the thoughtful consideration it deserved.

"This is a class for writers," said the novelist, stern, to the class at large. He brought his brows together in emphasis. "And do you know how we can tell who are the writers among us?"

It was, Hamilton figured, a rhetorical question.

"Writers," said the novelist, "are people who write." He beamed at them.

Hamilton couldn't imagine getting up to start writing at four o'clock in the morning. Hamilton wrote his poetry at night. He held the file folder in his hands, hefting it.

"Next!" cried the instructor.

Hamilton sighed deeply. Slowly he reached down. The objects dangling from his belt loops made a satisfyingly tinny jingle as he swept his knapsack off the floor.

"I'm a poet," said a woman wearing pink sweatpants and sweatshirt, with a heavy white cardigan slung across her shoulders. "And I'll always write primarily poetry. But lately I've gotten into short stories, and now I'd like to explore the possibilities offered by the novel."

Hamilton slid from his chair, slipped behind it, reached for the door handle.

"Lost your courage?" said the instructor, who was smiling at him from behind his glasses and his folded arms.

Hamilton imagined himself on the backseat of the novelist's car, hiding on the floor with a long metal skewer in his hand. One poke in the butt, he thought, when you're halfway over the Granville Street Bridge, and we'll see whose courage goes flying. He laughed out loud. Shaking his head, still chuckling, he left the room, letting the door close softly behind him.

Chapter 21

"You're a handsome girl," said Nadine. "Are you married?"

Maria nodded.

"Do you have any children?"

Maria nodded again. "A daughter. Belinda." It was difficult to speak.

Her mother hadn't taken her eyes from Maria's face. "I asked them what had happened to you," she said. "They wouldn't tell me. 'She's in a good home.' That's all they'd say. Were you in a good home?"

"Yes."

"Good."

The rain had lessened and was now sheeting down the windows in coats of transparent silver.

Maria asked, "Why did you do it?" She felt an astonishing flood of relief.

Her mother sat back on the wooden chair, lifting her disfigured hands into her lap. "When did you find out?"

Maria heard nothing in her voice. It was as dry as dust. "Yesterday," she said.

Her mother shook her head slowly and looked away. She was small, frail, crippled—it was hard to imagine her having the strength to stab anyone. But she had struck her husband in his sleep and the biggest child, too.

Maria put her arms on the counter and bent close to the wire. "Please."

Her mother glanced behind her, at the attendant who waited by the door through which they had entered.

"Please," said Maria. Her thoughts were in disarray. She tried to marshal them—she needed coherence. "Oh, God," she whispered, struggling for control. She felt the director's eyes on the nape of her neck.

Nadine looked at her impassively. "I don't know why you think I could answer that. Is it the only thing you want to know?"

Maria looked down, blinking rapidly, freeing her eyelashes of tears. "Yes. I guess it is." Nadine studied her, and Maria tried to see in her mother the young woman in Edward Dixon's photograph. "No. It isn't the only thing. Tell me about my father."

She watched pain flicker across her mother's face and wondered what Nadine had felt as she drove the knife into her husband's chest. Had his eyes opened? Had she wanted too late to change her mind?

"Did you love him?" she asked. Her mother continued to look at her but didn't respond. "What was he like?" Nadine gave an impatient shrug. "Please," said Maria, leaning close to the wire divider again. "I need to know."

"It's very unsettling to have to deal with you," said her mother irritably.

"But you must have expected that I'd show up eventually. You must have at least thought about it."

"For a while I did, yes. But not recently. Not for years."

The rain had stopped, and through the window Maria saw clouds rapidly scudding eastward. She didn't want to be here any longer.

Would she tell Richard and Belinda? Nadine wasn't anybody Maria wanted as a grandmother for Belinda. Though Richard might find her a more interesting mother-in-law than even Agatha had been, she thought.

She examined her mother, looking for familiar things. Would she, Maria, get arthritis, too? she wondered. Or would Belinda? Nadine had had heart attacks—would Maria and Belinda have them, too?

"Why are you still in this place?"

"Because I want to be."

"Why?"

Nadine looked at her with distaste. "I'd have to know you a hell of a lot longer than fifteen minutes before I'd—"

Maria slapped the counter and half rose on her chair. The attendant looked over at her but stayed where he was. "Listen! You took my family from me. I thought I was somebody I wasn't, because of you." She jabbed the air. "You owe me." She sat down again, slowly, trembling.

"I owe you what?" said her mother, with contempt. She sat stiffly on her chair, cradling her hands in her lap.

She probably suffers, thought Maria. Still trembling, she looked through the wire at her mother. She tried to remember Belinda's birth—but her head resonated with the sound of screaming. Maria put her hands carefully over her ears, pushing firmly, then took them away—and the sound was gone.

She probably suffers, she thought again, looking at her mother.

"Nothing," said Maria dully. "You don't owe me anything." She looked around for her handbag and picked it up from the floor.

"Wait." Nadine leaned closer, and Maria saw the pink skin of her scalp where her white hair was parted. "You asked about your father."

Maria put her handbag in her lap and faced her mother.

"Everything else you want to know—it's too late," said Nadine. "But—" She looked down at her hands, resting grotesque and helpless on the countertop. "Your father—" For the first time she spoke with an effort, and Maria thought there might be pain in her voice. "He was—strong. Healthy. Intelligent." She gave Maria a wry glance. "Good genes, on one side, anyway."

Maria was incredulous. "But how could you do it? How could you kill him?"

Nadine was silent.

"Why?"

"I didn't kill him."

Maria wanted to believe her. For a second she did believe, for a second she thought, I will spend the rest of my life finding a way to prove she's innocent. My mother. Innocent.

"I killed Ira Gage," said Nadine. "I didn't kill your father."

Maria sat there, across the counter from Nadine, looking at her through a wire divider.

"Tell me," she said.

THE PRESENT

Chapter

22

Alberg was sitting on the edge of his bed in a motel room in Calgary, the same motel he and Cassandra had stayed in just a week ago, when Janey had gotten married. The days had been blue and gold and the sun warm, a week ago; and now tonight the snow was falling here as it had fallen yesterday in Saskatoon. Alberg knew it wouldn't last. But next month it would.

He had come to Calgary in search of the hired man who had rescued Maria.

He realized that he was staring at an ashtray in which there was a book of matches with the motel's name on it. He moved it from the bedside table to the desk. But that was where the phone was. He moved it again, to the table on the opposite side of the bed—but that wasn't good enough, either. Finally he stashed the ashtray in the bottom of the chest of drawers, which he wouldn't be using.

Then he went to the desk and dialed Janey's number. The musician answered. Janey, he told Alberg, was not at home. Home, thought Alberg, marveling. Her home was with this musician, now. He left a message and then called Diana and got her machine. Finally he tried his own number in Gibsons, and here he had better luck.

"I'm sorry I had to make this trip," he told Cassandra.

"Look, Karl. I can't live the rest of my life in somebody's pocket. I've got to get over this, and I will."

"I know. But still. I'm sorry."

"It would be better if we were in another place."

Alberg's heart sank, despite the fact that he'd been steeling himself for this. Preparing for it. Even planning it.

"Every time somebody knocks on the door—"

"I know, I've been thinking the same thing." Not anyplace on the goddamn prairies, though, he'd decided, and he hoped she would agree.

"So when you get back," she said, "let's go house hunting. Okay?"

"House hunting?"

"Yeah. How about it? I'll sell my place and we'll buy a house together."

"A house? Where?"

"I don't know where. Here in Gibsons. Sechelt. Wherever."

"Are you sure?"

She didn't speak for a moment or two. "You mean you aren't? I thought you wanted to get married, for God's sake. Now you don't know if you want us to buy a house?"

"No no no." He stood up, but the cord was too short, so he had to sit down again. "No no no. No."

"Karl, what's wrong with you?"

"Nothing, nothing. I misunderstood you, that's all. Yeah. House hunting. Terrific! That's terrific!" He felt himself beaming.

"When are you coming home?" she said. "I miss you."

"Me too," said Alberg, still smiling. "I don't know exactly. It depends on the guy I'm seeing in the morning. It's possible I'll be able to get a flight back late tomorrow."

"Have you learned anything useful?"

He hesitated. He wanted to tell her the story, but there

wasn't enough of it yet. He was filled with expectation. He wanted to cradle that to himself, for the moment, until he knew more. "Yeah," he said. "It's been a useful trip."

Cassandra, standing in the darkened kitchen of the directors' house in her nightgown, said good night and hung up and stood there, listening to the rain pelting the window and the wind rattling in the eaves trough. She wondered if she wanted a glass of milk or a cup of tea.

She opened the fridge and had to smile: her mother had tidied up in there. Leftovers had been transferred from plates or plastic bags to proper containers, with lids. Jars of condiments had been wiped clean and replaced with all labels facing front. The drawers had been washed and lined with clean paper toweling. Cassandra took out a can of soda water and poured it over ice into a large glass.

She returned to the living room, where a rented cot had been set up in the corner behind Karl's wingback chair. A standing lamp sat next to it and its light shone upon the cot, a pile of books on the floor beside it, an opened book sprawled on the bed itself. Cassandra put the glass on the floor. She climbed into bed, adjusted the pillows, and turned out the light.

A few minutes passed.

"Cassandra?"

She turned her head and saw that her mother was sitting on the end of the sofa. She sat up quickly. "What's wrong?"

"Nothing. I couldn't sleep, that's all."

Cassandra pulled up the pillow and leaned against it. The sound of the rain on the roof had subsided to a shallow clatter, and she could no longer hear the wind. Her mother's robe was a splotch of white in the darkened room.

"I'm glad you asked me to stay with you. I'm glad I can be of some use to you, still."

"I'm glad, too, Mother."

"Are you and Karl planning to get married?"

Cassandra rested her head against the wall. "I don't know. Maybe." She looked over at her mother, whose face was still in shadow, but Cassandra could see her hands, in her lap, smoothing the fabric of her robe, a quilted white one with pink piping around the collar and cuffs. She tried to see if her mother was wearing her slippers, but her feet were hidden by the folds of the robe. "I was going to propose to him the other night, as a matter of fact," she said with a little laugh. "And then he told me he had to go out of town."

"For heaven's sake, Cassandra. What's that got to do with anything?"

"You know, Mom. I can't bear to be alone yet. That's no reason for getting married."

"But it wouldn't *be* the reason, would it?"

"No. But it would feel like it was."

Her mother leaned forward, and the faint light that filtered through the curtain from the street lamp touched her face. "This is such a difficult time for you. I wish I could help."

When it was all over, Cassandra had sat on the edge of her mother's bed and said, "A bad thing happened to me, Mom. I have to tell you about it." As she talked, her mother sitting up in bed by then, Helen Mitchell had had tears in her eyes. They ran slowly down her wrinkled cheeks as she touched Cassandra's face and gathered her in her arms. Cassandra had been very impressed with this, for her mother had never been a demonstrative woman, not even when Cassandra was a child.

"I remember," said Cassandra dreamily, "when macaroni and cheese was my favorite food, and I wanted to have it every day, for lunch."

"I remember that. It was before you started school," said her mother.

Cassandra heard a siren, far away, a mournful sound that brought Karl back into her thoughts.

"Your father didn't like macaroni and cheese. Neither did Graham. I did, though. Apart from not wanting to be by yourself—how are you?"

"I'm fine, Mother," said Cassandra. Helen Mitchell's face, in the dim light and at this distance, looked fresh and young. "I'm going to be fine."

The next morning Alberg parked his rented car in front of a house in southwest Calgary where Art Johnson lived with his son, who was divorced and childless and a few years younger than Alberg. The son was a chartered accountant who worked in a small office with a partner on Twelfth Avenue. Today was Sunday, though, and he would be at home.

Alberg had begun the search for the hired man in the town where the murders occurred. The woman who used to be postmistress, when there was a post office there, told him about Johnson's son, whose name was Thomas. "Thomas Hardy Johnson," said the erstwhile postmistress, "named after the Englishman who wrote *Tess of the d'Urbervilles*." He'd gone to university in Saskatoon, she said. Alberg traced him through the alumni association, to which Thomas Hardy Johnson had made regular contributions ever since his graduation.

Alberg climbed the steps and went through a screen door that led into a porch about half the width of the house. He knocked on the inner door and waited, shivering, for someone to answer. It was a very cold day—although at least it had stopped snowing and the sun had come out. There was a stack of folded-up lawn chairs in a corner of the porch, and several hanging baskets containing frozen flowers had been lined up next to it. Corpses, awaiting burial.

The door was opened by a tall, middle-aged man, balding, slightly paunchy. He presented Alberg with a wary expression, not exactly hostile, but certainly reluctant. This guy was not pleased to be opening his door to Alberg: maybe because Alberg was a cop, maybe because he was concerned for his aged dad—who could tell. But Alberg was not unaccustomed to this kind of reception and had learned not to let it bother him.

"Karl Alberg. You're expecting me."

"Right." Johnson stepped back to let him enter.

In the cramped hallway Alberg's eye was caught by a row of hooks, the kind he remembered from his schooldays. Two jackets hung there, along with scarves and toques. On the floor, on a rubberized tray, sat one pair of toe rubbers and one pair of ankle-high galoshes; weatherproof footwear with metal clasps. The floor was hardwood, with a rubber-backed carpet runner in the middle.

Johnson took Alberg's jacket and hung it on an empty hook. He appeared to be waiting for something. Alberg rubbed his hands vigorously and made a comment about the weather. Finally it dawned on him that his host wanted him to remove his shoes. "Ah!" he said. He leaned against the wall and toed off his shoes and followed Thomas Hardy Johnson in his stocking feet.

The hallway—which he thought of as a cloakroom—was dim, lit by a hanging lamp whose wattage ought to have been increased, a cramped and gloomy area, and he was pleasantly surprised by the living room. There was a window in the front, and two big windows on the side looked out into a large garden.

"Take a seat," said Thomas Hardy. "I'll go get Dad."

The narrow hallway widened into a circular area from

which a staircase led to the second floor. Alberg had noticed a dining room across from the living room. The back of the house would contain a kitchen and a bedroom—probably the old fellow's room, to save him having to climb the stairs—and there would be a bathroom down here, too, he thought.

He looked around the living room, which didn't look like a room shared by two bachelors. The furniture was covered in fabric striped in muted shades of blue and green—there was a sofa, an easy chair, and a wingback chair that matched. But over in the corner by the fireplace stood a big tweed chair and a scuffed leather footstool, with a standing lamp positioned for reading. And in another corner there was a padded, high-backed rocking chair, a TV set, and a potted tree, and from the ceiling hung a huge plant with long segmented branches dripping with red flowers. Alberg saw no sign of music, no CD or tape or record player, and no bookcases, either, although there was a pile of newspapers on the floor by the sofa, and a book lay facedown on the footstool.

He heard the two men coming across the hall and turned to greet them.

Art Johnson was much shorter than his son, but he was permanently bent over, so it was hard to tell how tall he might once have been. He was clean-shaven and almost completely bald, with a fringe of white hair that was neatly trimmed. He wore gray pants and a white shirt with a maroon vest on over it. His dark blue necktie had tiny white horses on it, and on his feet were leather slippers. His son stood close to him, and Alberg wondered just how tottery the old guy was and whether he usually used a cane, but not in front of strangers if he could help it. He could not imagine this man as a hired hand. We are talking about another world, he thought; another time, and about people who have slipped perhaps not easily from then to now, from there to here.

"Mr. Johnson? I'm Karl Alberg." He stepped close to the old man and offered his hand. "Thanks for agreeing to talk to me." He was surprised by the size of Thomas's hand and the strength of his grip.

Art Johnson moved to the wingback chair and sat down. What the hell has he got to tell me? thought Alberg, gazing at him.

Thomas Hardy said, "I'm going upstairs to do some work, Dad. Give me a holler if you want me."

"He wasn't even born when it happened," said Art Johnson, watching his son cross the room. "He probably works too hard. I know he works harder than he needs to." He turned to look at Alberg, who had stationed himself on the sofa. "He hasn't got much else in his life but work. I look after him as best I can. He's a sad person, Thomas is. Luckily, he's got me. I don't crack a lot of jokes. But I have a perspective on things that interests him. Now. How about a glass of sherry?"

Alberg hesitated. "It's a bit early, isn't it?" he said. "But what the hell. Sure. Good."

The old man pushed himself to his feet and shuffled out of the room. Alberg heard him in the dining room, opening a cupboard door, selecting glasses, pouring—a slow *glug-glug*—replacing the bottle, closing the cupboard door. Alberg forced himself to remain seated as he watched Johnson shuffle back into the living room, bearing a small brass tray on which sat two crystal sherry glasses filled almost to the brim. Alberg took one. Johnson put the other on the small end table next to his chair and turned to toss a small smile of triumph over his shoulder. He put the tray on the floor and sat down.

Alberg lifted his glass to him and took a sip. "Excellent."

Johnson nodded, pleased. "Now. What do you think I can do for you, Staff Sergeant?"

The sun glinted from the snow in the garden and fell summer-warm across the dove gray carpet and Alberg's sock-clad feet. "Maria Buscombe, once Maria Gage, has been murdered, in Sechelt, which is my patch. Part of the investigation into her death involves looking into her personal history."

"You're going pretty far back," said Art Johnson.

"Yeah. I started with the fact of her adoption, and one thing just led to another." Alberg shrugged.

"Things usually do," said Johnson dryly. He picked up his sherry glass, which looked small and fragile in his huge hand.

"I guess you're the end of the line, though," said Alberg. "According to Edward Dixon, anyway."

Johnson sipped the sherry but didn't seem to taste it. "Tell me about Maria," he said. "Did you know her?"

"No," said Alberg.

"She's just another victim to you, then."

"No. She's a puzzle, to me."

"The last time I saw her," said Johnson abruptly, looking out the window, "her little face was as white as that snow out there. Her eyes were shut, her cheeks were covered with . . . dried tears, she was lying in an apple box with a pillow in the bottom, covered up with blankets. It was just before they took her away from that house. She'd screamed herself unconscious."

"Tell me about her parents," said Alberg quietly.

Johnson turned back to him. "I'll probably dream about it tonight. If I do, it'll start with the screams." He put down the sherry glass. "Ira was hardworking. A worrier. Loved his kids. Doted on his kids. Loved Nadine, too, I guess." He stood up and shuffled around the chair. "My joints get stiff.

Gotta change position, every so often." He rested his forearms on the back of the chair. "It was a bloody hard life. First the Depression, then the bloody war. All the women putting together parcels for Britain, wondering if their men were gonna join the bloody army." He shook his head and stared into the sun splotch on the floor. "Still," he said softly. "There were good times, too."

"Did Nadine send parcels to Britain?"

Johnson looked blank for a moment. "Nadine? Well, she tried. See, Nadine—" He paused while he moved out from behind the chair and sat down again. "Nadine was different. People said it was having babies that made her go crazy for a while, what they call postpartum depression nowadays, I guess, but that wasn't right. Nadine was always crazy. No. Let me correct myself." He looked away, his face screwed up in thought. "Delicately balanced. That's what she was."

Alberg thought about this. "You mean more things than childbirth could throw her off."

"Yes. That's what I mean."

"And what happened," Alberg asked, "when she got thrown off?"

Johnson stared into the sunlight again, remembering. "She would become agitated. And then she'd either blow up, or she'd get laid flat by melancholy. Sometimes things would happen to calm her, like one time . . .

"She'd hung the washing on the line, it was a summer day, hot and windy, and along about noon the winds got stronger and a storm blew up and the washing got drenched in the rain that fell. I remember she was standing on the steps, looking at the rain that was dousing the clothesline. And her, too; She was soaked. She had one hand on her head, keeping her hair out of her face, and I was standing nearby, wondering what the hell she was gonna do, when the rain stopped and the sun came out. You know how sudden that can happen on the prairie, the wind just goes *whoosh*"—he made a sweeping gesture—"and the rain's gone. And there was a double rainbow. From horizon to horizon. Nadine put her hands together, like this, and watched the rainbow, and cried. And she was fine, that time."

"But other times?"

"Other times she'd walk off up the road and not come back for hours. Or else she'd throw things around and yell at Ira and the kids. And me."

"What was she like when she was—balanced?" said Alberg.

"As pleasant a woman as you're likely to meet. Smart, too. And she had a fine sense of humor. Wry. Ironic, like."

"Do you know what set her off, the night she killed her family?"

Johnson shook his head. "I've been over it and over it. What did we miss? I keep looking for it. Why couldn't I get upstairs faster? I keep trying again, in dreams. Fifty-four years ago, it happened, but when I dream about it, it's happening now."

"You saved Maria's life," said Alberg.

"Yeah. But it's the others I remember. That's just human nature." He took another drink of sherry. "She seemed to be fine that day. Calm, she was. She seemed calm, anyway. And then—ah, God. She was so strong. And slippery with their blood." He pulled a handkerchief from his pocket. "Yeah. I saved the little one." The old man looked at Alberg, moisture gleaming in his eyes. "But she ended up getting murdered anyway."

"Yes," said Alberg. "She did."

"I've got one thing to tell you that probably won't help you. I hesitate because it feels like gossip. Although it isn't. It's a thing I know to be true. I just don't figure it's relevant." He glanced away, then back at Alberg. "Nadine had a boyfriend."

Alberg had a vision of a woman on a tightrope. She was wearing an ankle-length dress, and her long hair flowed down her back—it was an image completely wrong for the period, but he was stuck with it. She held her arms away from her body, for balance, and there was such hesitant, tenuous grace in her carriage that he felt an ache in his heart. He was on her level, in this vision, but looking at her from the side and from a little bit behind her, so that he could not see her face. She was harshly illuminated from both sides and surrounded by darkness. The rope on which she balanced stretched back and forward into infinity.

"Did she, now?" he said softly.

"Uh-huh. I saw them together three times."

"How long had it been going on?" said Alberg.

Johnson shrugged and shook his head.

"Did her husband know?"

"Oh God, no."

"But could he have found out? And confronted her? Because that would have—set her off. Wouldn't it?"

"You'd think so." Johnson glanced toward the hall, hearing his son's footsteps on the stairs. "It's one of the things I wonder about."

"What was his name?" said Alberg.

"Stewart," said Johnson. "Alan Stewart."

"You two about ready to wrap it up?" said Johnson Hardy Johnson, from the doorway.

"Almost," said Alberg, his eyes still on the old man. "What can you tell me about him?"

"He was the doctor. He retired fifteen years ago, same as me. Only he went to the Coast."

"Where on the Coast, do you know?"

"Vancouver."

Chapter
23

Alberg spent the morning of Thanksgiving Day in his office, getting caught up. It was just before noon when he sat back with a sigh and took off his reading glasses. He studied the photograph of his daughters, which took pride of place on the wall next to his desk. He leaned closer, to peer at it more critically, and saw that it was time for a new one. This one was out-of-date. They'd gotten older again. And now one of them was married; by rights the musician ought to be in the picture, too. Alberg was very glad he wasn't.

Alberg looked restlessly around his office. He wanted some kind of big change in there, now that he no longer had to consider early retirement. He wanted to knock out a wall, or at least get a larger window, or maybe paint the walls yellow or some damn thing. In the meantime, he thought, picking up a file folder from his desk, he would vacate the place.

When he pulled up a few minutes later in front of Sid's house, Sokolowski was standing on the porch of the house next door. Alberg cut the motor and climbed out of his Oldsmobile as the front door opened. A young Chinese woman stood there, with two small children hiding behind her legs. Alberg wasn't close enough to hear what Sid said to her as he handed her something. The woman looked surprised but accepted it. Sid gave her a little salute and turned to leave, and Alberg saw that he had presented her with a dish of some kind. The woman disappeared back inside.

"Hi," said Alberg.

"Karl. What are you doing here?"

"What was that all about?"

Sid closed the gate, making sure the latch caught. "I gave her my specialty," he said. "Tuna casserole."

"You made it yourself?"

"Of course I made it myself." He threw Alberg a bitter glance. "There's nobody else gonna cook my meals that I know of. Not anymore."

Alberg followed him up the walk and into his house, which smelled like furniture polish.

"They just moved in," said Sokolowski, "those people next door." Alberg steeled himself for the inevitable pronouncement on race and/or nationality. "Clean people, the Chinese," said the sergeant, heading for his kitchen. "Quiet. Shrewd, though. Gotta watch them in business dealings. Not that I intend to have any business dealings with them." He stood looking out the window at his backyard. "I wish they'd moved in on the other side of me, though. That same old guy is there, Karl. With the leaves all over his so-called lawn, and the old car just dumped there, and dandelions in the spring." He sounded disproportionately distraught.

"You got any coffee?" said Alberg.

"Yeah." Sid got mugs out of a cabinet. "I was just gonna have some."

They took their coffee into the living room. Before he sat down, Sid stooped to pick something up from the carpet— a small dead leaf, Alberg thought it was.

"I wanted to talk to you about Maria Buscombe," said Alberg.

"Shoot," said Sokolowski. He was sitting on a big, deep recliner that faced a television set. Next to it was an end table on which he had placed his coffee mug. "Did you get anywhere with the guy in Saskatchewan?"

Alberg took his notebook from his pocket. "Yeah, I think so." Referring to his notes, he told Sokolowski about Edward Dixon and Art Johnson and Maria Buscombe's parents. "The mother died in the hospital about eighteen months after Maria went to see her there. I don't know if the doctor's still alive—or what he can tell us if he is. I'll start tracking him down tomorrow."

That picture materialized in his head again: a baby, screaming, clutching the rail of her crib, and across the hall in her brothers' room, her mother, a shadow, stabbing. Alberg had learned early how to achieve distance from his work. He was able to maneuver himself through bad stuff while remaining untouched by it, deftly keeping his mind absorbed in the problems it had created while keeping himself free of it emotionally. But sometimes an image got burned into his mind and he couldn't shake it loose.

"It's hard to tell what all this has to do with the homicide, though," said Sokolowski. There was no reproach in his voice, just a certain delicacy.

Alberg glanced at his notebook. He drank some coffee. "The woman takes off on her husband and daughter, Sid, leaving behind a note which says virtually nothing. If the husband can be believed. We know that she holed up in a basement apartment out in the Fraser Valley, for God's sake. And now we also know that every year for seven years she deposits a bank draft for twenty thousand dollars. Those two things are connected: her leaving, and the money."

"You don't know that for sure, Karl," Sokolowski said patiently.

"They are connected, Sid, by the photos in that album." He occupied the recliner as if it were a throne, Alberg thought irritably. "Somebody provided her with pictures of her daughter, one a year. Why? To show her that the kid was okay. Who? It's a fair guess that it's whoever was paying her the twenty thousand a year." He flipped the notebook closed. "Now we have to find out who benefited from her absence."

"Twenty thousand a year, it's not enough to desert your family for," said Sokolowski fervently. Alberg suddenly wondered if Elsie was supporting herself in Vancouver or if Sid was providing her—reluctantly—with financial assistance that enabled her to live apart from him.

"It was enough to live on," said Alberg.

"Well, be that as it may," said Sid. He drained his coffee mug and put it on the table next to him. "I can see you've got your work cut out for you."

"How about coming over for dinner tonight?" Alberg tucked his notebook back in his pocket and stood up. "Turkey, pumpkin pie, the works."

"Oh, I don't know, Karl." The sergeant got up to walk Alberg to the door. "It's a family-type thing, Thanksgiving."

"Right. And your family's hither and yon, and so is mine." He went out onto the front porch. "There'll just be Cassandra, her mother, me, and you. Six o'clock."

As he drove off he waved at Sokolowski, a big, brooding presence on the front step, and wondered if he'd ever again live close enough to his daughters to have Thanksgiving dinner with them every year. He also wondered, uneasily, what Janey's laconic musician would contribute to family gatherings.

Chapter
24

"There's a gentleman down the hall," said Helen Mitchell from her easy chair, "who's dying. He's been at it for several days now," she told Alberg, who had folded himself onto a chair that was too small for him. "Relations at his bedside and what have you," Helen went on, looking out the bay window at the evening that surrounded Shady Acres. "Taking turns. Spelling each other off." She adjusted the cushion that supported the small of her back. "The other day they brought a lunch with them." She looked indignantly straight into Alberg's face, her eyes flashing behind her glasses. "Kentucky Fried Chicken."

Alberg burst out laughing. He saw that this surprised her and was pleased when she decided to laugh with him.

"Thanks again for staying with Cassandra while I was away," he said.

"Thank you for Thanksgiving dinner," said Helen Mitchell. "And for bringing me home." She hesitated. "I want to talk to you. Why don't you get out of that chair and sit on the window seat."

Alberg did so.

He had always been slightly uncomfortable in her presence,

as if feeling criticized. Yet he thought she approved of him. He had finally decided that Helen Mitchell's take on life itself was critical, and that this emanated from her continually, like a vapor. It was Alberg's opinion that Cassandra, in overlong visits with her mother, inhaled too much of this censorious gas, which was why she sometimes came home suffering from depression and a headache.

"I don't believe I'm being disloyal to my daughter by telling you this," said Helen Mitchell.

Alberg remained politely attentive.

"Cassandra told me while you were gone that she recently decided to marry you. But that she couldn't do it after all. Because of her fear of being alone."

Alberg shook his head. "Yeah. Well."

"I'm not asking you to discuss this with me," she said. "I'm simply providing you with information."

"Okay." He nodded. "Thanks."

She was looking at him intently. "She's never going to 'get over' this. Oh, she'll put it behind her, and life will go on, and she will eventually be able to be alone again. But that dreadful experience will always be with her. You know that, don't you?"

He tried never to think about it. He'd rather have the image of the screaming infant stuck in his head than Gordon Murphy, the preening, psychopathic son of a bitch who had kidnapped Cassandra. "Yeah," he said reluctantly. "I do."

"So don't wait," she said, leaning toward him. "Don't let her put you off."

Alberg nodded. "Okay." He smiled. "I'll try."

She sat back. "I could offer you a glass of wine."

"Could you now?"

"Would you like one?"

"I would indeed."

She got up and took a bottle of white wine from the small

refrigerator in the corner of her room and two wineglasses from a cupboard above it. She filled the glasses, replaced the bottle, and handed Alberg his drink. "Happy Thanksgiving," she said, touching her glass to his.

"Happy Thanksgiving," said Alberg, and they drank.

She sat down and looked at him thoughtfully. "What was your punishment," she asked, "for striking that lunatic?"

Alberg, in a flash, saw it again: Gordon Murphy, in his gym clothes, sweating. Grinning. And he felt it again: the splendid satisfaction when his fist hit that dazzling smirk and shattered it.

He raised his eyebrows. "Strike? Me? Oh no, Helen. He fell down."

Cassandra was doing the dishes when Alberg got home. He joined her and picked up a dishtowel and started drying. It felt very good, very companionable, she thought, to be working together. They talked casually about Sid, whose gloom had lifted only occasionally during dinner, and about whether Elsie was likely ever to return to him. Suddenly Cassandra heard herself saying, "Karl. Will you marry me?"

His mouth fell open. He was stupefied.

Cassandra began to laugh.

"What?" he said. "What?"

She laughed harder, flapping the dishcloth in the air, spattering him with soapy water.

"You don't mean it," he said. "You're playing a cruel joke."

She dropped the dishcloth and wrapped her arms around herself, still laughing.

"Cassandra?"

She shook her head, helpless. "I do. I do mean it." Her laughter vanished, leaving brown mascara tears in its wake.

Alberg wiped them away with the towel he'd been using to dry the dishes.

"Say it again," he said.

She was unexpectedly aroused and consequently flustered. She wanted to look away, but she didn't. "Will you marry me?" she said, watching him smile.

And he said that he would.

1987

Chapter
25

M aria entered his name in her address book, printing it carefully, Alan with one "l," Stewart with a "ew," not a "u." Her mother watched her do this. Maria wondered if she was imagining the two of them meeting, the adult daughter and her elderly father. But Nadine's eyes were so distant that she might just as well have had dinner on her mind.

Maria thought about Agatha, who had made her Hallowe'en costumes and helped her learn to read, put up with her adolescent shenanigans and seen her through accidents and illnesses, while her real mother languished behind bars.

"What do you do here?" she asked Nadine, who suddenly looked tired. "How do you spend your days?"

"Why?"

"Because I'll think of you, from now on, and I'd like to be able to imagine what you're doing."

"Look." Nadine leaned forward slightly. "I've been in this place for forty-eight years. There's no room in your life for me, and no room in mine for you."

Maria, chastened, felt herself flush and looked down. The counter was made of wood that had been painted the dingy green that somebody once decided would be a good color for institutions. On Maria's side of it there was a cigarette burn from when smoking in public was allowed, and some of the paint had been chipped away by people waiting, nervously, as she had waited, and somebody had printed his name there—"Reggie" was printed there on the edge of the counter, and Maria wondered if Reggie had been the person who waited or the person who was waited for.

She lifted her head and looked hard at her mother, seeking signs of madness. But it had been a fleeting thing, Nadine's madness, or so Maria had been led to believe: a thing brought on by childbirth, a thing for which Maria herself was therefore partially responsible.

She didn't know what to say next. She chipped away at the paint with her thumbnails, clearing a small area around the word Reggie, saying nothing. Her mother was silent, too, apparently uninterested in Maria. But then, why not? If she'd been interested in her, she probably wouldn't have wanted her dead.

"Tell me about my grandparents," she said. "Your parents."

Her mother glanced behind her again, as if hoping the attendant would tell her it was time to go. "Why?"

"Did they—did they have a lot of kids? Or just you? Or what?"

"Oh, for God's sake," said Nadine, exasperated. She lifted her clawlike hands. "I'm not going to sit here and—"

"Have you got anything to give me? Letters? Photographs? Anything?"

"Nothing. Not a goddamn thing."

"What I—did they beat you?" said Maria. "Did they hurt you? Were they violent? Did your mother—was she crazy, too?" There were tears in her eyes, and she was gripping the edge of the counter. "You would've killed me, too, wouldn't you? Wouldn't you?"

Nadine looked at Maria, and through her, for a long moment. Then she placed her hands on the counter and slowly, painfully, pushed herself upright. The attendant behind her stood up, too.

"Maria. I don't remember that day. Maria. Go home." She turned and walked slowly away, and the attendant followed.

The next morning Maria went back to see Edward Dixon.

Then she drove out of Saskatoon, heading northwest.

It took her only a couple of hours to get there. It would have been a much longer drive, all those decades ago, when the roads were narrow and made of gravel.

The town appeared rather suddenly, as Maria came to the crest of a rise. It had spread comfortably across its piece of the plains, dominated by the ubiquitous prairie grain elevator: a calm and quiet place. Maria drove through slowly. She saw stands of lilac bushes. A steady breeze was blowing. Maria looked with a stranger's eyes at cars parked in the heat—a cat curled up beneath a porch—a boy riding a bike—a man coming out of the drugstore, dressed in a suit, carrying a samples case. It took less than two minutes to drive into the town, along the main street and out the other side.

She drove on for twenty minutes and turned west, then north, then west again.

"It's probably not even there anymore," Edward Dixon had protested. But she had ignored this, holding out paper and pen. "It's near to fifty years ago now," he had pleaded. "It's sure to be gone."

"Please," Maria had said. And finally he had drawn the map.

She drove along the road toward what had once been her mother's house, hot and sweating because she had rolled up all the car windows. She had locked the doors, too. Yet she found herself glancing involuntarily into the backseat from time to time, perhaps expecting to see her mother there, if not charging the car from the roadside. That arthritic crone, thought Maria, fighting her fear. I could knock her flat with a backhand; she couldn't even carry a knife in those crippled hands now, let alone stab anybody with it, she thought as she inched along the road, gravel crunching under the tires—sometimes there was no gravel left on the road at all; it was just bare, dry ruts.

Much more quickly than she had expected, she was there.

Several tall trees huddled together next to the road. Would they have been there forty-eight years ago? Maria didn't know how long it would take trees to grow that tall or what kind they were. She stopped the car opposite the trees and turned off the motor. She sat still for a moment, sweating, looking straight ahead at the road, which continued on and on until it was swallowed into its vanishing point.

She glanced quickly to her left and saw buildings and looked quickly away. Once a woman had come to their door in Vancouver and asked to see the room where years ago she had grown up, which had become Belinda's room. But what could Maria possibly say to the occupants of this house?

She flung open the driver's door and got out, and looked more carefully into the yard of the farmhouse. It took her a few seconds to realize that the place was deserted.

Maria had not considered this possibility. Either the house would be gone, she had thought, or it would be occupied.

She closed the car door and walked up the driveway. The farmyard was littered with rusted pieces of machinery that Maria couldn't identify. The trees growing next to the road sheltered an old barn whose roof had fallen in. There were two more small structures on the property besides the house, that Maria could see, all gray and weathered by wind and snow and rainfall and time.

The prairie wind chuckled in the treetops, and rummaged harshly in the litter of rusting farm equipment, and blew hollow through the collapsed barn.

Maria turned and faced the house.

It seemed to loom toward her and away again.

It was a nondescript two-story wooden house, faded and gray like the fallen-in barn, a perfectly ordinary place. Yet its presence struck Maria with the force of a blow: it seemed to be breathing. For the first time, staring at this house, she thought of the brothers she hadn't known she'd ever had. Of Thaddeus, who would have been Edward Dixon's age. Of Geoffrey, the middle child.

She must have heard it. She must have heard it. She shook her head violently, as if to dislodge a memory. But there were no memories.

She stood here now, of course, on a day in August. On her way Maria had passed lush fields of grain, and the trees behind her were luxuriant with leaves. The hot sun was molten gold, bleaching the sky of its blueness.

The day it had happened, all those years ago, was a day in December.

Maria, rigid, looked up at the house and saw Nadine young, strong in body, if not in mind. She saw her looking out into the cold, bleak vastness of a snow-covered world, saw her turning back to the house.

There must be memories, Maria thought. Stored somewhere in my brain. And I won't let myself have them.

It was very quiet in the deserted farmyard. Maria heard only the breeze causing the trees to murmur, and she felt it on her cheek, brushing.

And I won't let myself have them.

Chapter
26

(*. . . her hands on Belinda's shoulders, pressing—why? She didn't remember why, just remembered those bony shoulders beneath her hands and Belinda whimpering, "I'm sorry, Mommy, I didn't mean it. . . ."*)

Maria wakened abruptly and swung her legs over the bed. In the bathroom, in the dark, she splashed cold water on her face, in the dark, yes, it was dark outside, no sounds, maybe a car now and then. Maria wrapped her robe around her and opened the motel room door. She looked out at a parking lot, a phone booth, and the street, with big trees lining it on the opposite side, trees shaking in the wind. She held her face into that wind: it would scour her mind clean of dark dreams.

Maria arrived back home on Friday.

Ten days later she drove across the Lions Gate Bridge to West Vancouver.

She drove south from Marine Drive, crossed the railroad tracks, and eventually turned into a narrow, curving street. She found the house number she was looking for on the side of a small gray garage and parked her car and got out. She was trying not to think about what she was doing, for if she did, she probably wouldn't do it.

The fences and garages she saw were almost obscured by greenery, trees and hedges and bushes. It wasn't a manicured kind of look. What made this street special was not what had been constructed here, but the land upon which those structures stood. On the south side, the large lots extended to the ocean and had their own private beaches. Some of these properties, now worth millions of dollars, had been occupied by the same families for fifty years or more.

Maria walked across the street to the small gray garage. A low gray picket fence stretched across the width of the property: Maria went through the gate.

She was on a narrow walk that extended a considerable distance, crossing an enormous lawn and disappearing among a stand of rhododendrons. Curving flower beds had been established along the fences on both sides of the property, and behind the garage, and beneath the lilacs. To Maria's left as she walked was the wider part of the lawn and a gazebo covered with climbing roses.

When she reached the rhododendrons she saw behind them a rock garden sloping down toward a small gray house, and over the rooftop of the house the beach was visible and Burrard Inlet. The forests of Stanley Park rose to her left, and the Lions Gate Bridge, which linked the park with the North Shore. Straight ahead was Vancouver, with Point Grey extending westward—she could see some of the buildings of the University of B.C. From the house, the land dropped abruptly: there must be a path down to the beach, she thought, but she couldn't see it from where she was standing.

She followed the stone walk around the rhododendrons and through the rock garden and down to the patio that surrounded the house. Here she stopped and listened, and heard a medley of sounds: the water washing up on the beach, which was part sand and part rocks; birds; children shrieking and laughing; powerboats passing; a seaplane heading for Vancouver harbor; a lawnmower. But nothing from the little gray house, constructed of timber and stone, nestled comfortably into its domain with its face to the panorama and its back to the rest of the world.

Maria had given a lot of thought to what she was going to wear today. She should have given equal time to what she was going to say. But this had been impossible, knowing what she did about the man, which was next to nothing.

Lying sleepless in the night, she had felt suddenly much younger, as if finding herself in possession of a parent again had ripped years from her age.

She was exhilarated at the thought of confronting him. She was in a tumult—this was the phrase that had swept regularly through her mind.

She had no idea what he would look like, or sound like. And in the time she had spent searching for him she had selected a multiplicity of characteristics, physical and otherwise, and had fitted them together in a variety of ways. It was mental doodling. Now, looking at this small house, she wondered if he might be an elfin man, a trickster, a droll little fellow with bushy white eyebrows that stuck out from his face and gave him an expression of perennial surprise.

This is pointless, she told herself, gazing down upon his house.

Then she thought: Which of the qualities that make up the person I have turned out to be, did I inherit from him? This reflection filled her with wonder. It was an exquisite moment. Standing in the sun, with the fragrance of roses in the air, occupying territory belonging to her kin, Maria felt suddenly rooted and secure. It was a sensation that was false and treacherous, and she knew this, but in the instant that it possessed her, she was exultant.

She was wearing a dress, a yellow dress with short sleeves, a full skirt, and a matching belt, a dress that buttoned up the front with big round buttons and had no collar. She was carrying a small white handbag. Her shoes were white, too, and flat, and she had put on panty hose even though she hated them.

She started moving again, down the now sloping path to the patio, which she saw would soon be in shade. The rock garden tumbled all the way down to the patio on one side of the path, to Maria's right, but came to an end on the other side, where there was a six-foot drop in the hillside, and here there was a short flight of wide wooden stairs, weather-stained and weather-battered. Maria stepped down them carefully, touching the bannister.

The house sat on a plateau. It was encircled by a patio. More flower beds spilled between the patio and the hillside, to the right, and against the fence at the edge of the plateau. A second flight of stairs led down a fifteen-foot slope to the beach.

Maria looked in the small windows at the back of the house and saw a kitchen and a laundry room. Dishes cluttered the kitchen sink, and a basket of clothes sat on the floor of the laundry room. These signs of occupancy gave Maria a jolt. She felt a rush of immediacy and said to herself: No. I'm not ready.

She backed away from the windows and looked up, and started for the stairs leading up to the rock garden, thinking about her car sitting in the lane, waiting for her. She thought of Richard and Belinda, who didn't know where she was. Nobody knows where I am, she thought, and was for a moment absurdly frightened.

In the corner of the patio there was a toolshed, the door standing open. Inside, Maria saw a wheelbarrow sitting under a worktable on which garden tools and equipment were carelessly scattered. A garden hose hung on the side of the house, and a large green watering can sat beside it. It was an untidy, untended part of the property, this bit of patio workspace tucked in behind the house, and its privateness comforted Maria. A large overhang extended from the roofline, creating shade and shelter, and from it was suspended an enormous Christmas cactus.

Maria realized that she would never be ready to do this thing. That's why we need courage, she thought, from time to time: to do the things we aren't ready to do.

She moved to the side of the house and looked out at the water, imagining herself on Jericho Beach, looking straight across the same water in the other direction, toward West Vancouver. Maybe through binoculars she was watching herself, the yellow dress a tiny splotch of synthetic sunlight against the gray of her father's small house.

She knew from the city directory that he lived here alone.

She pushed herself forward, around the house to the front, which was all glass; she couldn't see inside because of the reflecting sunlight. To one side was a door, with a knocker in the middle, a brass lion's head, and this Maria lifted and struck against the brass plate beneath it. She heard it resound within the house, a strangely flat noise but a clamorous one. Then she waited, with her head bowed, looking at the "Welcome" mat beneath her feet, aware of summer and the sickening pounding of her heart.

She heard footsteps, and the door opening. It seemed to take her a long time to lift her eyes.

"Yes?" he said.

And then she was looking at him. Alan Stewart. A big man. Not fat, but flabby. She thought he was a disorganized person—there was something about the way he was dressed that suggested this.

Maria was locked on to him, like a searchlight or a laser

beam, staring straight into his eyes.

He didn't speak again, just looked back at her. Maria had no idea what to say. She opened her mouth in the hope that words would involuntarily say themselves but they didn't. They continued to stare at one another. Maybe, she thought, maybe he thinks I'm some kind of accident victim, somebody who had a car accident in his lane or fell on his beach.

"I think you're my father," Maria heard herself say. She watched him intently.

He took a deep, reflexive breath, like a sigh, and bowed his head. He looked down, at the floor, or at his feet, or hers. He clung to the edge of the door as he slowly pushed it closed, extracting his fingers at the last moment.

Maria watched the brass lion's head for a long time. She imagined him on the other side of the door, leaning against it, braced to keep her out, not daring to breathe.

She backed away. Clutching her white summer pocketbook in one hand and hanging on to the worn bannister with the other, she climbed the stairs to the rock garden. She stumbled through the rhododendrons. What now? What now? Her legs were trembling. She crossed the lawn to the gazebo and collapsed on a bench, and was enveloped by the fragrance of roses.

Chapter 27

"**Y**ou've been home for days and days, Mom," said Belinda, "and you've hardly told us anything."

They were at the dinner table. Dinner was the only time
they had real conversations, Maria realized. And it didn't
happen every day, either: when Richard had meetings, she
and Belinda ate in front of the television set.

"I told you about the photograph," said Maria. There
were flowers on the table, roses, floating in a shallow glass
dish. "The photograph of—of Nadine and Ira. I told you all
about that, how young they looked, how graceful. How loving." Richard cleared his throat. He had nothing to say but
wanted his presence to remain significant.

"Yeah, but I mean, what did you find out about them?"
said Belinda.

Richard wouldn't ask, of course. But Maria could see
from the pricking of his ears that he, too, wanted to know.

"Not much, I'm afraid," said Maria. She had made another chicken dish. Chicken today, salmon tomorrow—no,
maybe not salmon. It wasn't in season. Only the fish farm
salmon was available, and there was something about fish
farming that Maria didn't like.

"You went all that way for nothing, then," said Belinda. "Shoot." She pulled her hair to one side and divided it deftly into three strands. "You can't tell me one single thing about my grandparents?" she asked, beginning to make a braid.

(*. . . Belinda is restless, sitting on the edge of the chair, swinging her legs while Maria brushes, Maria, late for work, brushing that long, dark hair. Belinda squirms and writhes; Belinda whines and yelps: "Mommy, it hurts—ow!" Maria clobbers her with the back of the brush, whacks it against her head. Belinda cries out, and Maria hits her again. "Sit still—sit still!" shouts Maria, trying to drown out Belinda's wails. "Sit still!"—whack. She experienced the sound of it and the feeling of it as the same thing, as a whipcrack, a deep, satisfying whipcrack. . . .*) Oh bad memories, slipping into her mind like knives into butter. . . .

"Don't do your hair at the table," said Maria sharply, and pushed her plate away. "Of course I learned something. Of course I did. But it's nothing of interest to you."

She felt the violence of then seeping through the years toward her, like a black stain, like the inkstain in the hotel's desk drawer.

She stared at the roses, stolen from Alan Stewart's gazebo. Then she stood and began clearing the table.

Maria went back the next day, and the next. Finally Alan Stewart opened the door. He held it open, standing behind it, until she had stepped inside. "I'm sorry," he said. Maria didn't respond.

He led her into a large bright room that opened through sliding doors onto the patio that overlooked the beach. "Please sit down," he said, and she did, in the middle of the sofa. He lowered himself onto an easy chair. Newspaper sections were scattered on the floor next to it, and a mug sat on the end table. "Can I get you some coffee?"

Maria shook her head. "Are you healthy?"

"A bit of high blood pressure," he said after a moment. "Otherwise—yes."

"I have not known my genetic background, you see," said Maria.

"I think—they decided that would be the best thing to do. Have you start fresh. With a new family."

"Who decided?"

"I don't know. Your relatives. Ira's people." He had gray hair, thick and rumpled, and hazel eyes. His flesh was sagging, but his cheekbones were prominent and his jawline pronounced, and his back was straight.

"But 'Ira's people' weren't my relatives," she reminded him.

"Well," he said softly. "They thought they were."

In this large, sunny, skylighted room, Maria noticed small sculptures sitting on a cluster of stands in one corner; an Oriental carpet lay in another, beneath elegant black-lacquered chairs and tables.

"How did you, uh, find out about me?"

"I found out about my mother. My mother told me about you."

"You've been to see her?"

Maria could only nod. There was an obstruction in her throat that was preventing speech.

"How is she?"

Maria shrugged, and the man who was her father averted his gaze, reaching to pick up the newspaper and fold it neatly. "Did you ever go to see her?" she asked him.

"Yes, of course," he said, dropping the paper onto the coffee table. Maria saw that it was Saturday's *Globe and Mail*. He got up and crossed to the wall of glass and pulled open the sliding door, letting in the sound of the sea and the various clamorings of a summer afternoon. He stood there for a moment, looking out, and then returned to his chair, moving slowly, heavily.

Maria imagined him working in his garden, filling the big green can and watering the Christmas cactus. He obviously liked indoor plants, too. An enormous Boston fern cascaded from a hook in the ceiling. A jade plant and a couple of geraniums were clustered at the base of a weeping fig tree. On one of the lacquered tables sat a group of cactus plants and on another table near the sculpture collection, away from direct sunlight, several African violets.

She would never know much about him, Maria realized.

"She didn't seem crazy to me," she said.

"No. Well . . ." He rubbed the back of his neck. "Crazy. Not a good word. People are more complicated than that."

"What happened to her?"

"She—life became intolerable for her." He looked at Maria apologetically. "When she did it, she didn't know what she was doing. Literally."

"What was so intolerable?" The lump was back in her throat, making speech painful.

He studied her and sighed. "I'll tell you what I know. But I've got to have more coffee first." He picked up his mug. "Sure you won't change your mind?"

"I will change my mind, yes. Black, please. No sugar."

While he was gone she made a mental list of questions to ask once he'd told her what he wanted her to hear. But really, she had only two.

He came back and handed her a cup of coffee and sat down, holding the refilled mug in both hands, sitting forward, resting his forearms on his thighs. He was dressed in baggy corduroy pants, navy, a blue polo shirt, and navy socks and leather sandals. There was an obviously expensive watch on his left wrist and a ring on his right hand, probably a university ring, Maria decided.

He began telling Maria how he'd met her mother—he was the family's doctor. He had treated her for depression after each child was born and after the second bout realized that he had fallen in love with her. Maria watched him dispassionately and discovered that she wasn't really very interested. He droned on, talking mostly to the floor, and Maria decided that most of what he was telling her was true, that he had in fact felt guilty and still did, because he wasn't supposed to fall in love with his patients. . . .

"Particularly if they were emotionally fragile," he explained with a solemnity that rang false, "and particularly, of course, if they were married. But it was something I simply couldn't help," he said, "and neither could she."

Maria asked, "Was she the love of your life, then?" noticing the dry tone in which she delivered the question.

He thought about this for a while, probably trying to decide just how frank he ought to be, and then slowly shook his head. She listened for a while to his silence, large and ponderous among the noises that drifted in through the open window: somewhere nearby, people were apparently attempting to launch themselves out to sea in a rowboat.

"When did she tell you about me?" Maria asked.

"When she was pregnant with you." It was a part of his personal history that he was obviously reluctant to discuss. He sat back and drank coffee and frowned, gazing into the past. And Maria gazed back there with him. She saw him as a young man, dismayed and apprehensive, and saw her young mother dismayed, too: Nadine not wanting another child, no matter who its father was, just *not wanting to have it*—afraid of having it—afraid of what would happen if she had it. Maria felt that she and her mother were looking into one another's eyes, past and future meeting in Maria's present.

Nadine had been right, of course, to be afraid.

This man—Nadine's doctor—Maria's father—was talking

again, explaining, relating, reporting. Maria watched him and listened, without much interest.

"I visited her there three times," he was telling her.

Maria stood, abruptly, startling him. "I'd like to see you again," she said. "There are more things I need to know. But I can't listen to you any more today."

He got up to see her out.

When they reached the front door, Maria stopped. "Do I look like her? Do I remind you of her?"

He shook his head. "You remind me of my sister."

Chapter
28

The anticipation didn't keep him awake—he fell asleep quickly and easily, as usual—but it was there the instant he awoke in the morning: Hamilton Gleitman was fully alert as soon as he opened his eyes.

He postponed it for a while, teasing himself. He put on the coffee, he even had a quick shower. Then he browsed in the fridge for breakfast but saw nothing that held his attention. Finally he filled his coffee mug and took it and the portable phone into the living room, where he surveyed the view, his million-dollar view, all one hundred and eighty degrees of it. The world was gray today, everything gray, sea and sky and bridge, all gray. . . .

Shit, thought Hamilton, and he made the call.

Twenty minutes later he burst out the door of his apartment building and hurried down the block to the corner and up to Marine Drive. He strode past the health food store and the drugstore and a couple of boutiques and stormed through the door of Green Parrot Books. He found Everett perched on a stool behind the cash register, thumbing through a furniture store catalog.

"I didn't get the grant," said Hamilton. He felt as outraged and humiliated as the day he'd gotten arrested for embezzlement, back in the seventies. "That goddamn son-of-a-bitching Canada Council." He wanted to sweep the shelves bare of their books. He wanted to set a bonfire here in the middle of the store; he'd feed it books until all the books were gone, destroyed, burned, dead.

Everett was clucking his sympathy. "Did they give you a reason?"

"No they didn't give me a reason. They don't give reasons—they don't have to give reasons." He moved restlessly up and down the aisles, shouldering aside space, air; giving some attention now to the pain in his gut. He stopped and rubbed it. "Jesus. Shit. It actually hurts."

Everett put aside the furniture catalog. He got up from the stool and came out from behind the counter, a man of fifty-five who was wearing a plaid vest over his shirt and tie. His face was droopy, with eyes that sagged at the corners and cheeks whose flesh bent downward. He had a full head of hair, dark brown with plenty of gray in it. Hamilton had got talking to him a year or so earlier, when he'd first moved to West Van and had gone in search of a bookstore. The store Everett managed was an independent, so it actually had some good books, including even some poetry. Everett was familiar with most of the stock, too, and kept himself informed about what went on in the local writing community. It was Everett who had told Hamilton about the guy giving the writing course at UBC.

Everett leaned against the counter and folded his arms. Hamilton noticed that his pants were gray, with knife-edge creases in the legs, and his shirt was white, and the tie was also gray: the vest had been given top billing.

"Most people don't get a grant the first time they apply," he said.

"Ah, to hell with it," said Hamilton, rubbing his belly.

He'd had his heart set on getting that grant. Maybe he should take up crime again.

"Give yourself the day off," said Everett, throwing an arm around Hamilton's shoulders. "Do only things you feel like doing."

"I feel like sending a letter bomb to the fucking Canada Council," said Hamilton.

Everett ignored this. "Maybe go to the track," he suggested.

"You're the gambler here, Everett, not me."

"See a movie."

"Seen them all."

"How about a massage parlor, then?" said Everett. Hamilton threw him a disgusted glance.

A well-dressed man carrying a briefcase hurried into the store. He greeted Everett absentmindedly, picked up a *Vancouver Sun* from the pile by the open door, and dropped change on the counter.

Hamilton, hands in the pockets of his jeans, gazed, disconsolate, out at the street. "I'm going over to Flora's for some breakfast."

"That's a good start," said Everett.

Hamilton picked up a newspaper. Before he could pay for it Everett said, "My treat."

"Yeah, thanks," said Hamilton. He left the bookstore and headed across the street toward Flora's Place.

Chapter 29

Maria called the man who was her father a few days later. "I'd like to see you."

"Fine," he said. "When?"

"Today. This afternoon. I'd like you to come here this time." He didn't like that, but he didn't argue.

She went carefully through the front and back yards and the main floor of the house, removing all visible traces of Belinda. Then she tidied up the place, but not too much. She didn't know why she wanted him to see where she lived. It was a modest house in a modest neighborhood—nothing to be ashamed of, and she wasn't.

When he arrived she was struck by his size, probably because in this house she was used to Richard, who was medium-size verging on small. His own house—Alan Stewart's house—didn't have many rooms, but the ceilings were high. She wondered how long he'd lived there and asked him.

"Thirty-five years," he said, and Maria marveled at this, thirty-five years in the same house. "It's been done over several times," he added. He looked awkward, sitting on her sofa, hands dangling between his knees. She offered him coffee. He looked as though he wanted to refuse, in the hope that she'd let him go earlier if he declined refreshments, but he said yes.

She brought it to the living room on a tray, two cups and saucers, cream and sugar, and as she served it she noticed him regarding the piano at one end of the room. "It was my mother's," she told him. "My adoptive mother. Now it's mine."

"Do you play?"

"No."

There were two sofas in the room, facing each other, with a long, low coffee table between them. In the wall opposite the piano a large window overlooked the front yard.

"Tell me about my mother," said Maria.

He looked uncomfortable but resigned. Today he was dressed in tan. A monochromatic man, her father. Tan pants, tan jacket, tan shoes and socks. His shirt was white, though. He was rumpled and rheumy-eyed, out of his element. Maria wondered how good a doctor he had been.

"Well, let's see," he said, setting his coffee cup carefully back in the saucer. "She had dark hair, like yours, and dark eyes, like yours. She was shorter than you, though. She had a beautiful laugh."

Maria waited. He picked up his cup and took another sip and then held the cup for a moment, staring into space, before replacing it. Maria became aware of a murmuring sound and realized she had left the radio on in the kitchen. The old man sitting opposite her smoothed his thick gray hair and glanced at her from behind his spectacles.

"Didn't she love Ira?" It was something she'd forgotten to ask her mother. It seemed important now, and she grew tense, awaiting his reply.

"Oh yes, I think she did," he said softly, looking away. "I can't explain. . . ."

"Try," said Maria. "Tell me about the two of you."

"We—it was hard to get together," he said. "I had a car, but there were only three in the whole town, so everybody knew them. So mostly I went out to the farm. With kids, you can always find something to worry about, something to call the doctor about. And she was known to be a worrier anyway." He got up and went to the window and stood there looking out, one hand on the sill, the other in his pocket. "Ira and the hired hand would be out working in the fields," he said, "and we'd—sometimes we'd do it in the barn. Sometimes in their bed."

Maria, incredulous, stared at him, this aged accomplice in adultery, this baggy-fleshed stranger who had fathered her. "For heaven's sake," she said.

"I don't know what you want to know."

"Well, I don't want to know about your damn sex lives, that's for sure."

"What, then?" He turned around and half sat on the wide windowsill. "What?"

She had expected to love him, she realized.

"Why didn't you take me?" Her throat ached, and her chest was full of pain. "Why did you let strangers take me?"

He lowered his head and shook it slowly—she saw his jowls quiver. But he said nothing.

(. . . *Maria sees it happen, down the street where a clutch of girl children are playing hopscotch, sees the play stumble to a halt, and sees Belinda, hands on her hips, lecturing. The girl called Annette reaches out and slaps her, and Belinda staggers back, stares, turns, and sees Maria out in their front yard, working in the garden. Belinda pelts down the street toward her, crying. Belinda flies toward home, toward Mother, crying, her braids bouncing, arms outstretched, crying. Maria wants to go inside and lock the door against her, lock out this wailing child.* . . .)

They met for a third time at the end of August, in a café in

West Vancouver, a little place above a health food store. They sat next to a window and ordered lunch. Maria had a glass of wine, but not her father—coffee again, not even decaffeinated.

He pulled something out of his inside jacket pocket, several sheets of paper, folded lengthwise. "This is for you." Maria unfolded it. "It's a copy of my family tree," he said. He reached into another pocket and retrieved a notebook and a ballpoint pen. "My sister put it together. The one you remind me of. It only goes back to 1754. She planned to go to the U.K. to research back farther, but she died last year." He opened the notebook and rested his elbows on the table. "We need to add you," he said.

Maria studied the tree and its many branches. All those names marching backward. Connections. A strong foundation for Maria's life. And this was only one side, too. Her mother had said there was nobody left in her family, but Maria couldn't believe that. It wasn't possible, she thought, gazing at the pages that were Alan Stewart's pedigree and one-half of her own—all those names, all those people—it couldn't be possible that the other side of her family was entirely dead. But did she really want to know them, the family whose genetics had produced a child killer?

Her father, who in thinking to give her these pages had showed that he was at last getting the point, clicked his ballpoint pen, preparing to write. "You're married, aren't you? Do you have children?"

The waitress deposited lunch in front of them, a salad for Maria and an omelet for her father.

"Let's not talk any more for a while," said Maria. She wasn't ready to let this man have his granddaughter. He had yet to earn her trust. She put the pages he'd given her in her handbag, and they began to eat.

The window was open, and Maria smelled the sea, which

swept upon the beach a block away. She lifted her face to the breeze and took a deep breath: it would be nice to live next to the ocean. She picked up her fork, glancing out into the restaurant. Her eye was caught by a man standing at the top of the stairs, scanning the tables. Her father turned to see what she was looking at. He saw the man and looked back at her, his face suddenly smooth and empty.

The man had seen him and was approaching their table. He slid onto the empty chair next to Maria's father. "Thought I might find you here," he said. He looked at Maria. "Who are you?"

"This is Maria Buscombe," said her father. "My travel agent. I'm thinking of going on a tour. Maria, this is my son, Harry."

Chapter
30

She had known he'd been married, of course. He was described in the city directory as a retired doctor and a widower. But the city directory hadn't told her that he had children, and now Maria felt like a complete fool, gazing across the table at her father's son. She was suddenly alienated from the old man who was her father, a person for whom she had begun to feel an incipient—something. She wasn't sure what. Not tenderness or affection . . . perhaps a kind of comradeship, a feeling that someday maybe she'd be able to ask the things she couldn't ask now, and that by the time she got the questions out, he'd be able to answer them. Trust—that was it. Perhaps one day there could be trust between them: that's what she'd been thinking.

And now this. He didn't want her in his life, that was obvious. At least not publicly.

But then, she hadn't let him into *her* life, either, she reminded herself. Neither Richard nor Belinda knew yet that he existed, and he didn't know about them, either. Maria felt a thrill of excitement: it could be said that she was leading a double life. And as she studied this person opposite, she decided that at least for the moment, until her father had had a chance to explain himself, she would cooperate. But he'd better be prepared to do all the talking. Maria knew nothing about travel agents and tours to foreign places.

His son had the face of an overweight ferret, she thought.

"Where's he thinking of going?" the son asked her.

"He's considering several destinations," she said, and was pleased with herself.

"Where's the brochures?" said the ferret.

"Oh, we're past the brochure stage," said Alan.

Harry sat back on his chair and watched his father eat. The waitress came over and asked if he wanted to order anything, but he waved her away.

Maria hugged to herself her secret knowledge. It made her feel powerful. He was nibbling on the inside of his mouth, this man who didn't know he was her half brother, while he examined his father's profile. Maria was exceedingly curious: what could he be thinking about so furiously?

"When are you planning to go?" he said.

Alan shrugged and bit into a piece of whole-wheat toast. Maria thought that at least some of his teeth weren't his own.

"When's he planning to go?" Harry asked her, swiveling his head to inspect her with his black ferret eyes.

"Soon," said his father sternly.

Harry leaned close to him. "How come you didn't tell me, Dad?" he said with the echo of a whine in his voice. Alan made an impatient gesture, and Harry's right hand shot out to grip his left shoulder. Alan froze. At first Maria thought that Harry had hurt him, but it wasn't pain on his face, it was anger.

"Get your hand off me."

Harry waited a moment, to make a point, then sat back.

He glanced across the table and winked at Maria, who turned away from him to look out the window.

Harry knew that something was off kilter. Something was definitely being kept from him. Could the old man be having it off with the travel agent? He could feel many things in the air, beams of various kinds, like silent alarm systems, and he was the receiver. His dad's chin was ducked into his chest, and his shoulders were hunched; the whole body was shored up against something, and Harry knew it was shored up against him, against him finding something out.

She was looking at her watch, the travel agent. Harry was a bit surprised that she wasn't younger. A rich old guy like his dad ought to be able to attract some gorgeous chick, mid-thirties, max.

"I've got to go," she said, and picked up this big purse thing from the floor. Harry got up and scooted around to pull the chair out for her. She looked surprised but thanked him.

"Let me have one of your cards," he said, smiling at her. "I might want to go on a trip myself, one day."

"I don't have business cards," she said, and if he wasn't mistaken, a little blush was spreading across those aging cheeks.

"I wonder why?" he said, delighted, with a smile so huge that it hurt his face. He listened busily to the exchange that took place then, his father half standing up, clutching his napkin, stammering something meaningless, and the travel agent assuring him airily that she'd be in touch. Which Harry thought odd. He would have expected the old man to say that. Maybe he'd been trying to but couldn't get the words out. Harry looked at him swiftly, hopefully; maybe his father was finally starting to fail. But the travel agent left, and the old boy settled back onto his chair and started eating again; he seemed A-OK, unfortunately.

Harry's mind kept going back to the woman. He couldn't remember what name the old man had said when he'd introduced them, but it probably wasn't her real name anyway. His father was going to make damn sure they never met again, he was pretty sure of that. Harry hadn't worked out yet how this situation could benefit him, but he was damn sure that if his father didn't want him to know something, there was going to be something in it for him, once he found out whatever it was that he wasn't supposed to know. And then he suddenly had an idea.

"You're not fit company today, Dad," he said, and stood up to leave. "Take it easy," he said, waving, and hurried across the restaurant, down the stairs, and through the health food store.

He looked frantically up and down the street, and there she was, a cherry red dress weaving and bobbing through the crowd. He couldn't follow her—it was too late for that—but he'd try to catch up to her and get the number of her license plate. But shit, she was getting into a damn car now. He was running along the sidewalk—trying to run, but too many people were in the way. Finally he stood still, huffing and puffing, watching her car pull out into traffic. Damned eyesight, Harry fumed, squinting.

He'd have to follow the old man instead, he decided. He'd follow him everywhere he went, for a while. Find out what was going on here. What was up.

THE PRESENT

Chapter
31

"It went on for six months," said Alan Stewart. "Then she told me she was pregnant. And that the child was mine."

"Maria," said Alberg.

The old man nodded. He was sitting on a rocking chair, looking toward the ocean. Alberg noticed a hearing aid in his left ear.

"Did you believe her?" he asked.

Alan Stewart looked at him in surprise. "Of course. There was no reason not to. She didn't want to leave him— Ira. She just wanted me to know." He turned back to the window. "Murdered. It doesn't seem right. It's as if her fate just got postponed."

"I don't believe in fate," said Alberg.

They were sitting in Stewart's living room. Rain fell steadily from a silvery sky, erasing the horizon, streaking the window glass, drumming on the roof.

"Did you meet her family?" Alberg asked.

Stewart shook his head. "I went to her house once. But she was alone there. She had a husband, I know. Children?"

"A daughter."

Stewart shook his head. He looked suddenly thin and frail, as if Alberg's news had exhausted him.

"You must have been surprised," said Alberg, "when Maria turned up in your life."

"Surprised. Yes." Stewart lifted his coffee cup with a hand that shook slightly. Alberg figured he had to be more than eighty and was entitled to a hand that shook. The old man sipped his coffee and carefully replaced the cup on its saucer. "Certainly. Shocked, in fact."

"But you agreed to see her."

"Not at first. But—she was my daughter, after all. I lay awake that night, and . . . She was my daughter. So the next time she came . . . we talked."

"Did you like her?"

Stewart thought about this. "I don't know. It was uncomfortable. We hadn't gotten past the stage where she asked questions and I answered them." His eyes were watery behind the spectacles he wore. "Tell me about her daughter. She must be all grown up." He blinked and looked away.

Alberg glanced at his notebook. "So you saw Maria half a dozen times, and then she just stopped calling. Right?"

"That's right."

"Why didn't you call her?"

Stewart hesitated. "I think I was relieved," he said unhappily. "We hadn't had time to get to know each other. And she complicated things with Harry. So when she stopped calling me, I decided to let it go."

"Who's Harry?"

"Harry's my son." He announced this flatly. Gloomily.

"Your son."

"I didn't want to tell him about Maria. I knew he'd take it badly."

Alberg looked around the room, at the paintings and sculptures clustered in this house that was itself worth a couple of million bucks. "And did he?"

"I told him she was my travel agent." Stewart smiled, his face rearranging itself in a sea of wrinkles. "But finally I had to tell him the truth. He didn't like it much. He was an only child all his life, of course. Didn't like the idea of having a sibling." He shuddered. "Thank God she didn't show up while my wife was alive."

"Does Harry live with you?"

Stewart looked shocked. "Good God, no, of course he doesn't."

"You're on your own here, then?"

"Yes. But I get help, now, with the house, and the grounds. Not from Harry. Good God, no."

"Where can I find your son, Mr. Stewart?"

Chapter
32

"Your father and I were married in my mother's garden," said Helen Mitchell.

"I know," said Cassandra.

"A minister performed the ceremony, of course. He was my father's cousin, I think. A Methodist. Or was he Presbyterian? I can't remember now. It doesn't matter, because at some point they all got lumped together. Most of them, anyway. And called themselves the United Church."

They were sitting in Helen Mitchell's room at Shady Acres. Cassandra had interrupted a game of gin rummy in the lounge in order to give her mother the news in private. Helen seemed pleased enough, if a bit distracted.

"I wish I were still on my own, Cassandra," she said now. "I'd like to take care of the reception for you. Bake the wedding cake. Host the rehearsal dinner."

"Oh, Mother . . ."

"But then these tasks get divided, don't they, between the bride's family and the groom's. I can't remember who does what, it's been such a long time since Graham and Millie got married. I'll have to look it up."

"Mother, please, it's not going to be that kind of an event.

We don't want a wedding cake. And believe me, there'll be nothing to rehearse. Are you sure you don't want to go out for a while?" Her mother usually took advantage of every opportunity to leave Shady Acres, if only for a couple of hours.

"I don't think so," said Helen. "I'm a little tired today." Her room was crowded with possessions. Mismatched bookcases lined the walls and were filled with bric-a-brac and photos in frames as well as books. On the dresser, perfume bottles were neatly aligned, brushes and combs, too. There was a small rug next to the bed and a long narrow one leading from the doorway. Cassandra found it exceedingly depressing that her mother's bed, though covered in a bright spread and laden with cushions, was still a hospital bed, and that the bathroom had two mirrors, one at wheelchair height, and that there were two emergency bellpulls, one near the bed, the other next to the toilet. Her mother must expend a lot of energy ignoring these things, she thought, and focusing instead on the bay window looking out into the garden.

"I'm very pleased about this, Cassandra." Cassandra turned to see that her mother was smiling at her. "I like him. I think you're good for each other." Helen Mitchell leaned against the headrest of her easy chair and looked out the window at the rain that leaked incessantly from the dreary sky. "Are you staying for tea?" she asked.

Cassandra looked at her watch. "No, if you don't want to go anywhere, I think I'll get back to work."

"Is it likely to happen before Christmas, do you think?" asked her mother.

"I doubt it. We haven't really talked about it yet, Mom, but I don't think we could get ourselves organized that quickly."

"Then you and I could still go to Edmonton for Christmas?"

There was nothing, absolutely nothing, that Cassandra wanted to do less. But she discovered now that she had almost resigned herself to it. "Maybe. We'll see." She kissed Helen's cheek. "I'm off. I'll see you Friday."

"We'll have to go to town, you and I," said Helen, suddenly animated. "Shopping."

"Why? Shopping for what?"

"Why, for a dress! A wedding dress!"

Cassandra wondered if people her age ever eloped.

"Could we go outside, maybe?" said Belinda.

Alberg peered out his office window at the rain. He looked at his watch: he'd been given the name of the restaurant in West Vancouver where Harry Stewart had dinner every day and was intent upon tracking him down there. "Tell you what," he said to Belinda. "I'm going to catch the three-thirty ferry, but I've got time for a coffee first."

"Thanks," she said a few minutes later as the proprietor of Earl's Café and Catering set two mugs of coffee on the table. "I hope you don't mind," she said to Alberg. "I just hate that police station, for some reason."

"I don't mind. I'm not all that fond of it myself."

"I was rude when you came to the house to talk to me." She looked him in the eyes, and again he felt enveloped by an authority incongruous in one so young. It fascinated him. She was a little uncomfortable with the effect she had on people, he figured, because she often averted her eyes, never looking at anyone directly for long.

"That's okay," he said.

"No, it isn't. My mother—" Her voice faltered for a moment, then was strong again. "She used to say that good manners was what kept the world oiled and running."

"I think my mother would agree with her."

"Is your mother still alive?"

"Yes. I'm sorry."

Belinda laughed. "Don't be sorry."

"I'm not, I meant—"

"I know what you meant." She poured a great deal of sugar into her coffee and stirred. "Does she live here?"

"No. She lives in London. Ontario."

Belinda took a napkin from the chrome container that sat on the table between the sugar bowl and the salt and pepper shakers. "I've been going over it in my mind, that day that I saw her on the road. Reliving it, you know? Not on purpose. I just couldn't get it out of my head. But then I realized, there was something funny about it."

Alberg was listening politely, but his mind was on Alan Stewart's son.

"So today I really concentrated. I—it was like I was hypnotizing myself. Because there was something stuck in my memory, that I'd been ignoring."

"What?" said Alberg, checking the time.

She leaned toward him, across the table.

"There was somebody there."

Alberg shook his head. "I don't understand. There was somebody where?"

"In the bushes. A man. Watching."

Chapter
33

"I think we should go take a look around," Alberg said to Belinda. "Are you game?"

"Now?"

"Sure. Why not?"

"I thought you had to catch a ferry." He was as tall as Raymond, but bigger. Some of it was fat, but most of it wasn't. His hair was blond, and his eyes reminded her of her father. But the thing that interested Belinda most was that he looked open and sympathetic—so that you felt like telling him things—without giving away anything about himself. He was either very confident, she thought, or very guarded.

"I'll catch a later one." He put money on the table for the coffee, and they left the café.

He parked outside the place where the seaplanes landed on Porpoise Bay, and they walked up the road toward Belinda's father's house. At the maple tree, she stopped.

"She was behind this tree," she told him, feeling somewhat breathless. "When I came around that bend up there, she stepped out from behind this tree. I must have known who she was right away, because I was so shocked that I stopped walking. And that's when she pulled off this kerchief thing she had over her head and I saw that all her hair had turned gray."

She couldn't speak for a minute and had to turn away. This was much harder than she had imagined. Finally she cleared her throat and looked up the rise at the spot where she had stood, riveted, staring at her mother.

"Then what?" said Alberg.

"I ran away, like I told you before. I was going to run back to Dad's house. But then I changed my mind. I stood in the road up there, thinking, and then I ran back. But she was gone."

"Show me what you did then," he said.

Belinda walked fifty yards or so up the road and turned around. She stood still for a few seconds and then ran to the maple tree. She pressed the palms of her hands against the tree trunk and touched it with her fingertips. She remembered thinking that the tree might know something—like where her mother had gone—and maybe she had thought she could read its message there, the way blind people read braille.

She stepped back, looked down, and squatted to inspect the ground. Then she stood up and looked toward the parking lot, hidden by a bend in the road. "I was thinking that she must have a car, and that if I hurried, maybe I could catch her before she drove away—" She began to run. "And when I got here—" She stopped and held out her hand, pointing, but didn't turn her head. "That's where he was hiding. I know he was there. I felt him."

Alberg walked toward her, and together they looked into the thicket of blackberry bushes. It was taller than either Belinda or the policeman, and maybe five feet across. "Yeah," he said. "Something's been in here, anyway." He went closer. Belinda smelled ripe blackberries. She peered over his shoulder and saw that something had pressed hard against the vines; several were broken. Alberg got down on his haunches and examined the ground, where vines and berries lay.

"Are there footprints?" Belinda asked hopefully.

"Nope." He stood up. "Not exactly. Nothing that we can use. But somebody's been in there all right." He looked at Belinda thoughtfully. "Where's Raymond, Belinda?"

"Up the coast. He'll be back later today."

"What about your dad?"

"He's at the store. Why?"

"I want you to stay with your dad until Raymond gets home," he said. "I'm sure there's nothing to worry about. But I'd feel better. Okay?"

1987

Chapter
34

"Are you seriously considering going on some kind of a trip?" Harry asked the day before Labor Day, in his father's living room.

His father did some shifting around on his chair, which Harry found interesting. The old man mumbled something.

"What? What did you say?"

"I said I'm thinking about it," said his father loudly.

Harry didn't like it that there was this younger woman in his father's life. It was an eventuality that he wouldn't have imagined in his wildest dreams. Shit, the old man might end up rejuvenated.

Harry sat down, rubbing his thighs, which ached. He didn't know why, but they often ached, and so did his back and one of his shoulders. It's age, is what it is, he told himself. He'd be a doddery crippled old fool himself before he got to spend his inheritance. "Maybe you shouldn't," he said. "You're getting kinda old to travel, don't you think?"

His father looked at him dead on, not squirming, not mumbling, clear-eyed and contemptuous. Harry realized that they disliked each other. Usually he stepped around this knowledge—not ignoring it, exactly: aware of it, but not concentrating on it, staying out of trouble, like you avoid making eye contact with a big hostile dog. And his father normally did this, too. Harry was a little unnerved by his father's uncharacteristically steady gaze and after a minute dropped his eyes. Which capitulation caused his usually well-banked anger to sputter to life.

Harry couldn't afford to get angry. So he got up and walked outside through the sliding doors onto the patio and around the house, up the stairs, through the rock garden, and across the grass to the gazebo. He sat on the bench with his hands clasped between his knees, rocking back and forth, fixing his mind upon memories of his mother, trying to smother his anger with them; for she had been a soothing presence in his life.

After a while he lay full length upon the bench, his hands under his head, legs crossed at the ankles. He looked up at the roses that had grown through the latticework and distracted himself by trying to remember—without looking down at himself—what clothes he was wearing today. He recalled that he'd wakened that morning feeling hot and sweaty. It was almost noon, and the sun was shining directly upon him; he'd forgotten to close the curtains. He'd turned to look at the clock, aware of lots of aches and pains, untangled himself from sheets and blankets, and stumbled in his underwear to the bathroom. Thought about having a shower, decided against it. In the kitchen he'd put the kettle on for instant coffee and leaned on the refrigerator door, looking inside. He found nothing appetizing there, nor in the cupboards, either. Cereal but no milk. Bread but no butter. Orange juice—but the thought of drinking orange juice curdled his stomach.

Let's see, he thought: what had he done next? Decided to go out for breakfast. Back to the bedroom . . . and he'd climbed into the clothes he'd thrown onto the chair the night before, which were white cotton pants and a B.C. Lions T-shirt. "Shit," said Harry, lifting his head to look down at himself. Yeah. White pants, you shouldn't wear them more than one day, they were creased and grubby-looking. The T-shirt was okay. He ran his fingers over his hair and wished he'd done the morning thing better. No wonder the old man wasn't impressed.

Harry went back into the house, where his father was sitting in what used to be Harry's bedroom, centuries ago, when he still lived at home. Now there was a TV in there, and some bookcases, and a desk where his dad sometimes sat scrawling handwritten letters or adding up figures with the help of a calculator he'd gotten free with a subscription to *TV Guide*. The old man had the TV on, and he was watching *Jeopardy!* He didn't notice Harry in the doorway.

So Harry backed off to check out the kitchen. Frozen waffles. Tins of chicken noodle soup. The old man had programmed himself like a robot, eating exactly the same thing for breakfast and exactly the same thing for lunch every day of the week. Except, thought Harry, remembering, when he eats out. He wondered how often that happened, now that his father had a girlfriend. He sat down at the kitchen table to think.

It occurred to him that his father might go loopy over this woman, maybe even marry her. Jesus Christ.

He returned to what his father called his den and said, "You're short on supplies. Want me to pick you up some groceries?"

The old man's attention remained fixed on the TV. "No, thanks."

"What're your plans for supper?" Harry was determined to remain relaxed and cheerful.

"Don't have any."

"Mind if I have a drink?"

His father shrugged. "Suit yourself."

Harry went back to the kitchen and looked in the fridge for beer, finally settled for Scotch and water. He slugged down half his drink, topped it up, and wandered back down the hall. He leaned on the door frame, watching his father watch Alec Trebek. At the next commercial break he said, "I'm sorry I'm not more presentable."

His father looked at him. "What?"

"It's not respectful to show up at somebody's place looking like this." He spread his arms and looked down at himself, assuming an expression of distaste. "I didn't even think," Harry went on. "Just grabbed the first clothes that came to hand. I was in pain, you see," he said confidingly.

"In pain," his father repeated.

"Yeah. It's my gut. I get indigestion attacks."

"Indigestion."

"Yeah. Sometimes it's real bad. But—hey. There's worse things." He grinned broadly at his parent. "So. How about I go out and pick us up some Chinese?"

He returned with the food just as the Sunday night movie was starting. It was one he'd seen, but he pretended he hadn't, pretended to be rapt, with his father, pretended not to know that Jeff Bridges really had done it. When the movie was over he cleared away the dishes, rinsed them, and loaded the dishwasher.

Alan watched from the doorway. Harry was almost merrily ovoid in shape, with a small narrow head, narrow shoulders, swelling gut, flabby thighs, small feet. He had a high forehead, and his black hair, clipped short, was nonetheless almost always greasy. His eyes were unfriendly.

"What do you want, Harry?"

His son turned, startled. "What do you mean?"

"First you try to bully me, now you're all sweetness and light. What are you after?"

Harry folded the dishcloth and put it on the counter. "You want some decaf?"

"No."

Harry sighed. "I don't want anything, Dad. Except to see a little more of you. Get a little closer."

"Bullshit," said his father.

This startled Harry a little. He clasped his hands in front of him and looked down at his gut, which had gotten too big. "I better take off now," he said, trying to sound sorrowful. He glanced up, to catch the old man's expression— but his father had left the room. Harry heard the sound from the TV get louder. He might as well go home.

Richard hadn't asked Maria a single question since she'd returned.

Then on Labor Day morning, when Belinda had gone to work, he said, "We really should talk, Maria." He unfolded his napkin and spread it upon his lap. "Whatever you learned in Saskatchewan, it's preoccupying you. I think we should discuss it." He surveyed her, calmly, with his bright blue eyes.

Maria, sitting opposite him, remembered that when he was courting her she had mistaken his reticence for shyness and had thought his arrogance was self-defensive, a mask for uncertainty. But the sex had been good, she thought; and he had always tried, in his way, to be her friend.

"I'll tell you, then," she said, and knew as soon as she'd spoken how immense would be her relief.

"Well?" he said encouragingly, pouring milk over his cornflakes.

"My mother is still alive," she told him. "I saw her, talked to her."

"What's her name?" said Richard, cereal spoon in hand.

"Her name is Nadine. Nadine Gage."

"What about your father?" His eyes sparkled with curiosity.

"This is where things get a little complicated," she said. She started collecting Belinda's breakfast dishes because she didn't want to sit there being looked at. "My mother's husband died when I was an infant," she called out from the kitchen, her face flushing as if she were telling a lie. "But he wasn't actually my father."

"Good heavens," said Richard, with distaste.

She returned to the dining room. "I found him, too, my real father," she said, trying to sound calm and confident, even though she knew her face was burning. "I've been to see him several times."

Maria squinted at her husband, wanting to take his face between her hands and stare into it; she was seeking compassion and love. And maybe she did see love there. Maybe. But there was no compassion. In fact, finally she had to laugh, standing there peering at her husband, because his face was positively swollen with disapproval, and she hadn't even told him the bad thing yet.

So she didn't tell him the bad thing.

"You mean he lives in Vancouver?" said Richard, obviously dismayed. There was no room in Richard's life for Maria's tainted family. She could feel his censure in the air.

"That's all," said Maria, clearing the table. "That's all for now."

(. . . *Maria throws the infant child onto the bed, onto the double bed, and the shock of the fall for an instant creates a blessed stillness—and then the screaming begins, louder than ever, more desperate than ever. "Shut up!" Maria cries, clapping her hands over her ears. "Shut up shut up shut up! . . ."*)

She stood in the kitchen, shuddering, and then she left the house.

She wanted solace from someone, but only Belinda could have given it.

There was only one solace available to her. Only one that she deserved. Maria saw this suddenly, clearly, and with devastating calm.

Chapter
35

Harry, having breakfasted late at Flora's Place, was walking aimlessly along Marine Drive, preoccupied again with the travel agent. He'd tried and tried to get her name from his father, but no luck. "It's none of your business," was all his dad would say.

He'd hung around the vicinity of his dad's house for most of a couple of days, lurking in the street, waiting for the old man to sneak off to meet her. But he never budged from the property. Harry had watched him out there, weeding or whatever the hell he did in the damn garden—wielding the hose, whatever—and he never left.

In the late evening of the second day, just as dusk was falling and Harry, bored, was figuring he'd give up on the surveillance thing, a cop car had appeared, coming slowly along, crunching on the asphalt. It drew up behind Harry's car, and the cop got out, ambled around, and shone a flashlight on him, smack in his eyes.

"Can I see your license and registration, sir," said the cop.

Harry fumbled the license out of his wallet and the registration out of the glove compartment and handed them over.

"What are you doing here, sir?" said the cop, studying the documents.

"Spying on my old man."

This got the cop's attention. "Beg pardon?"

"My old man lives in there," said Harry, pointing. "He's getting kind of senile. I keep an eye on him."

"And why do you do this from the street?"

"Because he doesn't want me to look out for him. He doesn't think there's anything wrong with him, see?"

The cop climbed back in his cruiser and picked up the radio. Checking Harry out. Harry wasn't worried.

After a few minutes the cop returned and gave him back the license and registration. "You'd better find another way of dealing with your dad," he said. "We got a complaint about somebody loitering."

"Yeah, right, okay," said Harry.

He figured he'd be a lot better at shadowing than he was at surveillance. If only his father would damn leave, so he could follow him.

He peered listlessly through the window of Everett's bookstore, which was closed on Sundays. He could play pool in North Van with whoever happened to be around. He could go bowling with the guys over in Surrey.

He could go home and do his laundry.

He stood there with his hands in his pockets, looking at his reflection in the bookstore window. Wishing he were taller. More—svelte.

Maybe he'd buy some magazines, he thought. Or rent a dirty movie. Or both.

But he decided instead to drop in on the old man again. He'd offer to help him aim the hose around in the backyard, or maybe there was something in the house that needed fixing. And maybe while he was there his father would announce that he had an appointment, and Harry would leave, quick fetch his car, and poise himself to do a tail.

Laurali R. Wright

Morning had become afternoon while he wasn't watching, and by the time he'd turned into his father's narrow street he was hot and sweaty. He had tugged off his jacket and was carrying it over his arm, and his feet were slapping moistly around in his leather sandals. He went through the fence and across the yard, down the steps, and around to the front door.

The sliding doors were open, and martial music was issuing from the living room. Harry stepped inside and saw the old man lying on the floor, doing exercises. He wore shorts that revealed thin white legs, knobbly-kneed and unaccountably freckled, and an underwear vest. His eyes were winched shut, and there was sweat on his forehead. The sight of him lying there made Harry nauseated.

He tiptoed delicately backward onto the patio and arranged himself on a chaise longue that was next to the table with a big sun umbrella stuck in the middle of it. At least there was a breeze off the water—it had to be ten degrees cooler than in the village.

After what felt like a very long time, the music was turned off. Harry dozed on the chaise.

"I wish you'd wait for an invitation."

He looked up to see his father, who'd replaced his shorts and vest with a pair of old gray pants and a faded yellow T-shirt. He'd also donned a straw sun hat with a fraying brim.

"And I wish you were a darn sight friendlier," said Harry, "to your one and only son."

"I've got work to do." His father trudged past him and disappeared around the house.

Harry struggled up out of the chaise and followed him.

The old man was pawing through a bunch of stuff in the shed on the back patio. He came out of there with a carryall into which he'd packed several tools and a sprayer.

"How can I help?" said Harry.

His father gave a hoot. He climbed the steps, followed the paving stones through the rock garden, and took off across the lawn for the gazebo. He put down the carryall and unloaded it on the grass beneath a monkey puzzle tree that grew near the fence. Leaning his hands on his knees for support, he peered for a minute at the collection of tools spread before him, then selected a spading fork and turned to the rose garden. Harry couldn't see any weeds, only bark mulch. But his father got down on his hands and knees and ferreted some out, tossing them over his shoulder to land on the grass. Harry, watching, felt his restlessness growing, and his resentment, too. He didn't know how to get at this man: he felt as if he were poking around in a fog.

"Have you decided where you're going yet?" he said finally.

"I don't know what you're talking about," said his father, flinging weeds.

"You know, your trip. That you're setting up with the travel agent broad."

Curiosity killed the cat, his mother used to say, and someday it's going to kill you, too, Harry boy. He figured she was probably right. But it was a burning in him, his curiosity. It was exactly like the excruciating burning sensation produced by a urinary tract infection he'd once had. There was nothing he could do about it.

His father continued to root around in the garden, looking for weeds, ignoring Harry.

"Listen, I want to know who that woman is," Harry finally blurted. "I want to know what's going on there."

His father, astonished, sat back on his haunches and stared at Harry indignantly through his bifocals.

"I know you're going to tell me it's none of my business," said Harry, "but I want to know anyway." He heard the whine in his voice and hated it. He was rubbing the palms of his hands on his thighs, drying the sweat on the denim of his jeans while listening to himself babble away. Shit, he thought, humiliated. His father said nothing, of course. Harry finally allowed himself to wind down, and then he waited, aware that he was out of breath.

"She's your sister," his father said finally.

Harry laughed. Waited. Laughed again. Then crouched down so as to stare right into his father's face.

"She was a love child," said his father.

Harry squinted at him, as if narrowing his eyes might improve his powers of comprehension.

When he finally grasped what his father had said, it took him a full minute to regain his power of speech—and even then he couldn't think of a single thing to say.

Chapter
36

"**Y**ou mean you're *following* her?" said Everett, incredulous, on a Monday in mid-September.

"Yeah."

"Jesus, Harry—that's a dumbass thing to do."

"I disagree," said Harry, feeling hurt. "I needed to follow her. I know a lot of things about her now that I didn't know before."

"Like what?" said Everett

"I know where she lives. I know she doesn't go to work. I know she likes to drive—does she *ever* like to drive. Christ. I've been all over the goddamn Fraser Valley."

They were sitting on a bench next to the sea walk that stretched from Dundarave to Ambleside Park. Everett was having a cigarette. Harry, when he thought of it, waved the smoke away from his face in an exaggerated fashion. Everett paid no attention to this.

"But what's the point, Harry?" he said, puffing on his smoke. "Why does it matter where she lives, or whether she's got a damn job? Where *does* she live, by the way?"

"Kerrisdale. And it matters, Everett, because this woman is a significant impediment to my plans for a comfortable retirement." He looked unhappily out to sea, waiting for an elderly woman in a white sweatsuit and a straw hat tied under her chin to jog slowly past.

"You're talking about your old man's money, right?"

Harry turned to look at Everett, who was wearing a dark brown suit and a shirt the color of maple syrup. Everett's voice had a rich, confident, caressing timbre. It was his voice that got him his TV work. He was a quick study, though, too, which Harry figured also helped him land the TV commercials that kept him in gambling money. It always gave Harry a charge to see one of Everett's spots. Just that morning he'd turned on the TV and there, like an omen, was Everett galloping among a field of grandfather clocks on behalf of the Chrysler Corporation. Harry had laughed out loud. He'd whooped and slapped his knee and pointed to the screen. "Hey, Everett, hey, buddy!" He'd watched the commercial intently, and when it was over he'd shut off the TV, drawn open the curtains, and looked around for his sandals. Then he had ambled over to the bookstore and persuaded Everett to come out for a walk.

Except for the gambling, Everett was a down-to-earth, practical kind of a guy. Harry often needed another point of view, and Everett's was invariably sensible, if uninspired. Harry needed somebody to keep him earthbound. He knew that and appreciated Everett for having assumed this role.

"Yeah, I'm talking about his money," he said to Everett now. "What else would I be talking about?"

"He's not going to give your inheritance to some broad who, whichever way you cut it, she's a total stranger who's dropped into your life."

"Yeah. Dropped into it like a great big old cow turd," said Harry glumly. "You don't know the old guy, Everett. I think he's getting senile. He could be a pushover for her."

"What are you going to accomplish by spying on her,

though?" said Everett, pulling a pair of sunglasses from a case in his jacket pocket and fitting them over his nose and ears.

And Harry didn't know. He had at first had vague hopes about finding skeletons in her closet. But even if there were any, how the hell was he going to find them, driving around in her wake all day long?

"The old fool's going to think he owes her something," he said despondently, watching a Sheltie trot toward them, heeling expertly next to a guy in his twenties who was wearing only an eyeshade, a pair of shorts, and running shoes. Harry thought about the old woman who'd passed them a few minutes earlier, bundled incongruously in a sweatsuit, and his mind went on a temporary imagination binge, visualizing recording devices under the sweatsuit or maybe grenades strapped to the old lady's body; maybe she'd planned to throw herself on top of him and blow them both to kingdom come.

He groaned and massaged his temples. "It's hard on my brain, Everett, all this crap. But I *know* he's gonna think he owes her something. The only question is, how much?"

He drove over there again that afternoon and parked down the street from her house, parked under a tree that turned out to be a kind that dropped some kind of sticky gloop as well as its leaves. What kind of a damn tree is that, for God's sake? Harry wondered as he got out of his car. He pulled his handkerchief from his pocket, wet a corner of it with spit, and started rubbing delicately at one of the droplets clinging to the paint. But he soon discovered that this gloop had the consistency of varnish. He rubbed more vigorously and still got nowhere.

Suddenly a kid zoomed past him on a bike, giving him a curious glance, a teenage girl with long dark hair and a book bag on her back. He watched her pull into the driveway of the travel agent's house. Harry knew her name now, but he couldn't stop thinking of her as the travel agent even though if she ever had been one, she certainly wasn't working at it now. She probably retired, he thought gloomily, as soon as she'd tracked the old man down, and now she was just sitting back waiting for him to expire so she could scoop up her share of his wealth—completely unearned and undeserved—and live the life of Riley.

He brooded upon this thought, staring through slitted eyes at the house in which she lived, a big and slightly battered-looking house with a small front yard, what appeared to be a big one in back, and a single-car garage. The red Toyota was parked on the street, so the garage must be for some other car, which meant the travel agent probably had a husband. The teenager had dumped her bike in the middle of the driveway—

Then it dawned on him.

The teenager—it had to be her kid, of course: Maria Buscombe's kid.

Jesus, thought Harry, feeling sick. His goddamn father, he had himself a grandkid.

THE PRESENT

Chapter
37

F lora's Place was on Marine Drive, in that part of West
Vancouver known as Dundarave. Alberg slid onto a
chair at a table for two and looked around: he saw nobody
fitting Alan Stewart's description of his son.

There was a bell above the door that chimed whenever
the door was opened. On each table in the café sat a small
vase containing a single flower. The tables were covered
with red-and-white-checked cloths over which smaller
white cloths had been laid.

Alberg ordered coffee from a waitress who wore a denim
shirt, jeans, and a crisp white apron.

"You sure that's all you want?" she said. "We've got the
meat loaf today."

Alberg smiled. "No, thanks. Just the coffee, please."

As he waited, he watched a woman who was energetically
wiping a counter that extended across the back of the café. She
was in her mid-forties, with long, bright red hair affixed to her
head in a complicated series of loops. She was wearing a great
deal of eye makeup, skillfully applied. She glanced at Alberg,
and he knew she'd instantly made him as a cop: he acknowledged this with a little wave that she ignored.

When the waitress set down his cup of coffee, the aroma triggered a sudden craving for a cigarette. He knew it wouldn't last more than half a minute or so, but he felt resentful that it was there at all. In senseless retaliation he dumped cream and a huge amount of sugar into his coffee, which he had for a long time been drinking black.

What nobody had told him, he thought despondently, watching the door, was that even when he had managed to quit smoking, he would not be the same nonsmoker he'd been before he'd started. Cigarettes had changed him permanently. Time, for instance, would never be the same to him again. The shape of his days would never be the same again. Cigarettes had punctuated his life, constituting a rewards system that had snicked commas and periods and semicolons among the events of his days, smoothing his hours, sculpting his life, giving it—he thought now, looking back wistfully, enviously, at his former self—giving it an elegance, a deliberateness, that it now lacked.

He noted that the petulant little craving had subsided. These were easily dealt with, the physical remnants of his addiction. The psychological ties were much harder to break. He looked dismally at his creamed-and-sugared coffee, aware of the ten superfluous pounds around his waist.

Then the door opened, the bell chimed, and Harry Stewart swaggered into the café.

Alberg knew him immediately. A medium-size, black-haired man, egg-shaped, with small darting eyes and small hands, one of which clutched the handle of a worn briefcase. He was wearing jeans that drooped at the waist to accommodate a distended belly. They also bagged at the knees. Alberg felt a flicker of compassion, looking at the knees of the man's jeans.

The redhead swept from behind the counter. Alberg stood up and got to Harry before she'd finished whispering in his ear.

"Harry Stewart?" he said with what he hoped was a disarming smile.

"Yeah. What of it?"

"I'd like to talk to you for a few minutes."

"Who the hell are you?"

"My name is Alberg. I'm with the RCM Police in Sechelt."

"Yeah? So?"

"I don't want any trouble," said the redhead, who Alberg figured must be the manager or maybe the owner of the restaurant. Patrons at nearby tables were neglecting their meals to watch and listen.

"Whaddya mean, trouble?" said Harry Stewart indignantly.

"No trouble. I just need to talk to him," said Alberg. "Come on over here, Harry." He led the feebly protesting man to his table, and they sat down. "Bring him a coffee," he asked the red-haired woman.

"He doesn't drink coffee."

"Yeah, tea, Flora, bring me a tea. No, make it iced tea."

Alberg hadn't noticed how small the tables were until he was sharing one with Harry Stewart: their knees were almost touching.

"Oh, hey, Flora," Stewart called after her. When she turned, he said, "And the meat loaf, okay?"

Alberg was suddenly hungry. He told himself that he could eat on the ferry. Except that ferry food ought to be consumed only in emergencies.

"So what's this all about?" said Harry, crossing his arms and resting them on his belly.

Alberg, studying him, saw in his mind Maria Buscombe, lying on the floor of her apartment. He thought again how impossible it was to mistake a dead person for somebody who was merely sleeping, even without a whole lot of spilled blood all over the place.

"Where were you," he said, "on Sunday, October second?"

He saw a certain amount of bravura in Harry Stewart. He thought the guy was uneasy; he suspected that he lived a complicated sort of life. Alberg got this impression partly from the way he dressed. Harry Stewart was a middle-aged man who went around in baggy jeans and a T-shirt that had seen better days and a pair of running shoes, one of which had come untied. This was not a guy with an office job. This was not a guy with any kind of a job at all. Yet he was carrying a briefcase, a battered leather thing, with files and notebooks sticking out of the top. He was a jumpy person, too. He had clasped his hands together in his lap because whenever he let go of them they started crawling all over the tabletop.

"On October what? Second?" said Harry, frowning at his right hand, which was now clutching the salt shaker. "Jesus. I don't know. That was a while ago, you know. A few days ago." He shrugged and crossed his arms upon his belly again. "I got so much stuff happening in my life, it's pretty hard to remember."

The waitress put a glass of iced tea in front of him. "Meat loaf'll be up in a minute."

"Yeah, thanks, Regina." Harry dumped two containers of cream into his tea and watched it swirl.

"Maybe there's something in there that would help you remember," said Alberg, nodding at the briefcase.

Harry looked at it. "Yeah." He reached down and hauled the briefcase into his lap. He poked around inside and finally pulled out a pocket diary. He paged through it, frowning. "Oh, yeah, right. I had some business out in Surrey that day," he said to Alberg, looking relieved. He stuffed the diary back inside his briefcase and put the briefcase back on the floor. "What's this about, anyhow?" He picked up his iced tea and slurped some up through the straw.

"On a Sunday?" Alberg said disbelievingly. "What kind of business?"

Harry looked up into a far corner of the room. "Oh, you know. Business."

"No, I don't know. What kind of business?" said Alberg patiently.

Flora was approaching to personally deliver Harry's dinner. She bent to place it before him almost tenderly. She was dressed in an extremely short green skirt and a short-sleeved blouse with green stripes, and she smelled of perfume and sweat. "Enjoy," she said with a smile and a pat on Harry's shoulder. She gave Alberg not so much as a glance.

"The bowling business," said Harry, looking approvingly at his plate, where a large slice of meat loaf steamed alongside a mound of mashed potatoes and some sliced carrots. "I'm in the bowling lanes business, with a couple of friends."

"How well did you know Maria Buscombe?"

Harry didn't move for several seconds. He sat with his fork poised over the meat loaf, leaning forward slightly. Then he looked up, and he was panting a little, and his small eyes seemed to have become even smaller, to have shrunk. "Hardly at all." His voice was pitched noticeably higher.

"When did you see her last?"

"I dunno."

Alberg rested his forearms on the table, leaning into the aroma rising from Harry's dinner. "Think, Harry. Concentrate."

"I dunno. Why? It was years ago. Why?"

"Years ago."

"Yeah. Why? What's this all about?" He lowered his fork and put it down on the table, next to his plate. "How come you're asking me about her?"

"She was your half sister, right?"

"Right. Yeah. I only met her a couple of times, though."

"And then what?"

Harry hugged himself, shivering. "Jesus. They got the air-conditioning on full bore in here, don't they."

"You met her a couple of times, Harry. And then what?"

"Why, then she moved away, I think. I think she did, yeah. Although my dad, he'll be able to tell you more about that."

"Where did she go?"

"I don't know, for chrissake. She just up and went. Somewhere."

"Why?"

"Listen, I hardly knew the broad." He pushed his plate a few inches away from him, toward Alberg. "Jesus."

"It must have come as a shock. Finding out you had a sister."

"She's not my sister. Jesus. A love child, that's what he calls her. Christ."

"Not anymore."

He sneaked a wary look at Alberg.

"She's dead, Harry." This was obviously news to Harry Stewart. Alberg felt a pang of regret; of disappointment.

"Did she kill herself?" He blurted it, then lifted his hand and placed it with surprising delicacy over his lips. Alberg couldn't tell whether he regretted having spoken or was steeling himself for Alberg's reply.

Alberg shook his head.

"Cancer? Heart?" These were among the terrors that lurked in Harry's nightmares.

The cop shook his head again. He was staring at Harry so intently, it felt as though he could see right through his skull into his brain—but Harry knew that wasn't possible. "What, then?" After all, they shared some of the same blood, for God's sake: it was important that he find out how she died.

"Homicide."

For a second or two Harry couldn't make sense of this. He'd been expecting to hear the name of a disease.

Then he got it.

Later he'd swear to Everett that his damned heart stopped pumping at that moment. Everything, he'd tell Everett, just shut down. He felt his blood drain away, fleeing the surface of him, taking refuge in his nonoperational heart. He literally couldn't feel his face, or his fingers, or his toes. He wanted to stand up and walk out of the café, but he thought he'd crumple to the floor if he tried to move.

"Somebody beat her to death with a hammer," said the cop.

"Oh, my God." Harry picked up his briefcase and put it in his lap, and hugged it. He was intent upon not letting the cop see inside his brain. It was the most important thing he'd ever had to do. He would concentrate upon not letting the cop see in there, and if he kept his entire attention focused upon this, maybe he could keep Hamilton Gleitman out of his thoughts, and then it wouldn't matter if the cop saw them or not.

Chapter
38

Belinda had not gone to the Jolly Shopper as the policeman had asked. She had gone home and was now sitting cross-legged in the middle of the bed she shared with Raymond, looking out the wide window into the backyard, which was a rough tangle of untended greenery. The day was warm and summery; but the leaves of the lilac bushes were getting rusty, and the sweet peas were sparse upon yellowing vines. Belinda wondered where she would be exactly one year from today.

The book lying open on the bed in front of her had been published in 1974. She wished she'd noticed that before checking it out of the library. A lot of progress must have been made in twenty years.

She had always expected that her mother would return someday. At first, of course, she had expected her all the time. Every time she heard footsteps on the porch, even though she knew they weren't her mother's footsteps because her mother's footsteps were unmistakable, nevertheless, every time the mail was delivered or the paper; every time a neighborhood kid came by wanting bottles or cans for his hockey league; every time a representative of a religious sect knocked on the door to invite them to heaven; every single time, for a while, Belinda had thought, when someone came to the door, It's Mom. And when the phone rang, too, she had thought it would be her mother, with an explanation.

The book had a section entitled "Old Wives' Tales," which it said were "destructive" and "demoralizing." Belinda appreciated the controlled anger that permeated these paragraphs. She felt soothed by them, even though she hadn't heard any old wives' tales, and it wouldn't have mattered anyway: she was just browsing her way through this book on her way to the last chapter—"Induced Abortion."

Her father had never been willing to discuss it. He'd shown Belinda the note, which she had to agree was far from satisfactory. Her mother's handwriting had been shaky, but that was to be expected, Belinda was glad of it, because it wasn't a commonplace thing to desert your family, and a person's hand ought to shake while trying to explain it. She hadn't explained it, though.

Belinda drew up her knees and hugged them. Would she have to live the rest of her life without knowing why her mother had left her?

She pulled the book around to her right side and thumbed through some more pages. Ovulation . . . implantation . . . genetics: "What will your baby inherit? . . . The statistical chance of your baby inheriting any particular trait, good or bad, can be determined with reasonable accuracy." Belinda wished they would stop referring to "your baby." The growth inside her wasn't a baby, for heaven's sake. Not yet.

Her mother hadn't just died. Her mother had been murdered. Belinda knew that she hadn't actually accepted this. She understood what had happened, but this comprehension hadn't yet progressed beyond the intellectual to become part of her. She stretched out her legs and put a hand on her heart, curiously. It was amazing, how nonphysical anguish could produce actual physical pain. She had thought she was getting over it when all of a sudden she was pregnant, and this brought it all back. And then, to make matters worse, her damn mother had shown up, finally, and . . .

Belinda turned more pages in the pregnancy book. She came to some drawings, black-and-white drawings sketched with a surprising delicacy. She leaned closer. "Day 21." She couldn't make out what that drawing was supposed to represent. "Day 24." "Day 28."

Exasperated, Belinda turned to the text: "Fourth Week. The pregnancy is embedded and grows rapidly during this week so that by the twenty-eighth day, or at the end of the fourth week, it is just visible to the naked eye." Belinda shut the book.

She remembered a soft spring day when her mother had been gone for perhaps six months. Belinda had been sitting on the front step, waiting for something, she couldn't recall what, maybe waiting for her father to give her a ride to school or for a girlfriend to come by. Anyway. Waiting. Some daffodils were growing next to the porch. The branches of the maple tree were still bare, but the sun was warm on Belinda's bare arms. She was wondering how much time had still to pass before she would see her mother again when she heard a car, gradually became aware of its slow approach, and she launched into a daydream that this was her mother's car; her mother had gone off to make her fortune and was now returning—eagerly, full of joy—to Belinda and her father; she'd be driving a little red car, a Porsche, maybe. And then the real car came into view, and it was red. Belinda's heart leapt, and she stood, clutching the post that supported the porch railing. The car passed slowly across the screen of Belinda's vision, from right to left. It was driven by a gray-haired man. He glanced her way, and Belinda's gaze was so focused, her posture on the front step so tense, that the stranger lifted his hand in greeting as he passed.

Three and a half months. How many days was that? How many weeks? She opened the book again. The drawing labeled "Day 60" showed a baby sea creature; but Belinda was past day 60. "Day 80," she was past that, too, a humanlike creature, with ears, and eyes, and fingers, and toes. "By the end of the thirteenth week," read the text, "the baby is properly formed. . . . The remainder of the pregnancy is designed not only to allow the fetus to grow to a size at which it is capable of independent survival, but also to give all the vital organs in the body sufficient time to mature and develop the highly complex processes which are essential for independent survival."

Belinda turned another page: "Fig. 11 The Abdomen at the Twelfth Week of Pregnancy." She was sitting crosslegged again. She picked up the book and rested it on her ankles and studied the drawing of the tiny creature floating in amniotic fluid. It looked to be a genuinely restful place, the fetus floating free, there, kept safely anchored by the umbilical cord—like a dog on a leash, she thought, or a toddler in a safety harness.

"Sixteenth Week. By the end of the sixteenth week the limbs are properly formed and all the joints are moving. Vigorous movements continue but are rarely felt by the mother. The fingers and toes are normal, and fingernails and toenails are present. The head is still relatively large for the size of the body, but fairly rapid growth continues to enlarge the body. Primary-sex characteristics continue to develop, and the sex of the infant is now obvious to the untrained observer."

"A wonderful, terrifying adventure," her mother had said

when Belinda asked her as a child what it was like to have a baby. It seemed to Belinda, though, that there was a big unnatural separation between birthing a child and being a mother. You wouldn't think it possible that somebody could desert the baby with whom she had had this "wonderful, terrifying adventure."

She flipped to the last chapter and started skimming. "The termination of pregnancy before twelve to fourteen weeks," she read, "is usually quite simple. After fourteen weeks it may be much more complicated. . . ."

Belinda closed the book and lay flat on her back, legs stretched out, arms at her sides. She saw the afternoon light pooling on the ceiling and thought that she really ought to go outside and start putting the backyard in order. She closed her eyes, which caused tears to run down her cheeks. Shit, thought Belinda, I am so damn sick of crying.

"Belinda."

Her eyes flew open. Raymond was standing next to the bed.

"I didn't hear you," said Belinda.

"I walked from town. Had to leave the truck in the shop." He knelt on the floor next to the bed.

Raymond looked at Belinda intently, so engrossed in her that she almost felt embarrassed. She knew that he had seen the book lying next to her.

"Belinda, we can be different, you know."

She could tell that he wanted to touch her. She shook her head.

Chapter
39

On Wednesday morning Alberg was on the phone with the Surrey RCMP detachment, checking Harry Stewart's alibi. "He says he was doing business with a guy called Ron Philips," he said to the sergeant on the other end of the line, "and another one called Mason Godfrey."

"Say again?" said the sergeant, whose name was Nettie Pringle, she and Alberg had worked together, years ago, in Kamloops.

"Yeah. Godfrey. First name Mason." He gave her the men's addresses.

"Okay. Got it. But don't hold your breath."

"How long?"

"For you, Karl—a couple of days. A week, maybe."

"Come on, Nettie," he complained. "This is a homicide, for God's sake."

"Yeah, well, we've got a few of our own."

He hung up and made another call, leafing through the local paper as the phone rang and rang. When it was finally picked up he said, "You must be the only person in the world without an answering machine."

"I hate the damn things," said Alan Stewart.

"You've made a will, right?" said Alberg.

"You get straight to the point, don't you? Yes, I've made a will. A man would be a fool not to."

"And is your son, Harry, in it?"

Alan Stewart chortled wickedly. "I've left him an allowance. Enough to get by on. Barely. He's been stealing from me for years, did I tell you that?"

"No, you didn't," said Alberg. "How?"

"Taking pieces of my collection and selling them. He thinks I haven't noticed. Harry isn't too bright, among other things."

"Why didn't you call him on it?" said Alberg.

Isabella Harbud appeared in Alberg's doorway, worry scrawled in the frown above her tiger's eyes.

"I don't know," said Stewart. "It felt like too much trouble."

"Are you afraid of him?" Alberg raised his eyebrows questioningly at Isabella, who had sat down on the black leather chair opposite his desk.

"Of Harry?" said Stewart incredulously. "Of course not."

"What do you know about his friends?" said Alberg. He heard slow, heavy footsteps in the hallway. Isabella heard them, too, and got out of the chair. Sokolowski loomed into sight. Isabella gestured to him to come in, and when he did, she left.

"I don't know much about Harry's life, Staff Sergeant," Stewart was saying. "He hangs around in bowling alleys. He's got a friend who acts in TV commercials. That's about all I know."

Sokolowski had assumed his customary position on the leather chair: back straight, knees apart, hands on thighs.

"I'll just be a minute, Sid," said Alberg. "Can you tell me, Mr. Stewart, who's the major beneficiary, if it isn't Harry?"

"I was going to leave something to Maria," said Stewart,

"although I hadn't decided how much. But then she disappeared. So even though I hate dogs and don't care for cats, either, the SPCA gets pretty well everything, because they're about the only damn group in town who didn't ask for it."

"One more question and then I'll let you go for now. Does Harry know all this?"

"Nope."

"How can you be sure?"

"I don't keep important documents lying around. Harry's a snoop. Everything's with my lawyer."

"What does he think he's going to get?"

Stewart cackled. "Everything, probably."

Alberg hung up and turned to Sokolowski. "I don't know what the hell to think," he began.

"I'm okay," Sokolowski reassured him. His face was flushed, and Alberg thought he looked curiously fragile. His reading glasses stuck out from his shirt pocket at an awkward angle.

"That's good," said Alberg.

"I see you're looking at real estate," said Sokolowski, nodding at the paper on Alberg's desk.

"Yeah, that's the plan." Alberg folded the paper closed and tossed it on top of his filing cabinet, next to the pot of ivy that was Isabella's most recent contribution to his office decor.

"I'm thinking of selling my place," the sergeant went on. "I mean, what's the point. But I'm okay with it, Karl."

"Sid—what are you talking about?"

Sokolowski pushed himself out of the chair. "That vandalism thing; I got my eye on Frank Garroway's grandson, by the way. He's been coming over here on weekends since the beginning of summer."

"Sid, are you okay?"

"See, it's what I said all along. It's stable families that we need." He was at the door now. "The kid's parents split up. His mother works weekends. And the boy starts getting in trouble in Vancouver, where they live, and so he has to come to his granddad, and now I think he's getting into trouble over here," he said, his voice fading as he disappeared down the hall.

A minute later Isabella slipped back in.

"What the hell?" said Alberg.

"It's Elsie." Isabella's long graying hair was pulled away from her face and anchored firmly in a bun. It made her look exotic, Alberg decided. Now there was nothing to distract from her golden eyes.

"What about Elsie?" he said. "I'm getting fed up with Elsie," he added.

"She's been out on a date."

"Oh, great. And who the hell told Sid?"

"One of his kids let it slip, on the phone."

"Shit," said Alberg, gazing out his office door. "He looks like somebody hit him on the head."

Isabella sighed. "I guess somebody did, sort of."

1987

Chapter
40

Everett was right, thought Harry, pushing open the door to the bookstore, which caused a bell to jangle. His old man wouldn't disinherit him completely. But Harry didn't want even to share his inheritance. He didn't want this Maria person to get a single damn penny. There was only enough money to allow one person to live in total luxury for the rest of his life, and that person was going to be Harry.

In the bookstore he saw that Everett, who had summoned him here, was engaged in conversation with a customer near the shelves of paperback fiction.

There was a big bulletin board on one wall of the bookstore, covered with announcements from people who had things for sale or rent, people looking for work, people announcing swap meets or garage sales or lost pets. Harry wondered if he ought to put up an ad here for a woman who'd marry him and bear his child. It might be worth doing, he thought, if he could be sure she'd have a boy, thereby providing his father with his only grandson. And he was mulling this over, wondering how it might be possible to make it happen, when Everett emerged from a puddle of shadow: there were lights in each of the shop's several sections, but none that illuminated the whole place.

"I've been telling Hamilton about your situation," said Everett, dispensing with a greeting as he did with most formalities, and over there by the cash register Harry saw Hamilton Gleitman sitting on a stool.

"What? Why the hell did you do that?" said Harry, dismayed. He didn't know Hamilton well, but the guy made him uneasy.

"He might be able to help you out," said Everett. "He's a together guy, Harry. Got lots of smarts, lots of ideas."

"Shit," said Harry gloomily, staring over at Hamilton, who lifted his hand in a salute and started getting off the stool. Harry heard a jingling sound, made by all the crap that hung off Hamilton's belt loops.

It was really a collection of physical things about him that made Harry uncomfortable. First of all, he had gray hair, despite his youngish age; it was thick and wavy and totally gray. And under it there was this blank face, no lines on it at all, and these small eyes, gray they must be, though they looked silver—but that had to be the reflection of the hair or something. And then there was the body. Hamilton had these wide shoulders, and you could see the strength of his upper arms and his thighs right through the denim clothes he always wore. Yet he insisted that he didn't exercise. "It's all in the genes, Harry," he'd explained, grinning, when Harry asked how often he worked out. And he'd said it in a light, soft voice that went with the hair, but not with the eyes or the body.

"It's a great story, Harry," he said now, "about your long-lost sister." He took a pair of sunglasses out of his shirt pocket and put them on, though why he needed to wear sunglasses in a bookstore, Harry couldn't figure.

"She's not my sister," he replied sullenly.

Harry had seen Hamilton's work in various magazines, local and national, and he was reluctantly impressed by the fact that Hamilton's byline had appeared in some of these publications. He wasn't impressed with the stories, though. They were a lot blander than you'd expect from a guy like Hamilton.

"Half sister, then," said Hamilton. "It's still a great story."

"Not to me it's not," Harry said grumpily. "To me it's a pain in the ass."

A woman and a child, probably her daughter, came into the store. They slowed down when they came through the door, as everybody did; it was as if there were a sign that said "No Hurrying."

Everett smiled at the woman, who smiled back and drifted over to the bulletin board, while the kid plopped down on the floor in the children's section.

"Let's go get a coffee," said Hamilton, a hand on Harry's shoulder, "and talk about it."

Ten days later, Hamilton cut the motor and remained in his car, looking through the windshield at a house across the street. A strong voice was telling him to be very, very careful. He took this to mean that he must be alert and agile in all his senses and above all to make sure that when he left here, it would be possible for him to return. *In other words, don't screw up,* this voice was saying. Since it wasn't in Hamilton's nature to screw up, he concluded that his instincts had confirmed that Harry Stewart's half sister was— potentially—an extremely rich vein of exploration.

He wouldn't have believed, from the look of him, that Harry came from a family with money. But oh yes, Everett had insisted that his old man was rolling in it. And Hamilton's subsequent research had confirmed this.

Hamilton peered over at the house she lived in, which was big and messy and needed painting. It wasn't a falling-down kind of place, it just needed some work; it was untended, but not neglected. People had been careless with it, as if they'd lately been too busy, but one day they'd march out on a Saturday morning to mow the lawns, prop up the fence, paint the doors and the window frames, and by the end of the day it would look almost spick-and-span.

It was of no interest to him at first, Harry's moneyed background; not until Everett described Harry's predicament. Then a tiny flutter of interest had occurred, causing Hamilton's nerve ends to shiver. He began to see faint possibilities. So he had agreed to talk to Harry.

The city directory said three people lived in this house: the woman, Maria, who was supposed to have a job with a PR firm, although for an employed person she spent a lot of time at home; her husband, Richard, who taught high school; and a fourteen-year-old daughter.

As Harry had reluctantly laid out the situation, Hamilton had found it increasingly difficult to control his excitement. He had feigned disinterest, at first; pretended to listen more as a favor to Everett than for any other reason. Gradually Harry had loosened up, let his complaints flow more freely. And Hamilton had allowed himself to be persuaded to a sympathetic point of view.

"So whaddya think?" Harry said finally, peering at him with those eyes that made Hamilton think of some kind of rodent. "You got any ideas?"

Hamilton, who had plenty of ideas, smiled. "How much money are we talking about here, Harry?"

It was early afternoon on a Friday in late September, a pretty hot day, and some idiot across the street had the sprinklers on, watering a brown lawn. The green-and-white house that was the object of Hamilton's attention sat slumbering in the heat, blinds pulled against it. A rake leaned against the maple tree in the middle of the front yard, and he could see a skateboard on the porch. There was a wicker chair on the porch, too, but Hamilton figured it didn't get sat on much: this wasn't the kind of neighborhood where you sat in your front yard and watched the world go by. Here, you'd huddle in the backyard around your barbecue, behind your fence. He patted his inside jacket pocket, making sure the notebook was there, and climbed out of the car, carrying the jacket over his arm.

All Hamilton wanted up front was enough money to live on for a year. What he wanted was what he should have gotten from the fucking Canada Council.

Hamilton had dressed carefully for this occasion, in khaki pants and a short-sleeved shirt with narrow stripes of khaki, blue and white. Nothing hung from his belt loops today. He had brushed and polished his expensive brown loafers and removed his earrings, and there was an expensive gold watch on his left wrist. He crossed the street and strolled up the driveway and along the walk in front of the house to the porch.

The screen door was closed, but the inner door stood open. Hamilton looked inside. He could see all the way to the back of the house, where there was a room with big windows and lots of plants and some ironwork furniture. Between the porch where he stood and that room, which was quite bright—though not as bright as it would be later, when the sun was lower in the sky—the house was shadowy. Hamilton knocked on the edge of the screen door and waited.

There was no sound inside. Behind him a car passed, slowly. A breeze stirred the maple tree and sent some of its fallen leaves skittering across the lawn. Hamilton pulled open the screen door and reached inside to rap smartly at the inner door, then stepped back behind the screen again.

For a long time the house remained silent, and he began

to wonder whether anyone was home. But she wouldn't have left the front door standing open. Maybe she was in the backyard. Then he heard somebody—it sounded like someone treading slowly down a flight of stairs—and she emerged from around a corner into the heart of the house. For a moment she was a faceless silhouette against the brightness behind her; then she moved toward him, and the softer light from the front door fell upon her.

She was smaller than Hamilton had imagined, and there was a less angular cast to her features, and he realized that he had unconsciously expected a resemblance between her and Harry. He was smiling as she approached the door, but she didn't return his smile. She looked as if she hadn't smiled in weeks. And she said nothing, just looked at him through the screen.

"Are you Maria Buscombe?" asked Hamilton, still smiling. She didn't reply.

"My name is Hamilton Gleitman, Mrs. Buscombe. I'm a writer with *City Magazine*, doing a piece on adopted children."

She stepped back and reached for the inner door handle.

"I have the honor," said Hamilton quickly, "of being acquainted with Alan Stewart." He looked down, scraping the toe of his loafer against the flaking paint on the porch floor. Then he looked up and smiled again, warmly, appreciatively. "Who has made, if I may say so, an immeasurable contribution to his community." What a lot of horseshit, said the small, dry voice within him.

He saw the pulse throbbing in her temple. Her hands will be cold and damp, he thought, and a thrill pierced his body from groin to throat.

"I understand how sensitive these matters are," he went on. "And believe me, I would never interview anyone for this story who was the slightest bit reluctant to participate."

She stared at him in disbelief.

"Would you be kind enough," said Hamilton, "to give me a few minutes to explain what I want to do in the article?"

She began closing the door.

"Please think it over," he said quickly. She shook her head. "They're very interesting stories." He had stepped back. He was smiling at her again, his voice, his body, relaxed and unthreatening. "I'd like to tell you about them. The other people in the piece. They're anonymous, of course." There weren't any others, actually. If she turned out to be the first woman ever to check him out, Hamilton was dead meat.

She was looking at him intently, almost squinting, as if she weren't altogether certain that anyone was actually standing there. Hamilton began to feel somewhat less confident.

"Five minutes," he said. "That's all I ask." He smiled again, winningly, but she was closing the door. "Excuse me," said Hamilton. "Hey! Wait a minute. Hold it," he said, grabbing at the screen door. But the inner door shut, and he heard her turn the bolt.

"Damn," said Hamilton, amazed. He threw his jacket over his shoulder and crossed the street to his car.

"Shit," he said, furious, staring back at the house.

"Fuck," he muttered to himself, driving away.

Maria watched the reporter through one of the narrow vertical windows that edged the door. She watched until he'd driven away.

The she went into the living room and turned on the television. In the tranquillity of this cool, shadowy room, she shivered, rubbing her hands together, trying to find the voice inside her that could speak to her with wisdom.

(. . . Belinda has just become a teenager; she has shed the soft-ness of childhood and not yet gathered into her the roundedness of womanhood. Belinda is gawky and uncertain and doesn't see that she is lithe, handsome. Belinda looks at Maria sometimes with a doe's eyes. Maria stands up suddenly one day from the dinner table and moves quickly around to the stove, where something threatens to boil over, and as she passes behind Belinda, her daughter flinches—an instinctive reflex . . . and Maria erupts at the sight of her flinching. Maria has never been able to understand this—why Belinda's fear should provoke Maria's rage. . . .)

Maria found that she was standing up, clasping her hands, staring at the television screen, where a man ostensibly telling the world about a diet cola was actually speaking softly, intimately, persuasively, directly to Maria. She knew it was her own voice, her private inner voice, and hearing it, she bowed her head. Nodded. Hearing it, tears splashed upon her cheeks—the voice said yes. Finally. Solace.

Chapter
41

Three days later Hamilton and Harry were huddled in the back of the bookshop. Harry was in a squat, leaning against shelving that held self-help volumes, his briefcase by his side, while Hamilton sat on a stool, hands clasped between his knees. Everett was perched behind a circular counter with a hinged section that allowed him to go in and out: he was flipping the pages of a catalog from a stationery supplier. A mournful teenager was stationed at the till at the front of the store, leaning on the counter, his chin in his hand. Everett was sure that the kid's sorrowful countenance was what was keeping the place empty. But the lack of business suited Everett, whose attention was not on the catalog he was thumbing through, but on Hamilton and Harry.

"I told you it wouldn't work," Harry was saying bitterly. "What a stupid idea. I told you she'd never let you in."

"Shut up," said Hamilton. He lifted his head and aimed his bleak gray gaze at Harry. "Stop your damned whining." He continued to study Harry, thinking, while Harry snapped the suspenders that were holding up his jeans, and Everett chewed concentratedly at a hangnail.

"I just wish I knew what's her goddamn *plan*," Harry complained. He snapped his suspenders, first the right one, then the left one, then the right one again. "She's after his goddamn money. That's obvious. She's gotta be. What's her goddamn *plan*, though, that's what we gotta find out."

"I don't know," said Hamilton, still looking at Harry, mulling things over. "Maybe she hasn't got a plan. She seemed—not quite with it. Tense."

"Tense," said Harry. "Shit. *She's* tense."

"I think you should go talk to her," said Hamilton suddenly.

"Who—me? Why?"

"I want to know if she's told anybody else about your old man. Like her husband, or her kid. If she hasn't . . ." Hamilton grinned and lowered his voice. "We'll wage a campaign of terror, Harry, old son. That'll persuade her to fade out of the picture right quick."

"Hey, Hamilton," Everett protested. "What's this campaign of terror stuff? What do you mean by that, exactly?"

"Relax, Everett. It's a figure of speech," said Hamilton, smiling up at him.

"Yeah, well, go there and say what?" Harry said uneasily, wiping his hands on his jeans.

"Do the friendly brother thing," said Hamilton. "Or else yell at her, tell her she's upsetting your old man—play it by ear."

"I don't know," said Harry doubtfully. "Shit."

"Whatever happens," Hamilton told him, "you're going to come out of there knowing more than when you went in."

Maria had told him she was feeling sick. "It's nothing, really. Just a cold, probably. Maybe the flu."

"What are your symptoms?" Richard wanted to know.

"Oh, you know," said Maria. "Aches. I ache all over." Tears thrust themselves into her eyes.

"Maria," said Richard in surprise, looking down at her lying in bed, huddling with her pain. "Can I get you something?"

"No, no, nothing. I just want to sleep," she said, closing her eyes to prove it to him. She felt his indecision, then felt his kiss upon her forehead.

"You're hot," he said, putting his hand there.

"Yes, yes, I'll take an aspirin, but later," said Maria. "First I have to sleep. Good-bye, Richard."

She heard him leave the bedroom, closing the door behind him, heard him speaking in low tones to Belinda, persuading her not to go in there.

"I'll get someone else to take my shift at work," Belinda said clearly as she and Richard walked off down the hall, and then Maria could no longer hear her words. But she knew that Belinda would come straight home from school to look after her.

If she did it today, then, it would be Belinda who found her. She didn't want that. Oh she didn't want that.

When she knew the house was empty she threw back the bedclothes and got up. She put on an old pair of sweatpants and a sweatshirt and moccasins, because today was not to be her death day after all. But tomorrow would be. Tomorrow she would dress with care because she wanted them to know she had been serene.

She would have to write a note. But what could she say? What could she possibly say?

The front doorbell rang. Maria stood still in the bedroom, listening intently. The doorbell rang, and rang again. She rushed downstairs to the door and opened it.

"Good morning," said Alan Stewart's son, smiling at her uncertainly with his ferret face.

Maria closed the door. She threw the bolt and stepped back.

"Hey!" she heard him call. "Hey!"

She reached out and opened the door. He looked at her apprehensively. "Come in," said Maria.

She led him to the kitchen and told him to sit down. There was coffee; Maria poured two cups and sat at the table with him. He asked for cream and sugar. She fetched it. She sipped coffee. Several minutes passed before she became aware that he was speaking. She looked at him with interest, wondering what on earth he was saying, and decided to listen for a while.

". . . my dad?"

"What?" said Maria.

"Your husband. Your kid. Do they know about him?"

She shook her head vigorously and tuned out again, watching his lips move, and his Adam's apple, watching his eyes blink.

". . . he's an old man," the ferret was saying the next time she allowed herself to hear. "It's been a real shock to his system, having you loom up over his horizon."

What an odd figure of speech, thought Maria. She didn't care for it. She found it unsettling, the image of herself "looming," like some threatening presence . . . but of course that was what she was, wasn't it? . . .

"I mean, what the hell," he said, agitated. "Here you come straight outa nowhere to mess up his life. Mine too. Shit. Who gave you the right?" He banged the mug on the table, and coffee sloshed onto the white cloth. Maria stood, abruptly, and he stood, too. He shouted at her, his face dangerously flushed: "Leave him alone! Get out of his life! Go away, goddamn you!"

She saw herself doing it—fleeing—running for the hills—vanishing. But to where? She looked into the ferret's miserable, angry face . . . and her head was flooded with the image of a woman in a boarded-up room. She was a real woman, maybe a nun, a woman in Montreal a long time ago, a very long time ago, who had incarcerated herself in a single room: she had had herself boarded up in there, and there she had spent the rest of her life. She had done this for some reason Maria couldn't remember, except that it had to do with God.

Maria stared at the ferret. "I can't afford to."

He shut his mouth and frowned at her.

"I'd love to do that—oh, I'd love to do that." Tears flowed down her face, and she licked them into her mouth. "But I can't work. Look at me. I can't. I'm not fit."

Alan Stewart's son took a step back. Maria ducked her head and sat down, her hands in her lap.

"Do what?" he said. "You'd love to do what?"

"Leave. Go. Oh, God."

"Are you serious?"

She nodded vigorously. "I'm a danger to myself and others, yes," she said. She sobbed into her hands.

"Pull yourself together," said the ferret, trying to sound authoritative and achieving only a petulant bossiness. "I've gotta think." He looked around him, trying to do this. "You'd go away?"

"Oh, yes. Yes."

"For a long time?" said Harry severely.

"Forever," she said, using her hands to wipe her face, which Harry noticed with distaste was wet with tears and sticky with stuff from her nose.

"It wouldn't have to be for *that* long." Was this possible? he wondered. Could this possibly work? He couldn't decide. He needed to consult with Hamilton. "How much would you need?"

"I don't know," said Maria. "Enough to buy food."

"And shelter," muttered the ferret. He looked around and spotted the paper towels hanging beneath one of the cabinets.

He tore off a couple of squares and gave them to her. "It'd be only the basic minimum," he warned.

Maria nodded.

"I'll see what I can do. I'll get back to you."

"Today," said Maria. She wiped her face and blew her nose. She felt suddenly calm, immensely calm.

"Forget today, today's not possible," said Alan Stewart's son, shaking his head.

"It's got to be today," said Maria. "That's that."

"She's wacko," Harry told Hamilton. They'd been conferring for half an hour, and he was still worried. "What's to say she wouldn't change her mind and just show up one day, banging on my old man's door again? I mean, we can't be sure she's gonna stay where we put her, just because she says she will."

Hamilton looked like a big cat, lounging on Harry's sofa, a big, gray, athletic cat, capable of speed, infused with power. "You said she *wants* to go away," he said.

"Yeah, *now*, sure. But she might change her damn mind, that's what I'm saying."

"Don't worry about it." Hamilton stretched, bright-eyed and smiling, and moved to the edge of the sofa. "That's my job. I'm the one who makes sure she stays put. Remember?" In exchange for this, they had agreed that Harry would pay him thirty-two thousand dollars, half now and half in six months, and that he would cut Hamilton in on his inheritance, in due course, that amount still to be negotiated.

Harry studied him, uneasy. "What're we doing here, anyway?"

"Nothing illegal," said Hamilton. "Jesus, Harry. We're paying her money to stay away from your old man, that's what we're doing. And if she wants to use it to pull up stakes and ditch her husband, who cares? That's her business."

"She's wacko, though," Harry said in wonderment.

Hamilton slapped his knees and stood up. "I've got to get going." He'd offered to set up Maria Buscombe's living arrangements. "You get your ass in gear and come up with the money." He looked at his watch. "You've got two hours, tops, pal." He waited until Harry had bestirred himself out of his chair, then left and headed off on foot down to Bellevue Street and his own apartment building.

There was a bounce in Hamilton's step and true lightness in his heart. The only thing to worry about was whether Harry could pull off quickly enough the black market sale of several pieces of his father's art, which was how their enterprise was to be financed. But Harry's eyes had gotten so shifty when Hamilton quizzed him about this that Hamilton had decided he'd done it before and had good reason to be confident of his success.

Hamilton, whistling, rode the elevator to the sixteenth floor and recalled the woman in the parking garage, the subject of his first fear poem.

He liked the idea of Maria Buscombe curled up in a nest that was of his—Hamilton's—making.

In his apartment he picked up the phone and made the necessary arrangements.

Maria sat by the telephone in the kitchen, drinking coffee and listening to the sounds made by the house and by the world outside. The outside sounds trickled in through minuscule cracks and fissures, she thought, or else they seeped in through the skin and bones of the house, maybe transforming themselves into some other medium, able to become for an instant part of the house, then, once inside, themselves again. There could be no other explanation, she thought, for sounds occurring out there being audible in here, with all the doors and windows closed.

The kitchen clock said it was eleven o'clock.

Maria wanted to think about Belinda. But Belinda flew from her mind whenever Maria tried to consider her.

The phone rang. No—it didn't make its usual ringing sound, it actually pealed, like an enormous bell, extraordinarily loudly, so loudly that Maria was almost knocked off her chair. She watched it, astounded, expecting to see the receiver rattle around in its cradle, the sound was so thunderous. Finally, cautiously, she picked it up.

"Okay, it's all arranged," said Harry Stewart, sounding out of breath. "My partner and I, we'll pick you up at two o'clock sharp. Be ready." He hung up, and so did Maria.

She sat down at the kitchen table and looked out the glass doors into the garden. She sat there for a long time, listening to the quiet ticking of the clock and to the quiet voice inside her head, which was sometimes there and sometimes somewhere else and which told her now to be calm, to have faith in decisions taken: and she listened respectfully, for it was a voice that at least for the moment had saved not only Belinda's life, but Maria's, too.

She had to make a list, now, of things to take with her. She would take hardly anything at all.

> Dear Richard. Dear Belinda. You are all I have to love, but I have to leave you. I don't know where I'm going, but I have to leave you. I'm sorry.
> All my love,
>> Maria.

Hamilton rapped at the door and waited, rolling back and forth on the balls of his feet. When she opened it he stepped back and gestured toward the street, where Harry waited in his car.

"I'm his partner," said Hamilton, with a wink, and stepped into the house. "You all set?"

He wandered down the hall to the room with the iron-work furniture, which turned out to be a sunroom/kitchen. "Nice," he said approvingly, looking around at the potted plants. "Nice," he said to Maria as she entered the room behind him.

"I'm ready," she said hoarsely.

He turned and studied her, hands in his pockets. A small, thin woman in her mid-forties with long hair, black, beginning to turn gray, which she had tied back in an unflattering ponytail. She was wearing moccasins and gray sweatpants, a sweatshirt that was a lighter gray, and no makeup. Hamilton imagined her with her hair up, choosing a dress, standing in front of a huge closet crammed with clothes, standing there naked—he could see her pale smooth naked back—looking for a dress that would push up her breasts and cinch tight around her waist, a dress short enough to reveal the swelling of her thighs. . . . He became aware that she had spoken. "Excuse me?"

"Were you really writing a story about adopted children?"

Hamilton laughed.

Outside, Harry honked the horn.

"Come on," said Hamilton. "Where's your stuff?"

"You'll let me know how they are? You do promise?" She was hanging on to the door frame, clutching this great jeezly doll and looking exhausted, and behind her on the kitchen table in the basement apartment was a bunch of stuff in bags and boxes that they'd had to buy for her—food, and some china, and some pots and pans, because the place didn't come equipped with that stuff.

Harry was exhausted, too. "Yeah, yeah," he said irritably. He just wanted to get out of there.

"We promise," said Hamilton, and Harry turned to see him smiling at her. "Really. We'll give you regular reports."

"There's no phone here, though."

"They'll come with the money," said Hamilton. "By courier. You take care, now," he said warmly, and he and Harry started along the walk that led around the house.

"See, I told you," Harry muttered. "Wacko. She's wacko."

"She'll be okay," Hamilton said cheerily. Although he agreed with Harry, of course. The woman was not rational. He'd have to keep a close eye on her.

They got to the street and headed for Harry's car. Just before he climbed in, Hamilton looked up and waved at the landlady, who was watching from the upstairs living room window, and who happened to be his mother. She gave him a big smile as she waved back.

THE PRESENT

Chapter
42

Late Wednesday evening Cassandra was reading in bed. Alberg, too, was holding a book, propped up on pillows next to her. But his mind was elsewhere, pondering Maria Buscombe's photograph album as he watched his cats. They were curled up on a chair crammed between an enormous oak wardrobe and the closet. Whenever one cat stretched the other two wakened for a moment and waited, politely, for the stretch to conclude before repositioning themselves.

Suddenly there was a loud banging on the front door.

Alberg threw back the covers and got up, reaching for his robe. "Sit tight," he said to Cassandra.

When he opened the door Sid Sokolowski was standing on the porch. "It is for sure Frank Garroway's grandson Dave who's our vandal," he announced. "He got caught red-handed dumping the Morrisons' garbage two blocks away in Richard Greverman's backyard." The sergeant put out an unsteady hand and leaned against the wall.

"Uh-huh," said Alberg.

"So here I am reporting it, just as it happened. Wrote it down. Went home. Decided to tell you it in person."

A lamp went on in the living room, and Cassandra appeared at Alberg's elbow.

"Did you drive here, Sid?" said Alberg.

Sokolowski grinned. "No, I walked." He frowned. "Sure I drove here. Course I drove here."

"Come in, Sid," said Cassandra. "Bring him inside, Karl."

"No no no no," the sergeant protested. Alberg took his arm and pulled him into the house. "Now you're gonna make coffee or some damn thing, right?" he said.

"Right," said Cassandra.

"No no no. No. I'll just sit down here for a minute, then I'll be on my way." Carefully, with great concentration, he lowered himself onto the sofa. "There." He looked around the room, then sorrowfully up at Alberg. "The word is you're getting married."

"Yeah, I am. We are."

"Well, then congratulations are in order, I guess."

"I was going to tell you, Sid. I just thought—"

"I know. Me and Elsie." He swept his hand across his face.

"Yeah."

"Makes it awkward for you."

"Jesus. Sid? . . . Sid?"

The sergeant's face had crumpled, and he had begun to weep. Alberg looked frantically toward the kitchen. He could hear the tap running as Cassandra prepared to make coffee. He hurried to the bathroom for a box of tissues and hunkered down on the floor next to Sid. "Here." He thrust tissues at him. The sergeant pushed them away, then grabbed them back and mopped at his face.

"Ah. I'm sorry, Karl. Too many beers, that's all it is." He looked blearily at Alberg. "She's going out on dates now. God knows what'll be next." He took another handful of tissues. "She's everything to me, Karl. I didn't used to know it like I know it now."

"Have you told her that?" Alberg glanced into the kitchen; Cassandra was spooning coffee into the filter.

"Not in so many words. I don't think it would make any difference, anyway. Shit. I'm starting to sober up. Maybe I should have another beer."

"I don't think so."

"Yeah, you're probably right." He sank back onto the sofa, and Alberg stood up, pulling at his robe, which had gaped open, tying it closed.

"If I'd told her a long time ago, maybe," said Sokolowski, staring moodily into space. "But it's not something she wants to hear me say anymore."

"Maybe you should try it, though."

Sokolowski turned to him and tried to smile. "So. When's the big day?"

"We haven't decided," said Alberg.

Sid leaned toward him and spoke in a loud whisper. "Is she—okay? You know. After that—the ordeal she had. I mean—you know. Romantically."

Alberg looked at him, expressionless.

"Oh shit." The sergeant sat back, miserable. "I spoke out of turn." He put his hands on his knees and was still studying them intently when Cassandra came in with three mugs of coffee on a tray.

"You'd better drink it black, Sid," she said.

"I better." He drank some and held the mug in his huge hands. "Congratulations on your engagement," he said uncomfortably to Cassandra.

"Thank you, Sid."

"You gonna have a church do, or what?"

"Oh no," said Alberg quickly. "I don't know. Something informal."

"But there's gonna be a reception, right?"

Alberg shifted position uncomfortably, glancing over at Cassandra. "I don't know, Sid. We haven't decided anything yet."

"There'll be something," said Cassandra. "Maybe a reception. Maybe just a party. But something." She smiled at him. "Do you think you could persuade Elsie to come?"

Sid's face flushed. "I could try."

Alberg was awake long into the night. He was thinking again about Maria Buscombe's photo album. He saw her pleading figure by the roadside, as Belinda had seen it. He remembered Edward Dixon and the map he said he had drawn for Maria.

In the morning, he called Maria's daughter.

"Belinda," he said when she answered. "Did your mother ever hit you?"

There was a long silence. "Sometimes."

Alberg leaned against his kitchen wall and listened to the shower running in the bathroom. He was grateful for his mother, in London. He was grateful for his absent daughters. "She was different, wasn't she," he said, "when she got back from Saskatchewan."

"Yeah."

"Do you know why?"

"It's pretty obvious, isn't it? I always figured she found out more than she wanted to tell us."

Chapter 43

Hamilton Gleitman capped his fountain pen and laid it next to his notebook. He sat straight on his desk chair, groaning, and massaged the small of his back with both hands. He was temporarily spent. But—Christ! he felt good. He got up and went to his window and looked out at the view, stretching, loosening up his body, exultant about the work he'd done in the last ten days.

The killing had provided him with an enormous amount of material, emotional data by the bucketful. He had been euphoric ever since. The poet in him had been dominant since that night, the poet's needs central: he had put off or canceled every magazine assignment he had, in order to write himself out.

Hamilton went to the kitchen and took sliced ham, a tomato, mayonnaise and mustard from the fridge and a loaf of stale bread from the cupboard. He put on a Frank Sinatra CD and began to fix himself a sandwich.

First to be mined was the way he'd felt before the killing: cocky, excited; in his eagerness for this new adventure there had been something sexual. Then there was the deed itself: the stealthiness with which he'd made his way into the apartment; the thrill of creeping to her bedside, hammer in hand; the shock of having her waken; and the multitude of sensations that had accompanied the act of striking her . . . she had fought him. Fought him. He hadn't expected that.

Hamilton put the sandwich on a plate and took it and a can of beer into the living room. He sprawled on the sofa and ate contentedly, looking at the view, listening to Sinatra.

He had gotten out of there by the skin of his teeth, with blood all over his clothes, and spattered on his face, and in his hair. He had tucked the hammer inside his jacket and loped half a mile to the ocean, feeling invulnerable. He waded into the ocean, oblivious of the cold, and splashed around until he'd gotten rid of the blood. Then he heaved the hammer into the black reaches of the Pacific and waded out and jogged back to his car. By the time he got there his teeth were chattering and his balls had shrunk to the size of walnuts. He started driving, and as soon as the motor had warmed up, turned on the heater.

He had planned to at least check out the daughter, too, and if things had fallen together as they often did for Hamilton, he'd thought he might even get rid of them both on the same night. But no damn way, he'd told himself in the car, shivering, teeth clattering around as if he had a mouthful of marbles. He'd heard somebody out in the hall just as he was slipping out the glass doors. So the body had probably already been found, and he had to get out of there.

He had slapped the steering wheel, grinning to himself. Jesus, but he'd felt good. The poems were going to gush from him now, black billowings of blood and terror, the truth of them deftly concealed.

And they did.

He took his plate and the empty beer can back to the kitchen and returned to his desk to leaf backward through his notebook, its pages covered with black-ink scrawls. At his next work session he would copy the revised poems cleanly into a new notebook and shelve it until he had filled enough of them to send off to his publisher.

He got another beer and returned to the sofa to rest his aching back some more. He had used up the murder of Maria. It was time to turn his mind to her daughter.

It was also time, he decided, to bring Harry back into this thing.

Alberg was sweating over more paperwork when Nettie Pringle called from Surrey.

"Yeah," she told him, "your boy Harry Stewart was here on October second. Spent the weekend, in fact."

"Shit. Doing what?"

"Bowling."

"Bowling? He said he had some kind of a business deal going."

"That's a laughable concept, according to these guys. But he was here, no question."

"Shit. Okay. Thanks, Nettie." He was scowling at the surface of his desk when Sokolowski appeared in the doorway.

"Knock knock."

"Come in, Sid."

"I'm here to apologize," said the sergeant lugubriously.

"Forget about it."

"No, it's only right—"

"Okay. Fine. Apology accepted."

Sokolowski studied him. "You're a tad snappish today, Staff."

"Yeah. Sorry." Alberg slumped back on his chair. "Harry Stewart's in the clear, and I don't have a blind-eyed clue what to do next."

Sid sat down opposite him.

"Nobody else had any reason to get rid of her," Alberg went on. "Neither did Harry, for that matter, but he didn't know it. I know what you think, Sid—but if it was a break-in, why wasn't anything taken?"

"The neighbor lady heard the guy," said the sergeant. "He probably knew somebody'd heard him, and figured he had to split to save his hide."

Alberg was staring at the ivy, which had wended its way halfway down the side of the filing cabinet. "On the other hand," he said thoughtfully. Why hadn't he thought of this before?

"On the other hand what?" said the sergeant.

Alberg turned to him. "Our Harry is lazy, Sid. Too lazy to work. Too lazy to dress himself in clean clothes, even."

"So?"

"So maybe he hired himself a hit man."

Sokolowski considered this. "It's possible, I guess."

Alberg smiled. "I think it's time I talked to him again."

Chapter
44

Among Harry's reactions to news of Maria Buscombe's death was, of course, relief: his father had become noticeably absentminded over the past few years, but there was a limit to how many sculptures and rugs and paintings Harry could lift without being found out, and Harry figured he'd about reached it.

Mostly, though, her death created terror in him. He badly needed to talk to somebody, somebody who was familiar with the situation. But if he was right, and it was Hamilton who'd killed her, Harry didn't want to have anything to do with him. That left only Everett. Harry hadn't seen him in some time, because Everett was very busy for several months of every year, now that his circumstances had changed so dramatically.

Six years earlier Everett had gotten hired to do a commercial for an oil company. He'd played a rumpled character who was warm-hearted and in-your-face friendly, a little bit of an "aw shucks" kind of guy. In the middle of his spiel music started happening, and Everett's character broke into a soft-shoe routine, hands in his pockets, talking on about gasoline as if he wasn't even hearing the music and certainly wasn't aware that he was dancing.

The commercial turned out to be a big hit. So the oil company had the advertising agency do another one with the same character, and then another one, and soon little stories were appearing in the entertainment sections of the newspapers about Everett. One thing led to another, one job led to another, until Everett ended up getting a lead role in a TV series shot in Vancouver, about a muddle-headed private investigator and his sharp-tongued sister who kept house for him. And this had changed Everett's life completely, of course.

But the crisis of Maria Buscombe's murder occurred while the series (which had been renewed for yet another season) was in hiatus, so Harry drove up to his house, pretty sure he'd find him at home.

Everett, so as not to put his newly fecund career at risk, had joined Gamblers Anonymous but since he still felt the urge on a regular basis, he kept himself very busy in the off season. When Harry trudged up to his front step, carrying his briefcase, he saw Everett spraying and vigorously polishing the glass that made up the top part of the door. Harry picked up the doorknocker, a miniature of the Eiffel Tower, and banged it down, startling Everett, who'd been so intent on the smudges on the glass that he hadn't noticed Harry out there. He opened the door and let him in.

"I gotta talk to you," said Harry unceremoniously.

Everett led him into the living room and got them both a beer from the wet bar in the corner. Everett's house, which he had bought when the series got renewed the first time, and in which he took great pride, was high above Burrard Inlet and offered a magnificent view of the water and the North Shore mountains. But Harry wasn't interested in the view.

"Have you seen Hamilton lately?" he said.

Everett shook his head and drank some beer. He had set

the bottle of glass cleaner and the roll of paper towels on the bar. "What's with the briefcase?"

Harry looked down at it, sitting next to his feet. He loved that briefcase. He'd bought it three years earlier, on sale. Carrying it gave him confidence, gave a lilt to his walk and a lift to his chin. It contained every piece of paper in his life, including the notebook in which he'd documented his father's art collection. Plus he carried the current *TV Guide* in it, too. "I keep my important papers in it," he said. "When did you see him last?"

Everett thought about it. "He had a book launch. I think that was—yeah, four years ago. I'd just left the store, is how I remember. Why? What is this?"

"You remember that broad, my old man's love child?"

"I never met her," Everett reminded him.

"I know, but you remember, she—she went away? We paid her—I paid her off, and she went away? Remember?"

"Yeah, I remember. What about it?" Everett's eyes wandered to the glass cleaner and the paper towels.

"She's dead."

Everett lifted his shoulders in a shrug. "So? Your worries are over, then, right?"

"No, see . . ." Harry wriggled to the edge of the sofa he was sitting on and said, in a harsh whisper, "She's been killed. Murdered."

Everett looked at him piercingly, then shook his head. "I don't get it."

"I'm afraid it was Hamilton," said Harry miserably.

"Come on," scoffed Everett—but almost immediately he looked apprehensive. "But why would he?"

"See—I found this out from the cops—I got grilled, Everett, by the goddamn cops, over this thing—"

"Jesus," said Everett, appropriately sympathetic.

"—I found out that her husband and their kid live in

Sechelt now, and that's where she was killed, in Sechelt, in this apartment, Everett, that she'd rented there." He sat back and took a long swig of beer. "It was Hamilton's job to make sure she stayed in Abbotsford. He got paid to do this, that was the arrangement. I came up with the dough, for him and for her—on and fucking on, year after fucking year, for her. And Hamilton, he found the place where she was gonna live, and he was supposed to make sure she stayed there. That was our agreement."

"How was he supposed to do that?" Everett wanted to know.

"His old lady owns the house she was in. She was gonna keep him posted."

"So you figure his mom told him she'd left, and—"

"Yeah," said Harry grimly. "I phoned him up, nine, ten times since the cop talked to me, but all I get is his machine. 'Go away, I'm in seclusion,' that's the message on the thing. Shit." He wiped his forehead on the sleeve of his worn navy sweatshirt and in doing so got a whiff of body odor that took him aback. "Now, Everett," he said, "my question to you is, I'm not to blame for any of this, am I?"

"You mean, legally?"

"Yeah, legally."

"I'm no expert—"

"Yeah, but you're this TV detective now," Harry broke in. "Some useful stuff musta rubbed off, right?"

"Well," said Everett.

"Plus you did all that reading," Harry went on, "when you managed the store. You've read more books than anybody I know, including my old man. Some of them musta been legal books. Or detective books. True crime. Whatever."

"Yeah," said Everett, nodding, thinking. "I guess."

Harry thought hopefully that his friend might be conjuring up pages, or even whole chapters, in his brain. He must have an exceptional-type memory, Everett, in order to learn all those lines every week.

"Okay," said Everett. "So if he did it—" He stopped and looked hard at Harry. "You sure you didn't know about some of this? You sure Hamilton didn't tell you she'd left this one place and rented this other one over on the coast?"

Harry was shaking his head so vigorously that he felt his jowls quivering. Jowls. Jesus. He was getting fucking old, and still he didn't have his fucking money. "No way," he said fervently. "No way."

"Why the hell would he do it, though?" Everett said thoughtfully, gazing through the window, but Harry didn't think he even registered what was out there. He looked back at Harry. "You'd already paid him his money, right?"

Harry nodded.

"So I don't get it. Why didn't he just let her go? Tell you to fuck off? He's a tough character, Hamilton. He wouldn't find that hard. I don't get it."

Harry was silent under Everett's scrutiny.

"What else is going on here, Harry?"

Harry, who had been expecting this, spoke with the greatest reluctance. "I promised him part of my inheritance."

Everett's eyes became huge. "What, if he killed her?"

Harry almost laughed at the squawk in his voice. "No no no," he said nervously. "No. If she stayed away for ten years. Or until the old man crapped out."

"You mean," said Everett, "if he made *sure* she stayed away."

There was a silence. "Yeah," Harry mumbled.

"Did you by any chance put this in writing?"

Harry looked down at the floor. He tried to recall when he'd last had a shower. He was sweating, and the smell of his body was stronger. He wondered if Everett was aware of it, too. He looked over at Everett, sitting on his big black leather chair, one ankle crossed over the other knee. He looked crisp and stylish, as usual. There was a worried expression on his face, but Harry didn't think that was because he was smelling anything bad. Probably the good leather smell from the chair blocked out everything else.

"Sort of," Harry said finally. "Not really. It's a kind of an IOU-type thing I signed."

Everett looked at him sadly. "You're in shit, Harry. I just don't know if it's up to your knees, or your waist, or if you're about to drown in it."

An hour later Harry was sitting at his usual table in Flora's Place, his briefcase on the floor between his feet, going over his conversation with Everett in his head. He was sipping iced tea and keeping his eye on the door in case that damn cop showed up again. There was no reason to think he would: Harry just happened to have an ironclad alibi; the cop would check it out, and that would be that.

He had said he'd be back, though. Harry thought that was probably just for show, but you could never tell anything for sure with cops—they were a surly, sneaky crew in Harry's opinion—so he kept a wary eye on the door. He had resolved to be as officious as hell with the cop if the guy bothered him again. For one thing, he'd say, What the hell are you doing, questioning people outside of your jurisdiction? He had some other remarks prepared, too. He was all ready for the damn cop, yes sir.

So when the door opened and instead of the cop standing there it was Hamilton Gleitman, Harry felt lost, like a character in an episode of *The Twilight Zone*. Hamilton stood there grinning, and Harry sat there staring at him, and his brain was trying to persuade him that he did not know this guy.

"Hi, Harry," said Hamilton, sliding onto the chair opposite him. Harry was gray-faced and starting to sweat. "What are you drinking?"

"Iced tea. Chicken's on the way. Hi, Hamilton. Long time no see."

Hamilton sat back and poured a small pile of salt onto the table. "Is it supposed to be good, then? The chicken?" He licked his finger, stuck it in the salt and then into his mouth.

"It's one of their specialties," said Harry. "Yeah, it's good."

"How's your old man?" said Hamilton. He lifted his hand and got the waitress's attention.

"Failing," Harry said quickly. "Definitely failing."

Hamilton gave him a skeptical glance and told the waitress to bring him what Harry was having. He ate more salt. "I see from your face," he said to Harry, "that you heard the news from Sechelt."

"You said you could keep her out there in the Valley," Harry blurted. He glanced quickly left and right and lowered his voice. "That was the deal. That was your part of the deal."

Hamilton felt his good mood beginning to fracture. "Shut your face, Harry," he said coldly. He watched Harry settle back on his chair. He had a little more color in his face now. "It's always a mistake," said Hamilton, his tone once more conversational, "to look back. Much more productive to look forward."

The waitress delivered Harry's meal and gave him a pat on the shoulder. What was it about this guy, Hamilton wondered irritably, that made women feel sorry for him? He leaned forward and sniffed. "Mmmm. Smells good. What did you tell the cops, Harry?"

Harry paled again. "What cops?"

"Come on," Hamilton said impatiently. "They were bound to wend their way to you eventually."

"I didn't tell them shit. Nothing," said Harry defiantly, his little eyes gleaming. "Why the hell would I?"

Hamilton studied him, brooding. Then he said, "Eat, Harry. Dive in." Harry picked up his fork and took a bite of mashed potatoes and gravy. He was wearing baggy jeans, of course, and a T-shirt under suspenders. Jesus, thought Hamilton in disgust, they were probably the same jeans, the same T-shirt, he'd worn that day seven years ago when they'd escorted Maria Buscombe to her new home.

He wet his finger and helped himself to more salt. "Failing, you said," he mused. "And just how imminent is your old man's departure from this earth, do you think?"

"I don't know," said Harry plaintively. "It could be anytime."

"Yeah, and it could be fucking years." Hamilton brushed the rest of the salt off the table and onto the floor. "I'm losing my patience, Harry." He rested his forearms on the table and skewered Harry with his metallic gaze; he was aware that his gray eyes seemed cold and empty, like a sunless sky. "I need bucks. I am sick to death of doing crappy stories for crappy magazines when I ought to be writing poetry."

"It's good stuff, you're right, Ham," said Harry, nodding. "I told you that. I read your book, and it's genuinely good. Should've won some kind of prize." He glanced at Hamilton. "Did it?" he said uncertainly.

"Nah," said Hamilton, as the waitress arrived with his dinner. He began eating immediately, realizing that part of his vexation was due to hunger. He was ravenous again. "Yeah," he said finally, "I know it's good."

"He's over eighty," said Harry. "He's bound to go soon."

"The old geezer's in some kind of nursing home, I guess,"

Hamilton said around a mouthful of chicken. He watched Harry consider lying and saw him decide against it.

"No," Harry said. "He still lives in his house. But he can't clean the place anymore," he added quickly. "Or do the gardening. He needs a lot of help."

Hamilton contemplated Harry thoughtfully, looking deep into his small, dark eyes, noting the flabby shape of him, wondering about his determination, and trying to assess the extent and the nature of his desperation. He leaned across the table toward him. "I'll do the daughter," he said quietly, "if you'll take care of your old man."

Harry felt sweat break out all over him. He could almost see waves of his body odor sweeping out across the restaurant. How the hell had he ever gotten mixed up with this guy? That damn Everett, he thought; it was all his fault. He made a bleating sound that he hoped Hamilton understood was a big "no," but looking into Hamilton's cold gray eyes, he knew it didn't matter what he said: that girl was going to die, and Harry's old man, too, because if Harry wouldn't kill him, Hamilton would.

Harry clung to the edge of the table, hanging on as if it were a mountain ledge and to let go would send him plummeting to his death. He made another sound—Hamilton was starting to look impatient, darkly impatient—and then over Hamilton's shoulder he saw the door open, and the cop was there. He pointed, words churning in his throat, and Hamilton turned, frowning.

"What?" said Hamilton.

At first Alberg thought Harry was having some kind of attack. His tiny black eyes were three times their normal size, and his face was the color of soapscum. He looked like he was trying to stand up. He was pointing at Alberg and making gargling noises. His gray-haired friend stared at Alberg over his shoulder with a look of exasperation.

Alberg went to their table and sat down next to the stranger, across from Harry. "You don't look well, Harry," he said, and shifted his gaze. "Who's your friend?"

"Who the fuck are *you*?" said the gray-haired guy.

They both looked at Harry.

"He did it," said Harry, struggling to his feet, pointing to Hamilton. "He did it," he said, starting to cry.

"He said that? He pointed at the guy and said, 'He did it'?" said Sokolowski.

"Yeah," said Alberg.

"So what did the guy do?"

"Hammered him."

Sokolowski bent over on Alberg's black leather chair, laughing. "Oh oh oh," said Sid, laughing.

"Yeah, right, it was real funny," said Alberg. "I had one hell of a time getting the cuffs on him."

"Oh oh oh," said the sergeant, sounding like he was in pain.

"I've got cuts and bruises all over me," said Alberg indignantly, "and you sit there laughing." He watched Sokolowski guffawing, red-faced, and wished Elsie was there to see this.

Chapter
45

Two days later Belinda sat next to her father on the red-and-white-checked sofa, looking at Maria's photograph album, which Alberg had given her.

"Belinda, at about one year," her mother had written on the first page. *"She is sitting in a tree. Richard is holding her there; only his hand shows in the picture, which is in black and white. Belinda is wearing a white sweater, I remember, and there is a dark curl of hair on her forehead. Her eyes are squeezed shut, and she is laughing."*

"I could have found her, if I'd tried," said Belinda's father.

"Maybe not," said Belinda. She turned the page. *"Belinda on her third birthday. She is wearing shoes with little bells on them and a dress with light blue, dark blue, and white stripes. Her hair is in a French braid. She looks very solemn."*

"I wish I'd tried. I should have tried." He ran his hand wearily over his head.

Belinda continued to turn the pages, reading descriptions of photographs her mother had left behind. The last one was Belinda at fourteen, only a few months before her mother left, wearing her McDonald's uniform: *"Belinda's first job,"* her mother had written.

On the next page was mounted an actual photograph: Belinda climbing onto her bike in the driveway of the house in Vancouver. It was followed by five more, taken about a year apart.

Here was one of her and her father getting out of the car. Another of Belinda in the backyard in Vancouver, mowing the lawn. The rest had been taken after she and her father had moved to Sechelt: Belinda in her father's store—in the hospital parking lot—with Raymond going into the Super-Valu. The last one showed Belinda outside the doorway of the Jolly Shopper.

Belinda closed the album and put it to one side. She felt somber and shaken.

Her father got up and went to the window, where he stood looking out, his hands in his pockets. They were quiet for several minutes, the two of them.

And then the policeman knocked on the door. An old man stood beside him.

Belinda said, "What do you want?" She sounded inhospitable, maybe even slightly hostile, but she didn't care. She had no more time for murder, and police.

"I've brought someone to meet you," said the policeman. "This is your grandfather, Belinda," he said.

Belinda looked at the man intently. He was extremely old.

"I'm your mother's father," he said, blinking. "My name is Alan Stewart."

She felt her father at her elbow.

Belinda didn't know if she wanted a grandfather. He looked harmless enough—but gazing into his wrinkled face filled her with apprehension.

"You look a lot like Maria," he said. "Except you're bigger."

"Please come in," Belinda's father said quietly. Belinda looked at him in surprise.

"I'll pick you up in half an hour or so," Alberg said to Alan Stewart, who was looking frail and uneasy, "and take you home."

Alan Stewart stepped away from the door, tugging at Alberg's sleeve. "How much should I tell them?"

Alberg shook his head. "I don't know, Mr. Stewart," he said wearily. "It's your call."

Cassandra was working late that night, so when Alberg got home from West Vancouver he fed the cats, set the table, and started dinner. Then he sat on his wingback chair with a Scotch and water, brooding, watching the cats at play.

Eventually he realized that Cassandra was considerably later than usual. He was instantly filled with unease and went to the phone: he'd call the library first, then Phyllis, then Cassandra's mother . . . and then he heard her car pull up in front of the house.

It was dark by now; he turned on lights, waiting for her to come inside.

She burst through the door, her face alive with excitement. "I've found the most wonderful house," she said, tossing her handbag onto the sofa. She rushed to him and hugged him tightly. "You're gonna love it. It's right on the water."

"Oh, Cassandra," he said, dismayed, but hugging her back. "We can't afford anything that's on the water."

"Yes, we can," she said. She stepped back, smiling at him. "How?"

"There's a mortgage to pay off on this house, true. But there's no mortgage on mine."

"There's no mortgage on your house?"

"I own it free and clear."

"You own it—?"

"My God, Karl. No wonder Maura married an accountant, after twenty years with you. Come on," she said, grabbing his arm. "Let's go see it."

That night in a dream Belinda saw her mother, her head bent low, hands limp at her sides, dressed in something white. Her hair, which was black again, covered her face. She was crying. She wept quietly, streams of tears cascading silver from beneath the fall of her hair. Belinda, in the dream, was whispering to her mother, wanting her to lift her face and look at her. Belinda's whispers were soft but urgent, trying to persuade. And then the tears lessened, and her mother's head began ever so slightly to move, to lift— and Belinda was filled with terror. She stumbled backward, wanting to turn around and run but unable to move except in slow motion. Her mother's head lifted higher, and higher, her hair began to fall away. . . .

Belinda's eyes flew open. "No!"

Raymond woke and held her. He didn't say anything, he didn't even make murmurs meant to be comforting.

After a while Belinda pulled away and turned on her bedside lamp. She looked into Raymond's face for a long time. She shook her head. "I don't know, Raymond. I'm really afraid of this."

"Me too."

"My dad—"

"I'm not anything like your dad."

"You aren't, are you." She touched his eyebrows, his forehead, the bridge of his nose. "Okay, Raymond. Okay."

Raymond closed his eyes. "We'll get him a dog," he said. The smile he smiled then was the loveliest thing Belinda had ever seen. "Moe Two," Raymond said dreamily.

Belinda turned off the lamp and lay beside him, and watched moon shadows flickering across the bedroom wall, and listened to the autumn breeze in the acacia tree. There were things she could never understand. But there were other things that someday she would know, inside herself, when she had lived long enough and loved well enough. Belinda rested her hand palm down on her belly and whispered in her heart to her baby.

About the Author

Laurali R. Wright won the prestigious Edgar Allan Poe Award for best novel for The Suspect. *Her other Karl Alberg novels include* Sleep While I Sing, Fall from Grace, Prized Possessions, *and* A Touch of Panic. *She lives in Vancouver, Canada.*